Security Breach

REBECCA DEEL

Copyright © 2020 Rebecca Deel

All rights reserved.

ISBN-13: 9798642485965

DEDICATION

To my amazing husband. I love you.

ACKNOWLEDGMENTS

Cover design by Melody Simmons

CHAPTER ONE

Emma Tucker sat up, heart drumming against her ribcage. In the darkness of her bedroom, she listened in utter stillness, waiting, praying the noise was the house settling. Seconds ticked away with nothing but silence in her small, temporary home. Must be her imagination. Again.

She sighed as her heart rate settled into a normal rhythm, frustrated with herself. How many times had weird noises in the night startled her awake in the past 18 months? More than she wanted to remember.

Emma rolled onto her side, eyes burning with unshed tears. She longed to go home, but couldn't. How soon would the FBI catch the serial killer who murdered her family and still scoured the country looking for her?

Her gaze shifted to the backpack propped against the wall within easy reach. Inside was money, false ID, two charged disposable phones, two changes of clothes, and a gun along with two magazines filled with ammunition. She prayed she never had to use that weapon.

Emma tried to sleep, but the effort failed. She sighed. Time to make herself a mug of hot tea.

Wood creaked.

She sat up, heart in her throat. That wasn't her imagination. She recognized the noise. One wood plank in the hallway always groaned when she stepped on it.

Thankful she'd slept dressed to run, Emma slid out of bed, jammed her feet into her tennis shoes, grabbed her jacket and pack, and hurried to the closet. Her bedroom door was already locked, saving her time. Silently closing the closet door behind her, Emma turned the lock and hurried to the entrance of her escape route.

After punching in the code, the door unlocked with a soft snick. Knowing the intruder would arrive at her bedroom door in seconds, Emma ducked inside and relocked the entrance.

She rushed through the small corridor, careful to keep her pack from brushing the sides of the narrow enclosure lest the noise give her away. After two hundred feet, the corridor angled downward to another entrance, this one blocked by a steel door with another access code.

Emma entered the number, twisted the knob, and slipped into the interior of the second tunnel.

She locked the door and ran. Was the Butcher responsible for her late-night visit or was this a run-of-the-mill thief? Either way, the Marshals would have to move her again.

Fury at the unfairness of her situation filled her. While she hid in fear for her life, the serial killer roamed free, targeting and killing more people. The Butcher had killed her parents and sister. Her grandfather, Isaac Watts, was her only living family member. Even though she would give anything to return home to Maple Valley, she didn't want the killer to hurt her beloved grandfather.

Emma swiped at the tears trickling down her cheeks. She also didn't want the man who owned her heart to be in danger because of her. If he was home. A Navy SEAL, David Montgomery served his country with skill and dedication, and was frequently deployed.

Someone must have told David about the deaths of her family and her disappearance. Her heart clutched anew at the knowledge that David must think she was dead. She'd begged the Marshals to contact David and her grandfather. They'd refused, saying their safety depended on them believing she was dead.

Emma reached the tunnel exit, a cave on the far side of the hill behind her house. She had a short window of time to disappear into the darkness. If the Butcher had found her again, he wouldn't stop until he ran her to ground unless she eluded him now.

Knowing the path by heart after multiple practice runs, she sprinted toward the cave entrance. Stopping near the opening, Emma forced herself to wait and listen. Nothing, including a lack of normal night sounds.

Dread built inside her. Not good. Someone was out there. Was the person close enough to harm her? She couldn't hover in the cave entrance in indecision. Praying she wasn't making a huge mistake, Emma dragged on her jacket and shrugged into her pack.

Time to go. As soon as she found a safe place, she'd call her handler and request an extraction. She eased to the entrance and peered out. Nothing moved in the still night, but her skin crawled.

Emma jogged down the hill, sticking to the shadows as much as possible. Ed Rafferty, her handler, had insisted she practice escaping from the house in daylight and at night in case something like this ever happened. She'd listened, and his advice was paying off in spades now.

When she reached the tree line, Emma turned left and ran toward the center of Rock Harbor. Five places were designated as safe havens. All she had to do was reach one and call Rafferty. Emma jogged toward the first destination on her list.

The coffee shop on Main Street was closed for the night. Why was a 24-hour coffee shop closed? Dismayed she scanned the hand-written note on the door as she walked past en route to her second choice. No water on the one night she needed to get lost in a crowd.

Emma turned left at the next corner and hustled toward Mel's Diner. The parking lot was more full than usual. She breathed a sigh of relief. Perfect. She'd be able to blend in with the crowd while waiting for Rafferty to arrive.

She walked inside the diner and headed toward the back of the restaurant. Emma slipped inside the women's restroom, breathing easier now that she was away from the large windows at the front of the diner.

After confirming that she was alone, Emma slid her pack from her back and grabbed one of her phones.

A moment later, Rafferty's deep voice sounded in her ear. "Rafferty."

"It's Emma. I'm in trouble."

"Where are you?"

"Mel's Diner."

"Are you safe?"

"For the moment. The place is crowded."

"I'll be there in 20 minutes."

Emma swallowed hard as she slid the phone into her pocket for fast access. So much could happen in 20 minutes.

Glad Mel provided two chairs in the restroom, Emma sat down to wait for Rafferty. She didn't want to join the crowd of people in the dining room. The last thing she wanted to do was endanger innocent people. Rock Harbor had been her safe haven for six months. While she hadn't gone out of her way to make friends, the residents were kind to her. They didn't deserve to have death brought to their doorsteps because of her.

After what seemed like an eternity, her cell phone buzzed with an incoming text message. Emma glanced at the screen and jumped to her feet. Rafferty had arrived. Thank God.

Shrugging into her backpack, she opened the door and peered into the hallway. Laughter and the buzz of conversation reached her ears from the dining area. No movement in the hallway.

Hoping she'd eluded her intruder, she continued down the hall and turned right toward the exit door beside the kitchen that led to the back parking lot where Rafferty waited for her.

Two kitchen workers glanced Emma's way when she reached the door, but didn't stop her.

Rafferty had parked the car a few feet from the back entrance. He hurried toward her, car still idling. Scanning the area, he gripped her upper arm and hustled her toward the vehicle.

After assisting her inside and setting her pack at her feet, Rafferty circled the front of the vehicle. As he opened the door, a shot rang out.

The Marshal grunted and fell to the ground.

"Rafferty." Emma scrambled to the driver's side. Her handler dragged in a ragged breath. Blood pooled beneath him. "Rafferty."

"Run. Take the car."

"You need help."

"Go," he whispered.

More shots rang out. A second bullet slammed into the man who had watched over her for six months. His breath petered out and stopped.

Tears streaming down her face, Emma shut the driver's door and threw the car into gear. Although she hated to leave Rafferty, his death would be in vain if she didn't go.

She took as many side roads as possible on her way to the next town where she would join other early-morning travelers on the interstate. As Emma drove, one thought kept circling through her mind. If the Butcher had found her in WITSEC, no place was safe.

CHAPTER TWO

David Montgomery, sheriff of Morgan County, Tennessee, turned on the light in his office and frowned at the new mound of paperwork. He'd cleared the top of his desk before going on patrol six hours ago. If he didn't know better, he'd swear paperwork had bred like a pair of rabbits in his absence.

He glared at the offending pile of white covering the scarred surface. If his assistant hadn't already gone home hours ago, he'd have sent the scalding look her direction. Not that his ire would have fazed the grandmother of six. No, Iris had a spine of steel and the discipline of a drill sergeant.

After covering a shift for a sick deputy, David was due to report in for work in four hours. No point in tackling this paper blizzard at two in the morning. He was too tired to deal with the mess. Maybe he could just use the pile of paper for kindling in his fireplace.

He grimaced. If he chose that route, he'd have to contend with Iris fussing at him for hours. After that, the efficient woman would reprint everything he needed to handle. Annoying the lady was not good for his health or stress level.

Following a short conversation with the night dispatcher, David called it quits on his 20-hour day. His brother, Levi, was on duty until six a.m. along with the night deputy and a detective if the need arose. If the detective was sent out to a scene, David would be called in as well. Praying for a few hours of uninterrupted sleep, he left the building housing the sheriff's department.

He climbed into his SUV, cranked the engine, and headed for the Rocking M, his family's ranch. His route home took him past the Tucker place. As always, the sight of the empty house caused an invisible band to tighten around his chest until he could hardly breathe for the pain.

The sweet family had been murdered while on vacation. Worse, Emma Tucker, the woman he'd been dating, disappeared the night her family was murdered and was presumed dead.

David looked into her disappearance when he left the Navy and his SEAL team and came up with nothing. People didn't disappear without a trace for 18 months. He could have done it. Emma? No way.

Grief hit him anew at the knowledge that the woman he'd been falling in love with was most likely dead by the hands of the man who killed her family.

In recent weeks, David's friends and family had dropped hints, subtle and not, that it was time for him to jump back into the dating pool. He'd responded kindly to his friends and snarled at his brothers. Each time his response was no, the same response he gave to the single or widowed women around the county who approached him with an offer of dinner or coffee. Irrational as it was, he couldn't go on dates with other women when the only woman he wanted was Emma Tucker.

Fifteen minutes later, he turned into the long, winding driveway of the Rocking M. As he parked in front of the family home, his cell phone rang. Biting back a groan,

David answered without glancing at the screen. "Sheriff Montgomery."

"Sheriff, this is Special Agent Craig Jordan."

His head dropped back against the head rest of the driver's seat. Fantastic. His least favorite federal agent. Great way to end an endless day. "You're up early."

A snort. "Some of us don't have cushy 9 to 5 jobs. I'm awake because I haven't been to bed yet."

Join the club, buddy. "What's this about, Agent Jordan?"

"We need to meet."

"About what?"

"Not something to discuss on the phone."

He scowled. "My phone is encrypted." Something he'd insisted on when he was elected as sheriff of his home county. Strained his budget, but unsecured phones could be compromised.

Jordan rattled off the address of the FBI field office in Nashville. "Meet me in two hours."

"This can't wait until the sun comes up?"

"Depends on how fast you want a response to your next request for assistance from the FBI."

"Blackmail, Jordan? That's a low blow."

"Two hours," the agent insisted and ended the call.

Growling, David sent his brother Owen a text, asking him to cover his shift in the morning. He had no idea what Jordan wanted, but the sooner he went, the faster he could return home and sleep.

Somehow, he had to convince the citizens of Morgan County that he needed more deputies to protect the growing population. Being short-staffed led to mistakes and endangered his deputies and the citizens of Morgan County.

After a quick stop at the gas station to fuel up and purchase the biggest cup of coffee the store sold, David drove to the FBI field office in Nashville. He maneuvered through early morning commuters, amazed at how many cars were on the road at this hour. Thank goodness his county was distant enough to escape the urban sprawl and exploding population of Metro Nashville.

He parked in the underground garage as he'd been instructed by Jordan. After taking a few seconds to stretch following the drive, David strode toward the elevator. In less than a minute, the car stopped at the lobby and the doors slid open.

When David stepped out, a tall man with a broad chest and an impatient expression on his face strode toward him.

"Come with me, Montgomery," Agent Jordan said, his words clipped.

He fell into step beside him. "What, no small talk? I'm hurt."

The other man slid a glance his direction. "Fine. What took you so long? Did you have to kiss the little woman goodbye?"

Irritation washed over him. The only woman he wanted to kiss was no longer in his life. "You wanted me here. I'm here. What's so important that we couldn't talk about it on the phone?"

"You'll find out soon enough." Jordan continued to move deeper into the bowels of the building. Deep in the inner core, he turned a corner and strode toward two men standing guard in front of a room. "Unlock the door."

After one of the men did as ordered, Jordan looked at David and inclined his head toward the room. "Go on in. I'll return in a few minutes to answer your questions. Agents Wallace and Kinski will stay on watch in the hall. You're safe here." With that last enigmatic statement, Jordan retraced his steps down the hall.

David frowned. What did he mean by that? Even if these two agents weren't on the door, he was more than capable of protecting himself. Besides, who would be foolish enough to launch an attack at an FBI field office?

He twisted the knob and opened the door. Inside the room, a dim light illuminated the interior. Once his eyes adjusted, he noticed someone standing at the window, peering out at the cityscape visible through the glass.

A woman. Why hadn't Jordan announced him? When he moved further into the room, one of the agents in the hallway closed David in and locked the door. What was going on?

He shifted his gaze to study the woman standing with her back to the door. Something about her was familiar, but the lighting made it difficult to pinpoint what.

"Did you find him, Agent Jordan?" the woman asked with a soft voice.

David froze. No. It couldn't be Emma, no matter how much he longed for her. "I'm not Jordan."

She gasped and spun to face him. "David?" The woman took one step, two. She moved into a pool of light bright enough to finally reveal her face.

Shock ricocheted through his body. "Emma." His heart rate skyrocketed.

With tears pouring down her face, Emma Tucker raced across the room and launched herself into his open arms. "You're here. I can't believe you're here."

He tightened his grip, holding Emma close as he'd longed to do for months. She was alive. His Emma was alive and in his arms.

When David couldn't handle her tears any longer, he did the one thing that always distracted her. He tilted her head up and captured her mouth with his. What started out as a kiss of comfort quickly turned into one of white-hot passion. Man, he'd missed this woman. Missed her touch, her taste, the feel of her in his arms.

Silently asking for and receiving permission to deepen the kiss, his tongue twined with hers. Tilting her head, he quickly found the perfect fit that made her sigh in pleasure.

Oh, yeah. That sound confirmed the truth. Emma was vibrantly alive and locked in his embrace.

Long minutes later, David broke the kiss and reached into his pocket for the handkerchief he always carried. He pressed the white cloth into one of her hands and settled her against his chest again, savoring the privilege of holding her.

She gave a watery laugh. "You still carry these?"

"Mrs. Grady would have my hide if I didn't." The housekeeper had served as a surrogate mother to the five Montgomery brothers after the death of their mother from cancer. One of the lessons she'd taught each of them was to carry a handkerchief.

Emma blotted her face dry. "I missed you so much, David."

He used his free hand to stroke her back. "I thought you were dead."

"I know. I'm sorry. I wanted to tell you I was alive, but the Marshals wouldn't let me."

Marshals? In a flash, he put a few pieces of the puzzle of her disappearance together. That explained her ability to stay off the radar for so long. She'd been living under a new identity since she disappeared. "You're in WITSEC."

"Forgive me. I didn't want to hurt you." More tears trickled down her cheeks.

His heart turned over in his chest. "You're killing me, baby. Please, don't cry. Besides, I don't have another handkerchief handy."

A small smile curved her mouth as the waterworks slowed to a stop.

Exactly the response he wanted. "I've missed your smile." And everything else about her. David cupped her cheek, brushing his thumb over her cheek bone. "There's nothing to forgive, Emma." He winked at her. "I'll just treat the absence as though you were the one on an extended mission this time instead of me."

She bit her lower lip in a familiar gesture. "Will you be in trouble with the Navy for coming to me?"

"I'm out of the military now."

She stared. "But you loved the Teams, David."

"I did." When he thought he'd lost Emma, he no longer had a heart for the job. "We'll talk about that later."

"I want to hear everything. I've missed Maple Valley and the townspeople. But first, tell me about my grandfather. I can't wait to see him again."

David stilled. Oh, man. The Marshals hadn't told her about Mr. Watts.

Emma leaned back to see his face. Her smile faded. "What's wrong? Grandpa is all right, isn't he?"

"I'm sorry, Emma. He's gone."

"No." Anguish filled her eyes. "Oh, David." She buried her face against his chest to muffle her heart-wrenching sobs.

As he hugged her tighter, anger flooded him at the callousness of the Marshals. They could have at least told Emma that her only remaining family member was dead. Instead, they'd left the task to him. She'd be devastated when she learned the truth about her grandfather.

David murmured words of comfort in her ear, one hand cradling the back of her head, the other coasting up and down her back.

When she quieted, she whispered, "When? How?"

"Two months ago. There's no easy way to tell you what happened to him, Emma."

She stiffened. "Just tell me the truth."

"Someone broke into his house in the middle of the night and beat him to death."

Emma stood motionless in the circle of his arms for long minutes before she finally spoke. "Who killed him?" she asked, voice filled with fury.

Pain and guilt speared him. He'd searched for answers for months and come up with nothing. "I don't know. The

case is still open. I'll find out who killed him and put him behind bars. You have my word on that."
"You sound like law enforcement."
"I'm the sheriff of Morgan County."
Her eyes widened. "Oh, wow. We do have a lot to catch up on."
"Later. We have time."
Emma's arms tightened around him. "Not as much as I want."
What did that mean? Before he could ask, the doorknob rattled. Between one heartbeat and the next, David turned, placing his body in front of Emma's, weapon in hand and aimed at the door.
Agent Jordan walked into the room, pulling up short when he saw the barrel of the Sig aimed center mass. He glared at David. "We're on the same side."
"Are we?" He slid his weapon into his holster. "You could have fooled me." He clasped Emma's hand and led her to a chair at the conference table. Although she was trembling, David was amazed at Emma's strength in handling the blows that just kept coming. David waved the other man to a chair across the table while he seated himself beside Emma.
"What's that supposed to mean?"
"I'm a cop, Jordan. You could have told me Emma was in WITSEC."
"That information was on a need-to-know basis, and you didn't need to know. You don't have the necessary security clearance."
"Oh, come on. I was a SEAL. My security clearance is probably higher than yours."
The special agent's face flushed as he dropped into a seat across from them. "Then you should understand that the more people who know the location of a witness, the greater the risk of a leak."

"Emma's mine, and I know how to keep secrets. If I didn't, I'd have been drummed out of the Teams. Tell me what's going on. Why is Emma in WITSEC?"

"Jordan's eyes narrowed. "She hasn't told you yet?"

"Not enough time." He glanced at Emma and gave her a slow smile. "We were distracted." Even in the low light, he saw color tinge her cheeks and felt a surge of satisfaction at her reaction.

Jordan scowled at Emma. "You expect me to explain why you've been absent for so many months? He probably thought you were shacking up with another guy. Did you even ask if he's found someone else?"

Emma drew in a sharp breath.

David cut in before she could respond Jordan. "Insult her again, and you'll be flat on your back. Why didn't the Marshals tell Emma about the death of her grandfather?"

The agent sneered. "What was the point? She couldn't attend the funeral without endangering her own life and the lives of everyone around her, including you."

"I'm not stupid, Agent Jordan." Emma frowned at him. "At least I would have known the truth and been able to mourn his loss. Instead, David had to tell me the devastating news. I deserved to know the truth."

David tightened his hold on Emma's hand. "Tell me what's going on, Jordan, or I walk and take Emma with me."

"If you want to walk, there's the door. Ms. Tucker is in WITSEC and will stay there until we catch her family's killer."

He raised one eyebrow. "First, stopping me would take more than you and the two agents at the door if Emma wanted to leave with me. Second, Emma can seek other options aside from WITSEC."

Jordan's expression darkened. "If she does, she'll die. Is that what you want?"

"Your sole motivation is making your case. Why has Emma been in hiding for the past 18 months?"

"The man who killed her family is scouring the country for her. He wants to finish what he started."

"Explain."

"The killer was interrupted before he finished the job on Emma. He wants to remedy that failure."

Finish the job? Rage flooded his veins. The killer had hurt Emma. David closed his eyes for a second. When he got his hands on the killer, he'd regret touching Emma. Catching this guy and putting him in prison or in the ground was going to be David's new mission in life.

"Yeah, you're right," Jordan continued. "I want to make my case and put this creep behind bars. I also want to keep your girlfriend alive. This man is a stone-cold killer, Montgomery. He enjoys stalking and killing his prey. The reason we haven't caught him before now is he doesn't leave witnesses behind." He inclined his head toward Emma. "Your girl is the only victim to survive his attack. He won't stop coming after Emma until he silences her permanently."

CHAPTER THREE

The knot in David's gut drew tighter with each of Agent Jordan's revelations. "Who is he?"

"We call him the Butcher. The perp beats his victims until they're unconscious, then stabs them to death."

Frowning, he studied the agent. "If you had her tucked away somewhere safe, why is Emma here now?"

Emma shuddered. "He found me again."

Again? David stiffened. The Butcher had found Emma in WITSEC? "You saw him, Em?"

She shook her head. "Someone broke into my safe house while I was sleeping. I escaped and called my handler for an extraction. When he arrived, Marshal Rafferty was gunned down in front of me. With his dying breath, he told me to run. I took his car and fled, then called the FBI for help. Agent Jordan came with a team of agents to meet me and bring me here."

"Why are you here instead of another safe house?"

"I refused to cooperate unless I saw or talked to you." She leaned her head against his shoulder. "I missed you so much."

Unable to resist, David brushed her lips with his. Although relieved to know she was still alive, the risk

Emma took worried him. She was lucky the killer didn't attempt to take her out before the FBI team showed up.

Jordan cleared his throat. "We don't have time for this. I secured another safe house for you, Ms. Tucker. We need to leave before the sun rises."

Emma shook her head. "I need more time with David. Please."

"You don't have it. I'm trying to keep you alive. You're not helping yourself or my team."

"Give us a few minutes," David said when Emma's eyes filled with tears. Those tears gutted him. "You can wait ten minutes."

The agent glowered at both of them, then stood. "Fine. Ten minutes, but not one second more. I'm not running a dating service. I have a job to do, and your lady isn't making my task easy." He strode from the room and locked the door behind him.

David tugged Emma to her feet and gathered her into his arms. She held him tight. "Are you okay?" he murmured.

She shook her head. "I don't want to leave you."

"You can stay with me."

Her head popped up. "Are you serious?"

"Do you want to be with me?"

"I've thought of nothing else since I went into hiding." Her shoulders slumped. "I can't, though."

"Why not?"

"The Butcher will find me again. He always does. I don't want him to hurt you."

"I can take care of myself and you."

"You don't know what he's capable of. That man is pure evil. I don't want you in danger." Her voice broke. "I'm already responsible for the death of a Marshal tonight. I won't risk losing you to the madman stalking me. If he killed you, it would break something inside of me."

"I'm not going to die."

"You don't know what he's capable of, David."

Not yet. He would. "You have a decision to make. You can go to another safe house." And risk having the Butcher unearth her location again. That was something else he intended to look into. How was this guy learning where Emma hid?

"Or?"

"Come with me."

She was silent a moment. "Will you be angry if I go with the Marshals?"

"Not angry. Disappointed. If you return to WITSEC, we'll be separated until the Butcher is behind bars." He wouldn't know if she needed him, if she was safe.

"It's been 18 months, and they don't have any idea who this man is. What if they never find him?"

"No matter what decision you make, I'll dig into this on my own. I also have well-connected friends who can help. Whatever your choice, we'll find this guy and take him down." He cupped her cheeks, willing her to give him the chance to bring her nightmare to an end and keep them together. "Trust me."

"You can't watch over me 24 hours a day. You have a job."

"My brothers are also out of the military and living at the Rocking M." David looked into her beautiful face. "Between the five of us, you won't be alone. If we need backup, we have options."

"The killer will look for me in Maple Valley. If he does any research, he'll connect you to me. You would be the only person I'd run to if I was in trouble. Not only that, but gossip is Maple Valley's favorite pastime. The town has its own Facebook page manned by the biggest gossip in Morgan County. My return from the dead will make a huge splash."

The door opened again, and Jordan strode in with two agents on his heels. "It's time, Ms. Tucker. Marshals

Cosgrove and Denton are your new handlers. Kiss Montgomery goodbye, and get going."

Emma looked at David. "Are you sure?" she whispered.

"Trust me," he repeated.

Emma turned to Jordan and squared her shoulders. "I'm leaving WITSEC and going with David."

Relief swept over him. Thank God. He would have abided by her wishes if she'd chosen to go with the Marshals. He was grateful he didn't have to trust her safety to anyone else but his brothers and maybe a team of Fortress Security operatives.

He'd take her to the Rocking M for at least a short while. He wanted to consult with his brothers and get their take on things.

David could request a leave of absence and take Emma off the grid himself with a Fortress team along for backup. David's brothers were capable of handling his duties as sheriff if necessary.

Jordan scowled. "Are you out of your mind? The Butcher will kill you and your stupid boyfriend while he's at it. Everyone you come in contact with will be collateral damage. You know how this man operates. If he thinks one person in Maple Valley knows where you are, he'll beat the information out of them, then kill them for the fun of it. Do you really want that on your conscience?"

"My mind is made up."

"What about testifying?"

"I'll be there when it's time."

David nudged her forward with a hand on her lower back. The sooner they got out of here, the better. His skin was crawling, a sure sign of trouble heading their way.

As they stepped into the hall, Jordan called out, "Wait! How will I contact you, Ms. Tucker?"

"Call my cell," David said. "Keep me updated on your progress. I'll do the same from my end."

"What does that mean?" the agent snapped.

"Your attempts to find this guy has been abysmal. Do you think I'll sit back and leave the hunt in your hands?"

A glare. "This is my case. I won't have you or anyone else interfering. If you impede our investigation, I will have you brought up on charges."

"We're on the same side. If you want to keep Emma safe, have her security detail carry on with their plan as though she's in the vehicle with them. Later, Jordan." David escorted Emma to the elevator as Craig Jordan uttered a continuous stream of furious curses behind them.

Behind the closed elevator doors, Emma sagged against David. "I didn't think he would let me leave."

When the car neared the garage level, David nudged Emma behind him and drew his weapon.

"Aren't we safe here?"

"No safety measures are foolproof. If the Butcher is desperate, he won't balk at targeting you in a garage." When the silver doors slid open, David reached back for Emma's hand. "Stay behind me."

He scanned the cavernous concrete interior. Although a few more cars were parked in the garage, none of them were parked near his SUV.

With Emma tucked against his side, he headed for his vehicle at a fast clip, alert for trouble. After helping her inside, he murmured, "I'll check the SUV for signs of tampering. While I do that, push your seat back far enough that you can sit on the floor."

When she nodded, David closed the door and searched the exterior of his vehicle, then dropped to the ground to check the undercarriage for signs of a bomb and tracking devices. Nothing. Excellent. Time to get his girl back on familiar turf.

He climbed behind the steering wheel and cranked the engine. "Ready to go home, Emma?"

"I've been ready for months."

David squeezed her hand. "I want you out of sight and on the floor. Even though I hope the Marshals will cooperate, I'm not holding my breath."

Without protesting, Emma slid to the floor.

"Did you bring anything with you to the field office?"

"I brought a Go bag. Should I go back for it?"

"Is anything inside that you can't do without?"

She shook her head. "I transferred money to the pocket of my jeans. The Go bag has two changes of clothes, two burner phones, and a gun."

His head whipped her direction. "You never wanted to touch a gun." He'd tried to persuade Emma to let him teach her to handle a weapon each time he was home on leave or when she'd visited him at the base.

A wry smile curved her lips. "Constant fear of the Butcher changed my opinion. Rafferty taught me to shoot. I'm not in your league, though."

Huh. "I don't want you to take anything provided by the FBI." Just in case.

"All right. I'm ready to go home, David."

"Yes, ma'am." He backed out of the slot and headed for the exit. At the street, he eyed the two-vehicle caravan passing the garage entrance. As the vehicles neared an intersection a block away, the vehicles exploded.

CHAPTER FOUR

Emma jerked at the loud boom. "What was that?"

"Hang on." David's voice sounded grim. The next instant they were in motion again. "Stay on the floor, Em."

"What's going on?"

"The Marshals' vehicles exploded."

Blood drained from her face. "A bomb?"

"Oh, yeah." He slid his phone from his pocket. A moment later, he said, "It's Montgomery. That explosion was a bomb in the vehicles driven by the Marshals." A pause. "Yeah, Emma's safe. I'm going to keep her that way." He ended the call.

A mixture of grief and fear hit her, grief for the families of the Marshals killed and fear for David. "How could the Butcher follow me here without one of the FBI agents seeing him?"

"That's what I want to know." David's knuckles turned white. "One of them should have spotted him."

"What should we do?" Emma asked.

"Stick with the plan. I'm taking you home."

"I'm a danger to anyone in my vicinity. If anything happened to you or one of your brothers or Mrs. Grady, I'd never be able to live with myself."

"One thing at a time. First, we need a safe place to sleep. After that, my brothers and I will figure out the best plan to protect you and catch the Butcher."

"He'll come for me."

"We'll be ready."

Such confidence David exuded while she was a quaking mess waiting for the next disaster. Man, she was so tired of being afraid all the time, and although she longed to be free, she didn't want anyone else in danger to attain that goal.

"I know you're uncomfortable, but I need you to stay on the floor for a while longer."

"I'm fine." Emma lapsed into silence, unwilling to distract David when he needed to remain alert. As the minutes stretched out, her thoughts circled to Agent Jordan's comments.

She studied David's profile. Was he right about David moving on to date another woman? Emma couldn't blame him if he had. After all, he thought she was dead. Why would he remain faithful to a dead woman?

She should have waited instead of kissing him as though nothing had changed between them. While she'd been frozen in amber for 18 months, David life had continued to move forward.

Then again, he was an honorable man. If he was dating someone else, David wouldn't have kissed her. Her cheeks flushed at the remembered passion of his kiss.

As though feeling her gaze on him, David glanced at her before returning his attention to the road. "Is something wrong?"

"Besides having a crazy killer after me?"

His lips curved. "Besides that."

"What I want to know can wait. I don't want to distract you."

"The answer to your question is no."

She blinked. "What question?"

"You want to know if I'm dating someone else. The answer's no."

Thank God. "But I've been gone over a year."

"Believe me, I know exactly how long you were missing." He sent another quick glance her way. "How about answering the same question for me."

"The answer's no, but the situation is not the same. I assumed you were alive and well in the military. You had no idea I was still breathing."

His lips curved. "I'm glad to know I don't have to convince another man that I have first rights to date you."

"You still want me even though I'm bringing trouble with me?"

"I'll always want you, trouble optional."

She stared. Did he mean that? "Same. You have no idea how hard I had to fight the need to call you from one of the burner phones just to hear your voice."

He reached over and squeezed her hand. Long minutes later, David said, "It's safe for you to get up now."

"Thank goodness. My muscles were starting to cramp." She climbed into the seat with a sigh of relief. "Where are we?"

"In a part of Rutherford County with less traffic. I wanted to be sure we didn't have a tail before I let you sit in the seat."

"Do you think the Marshals are okay?"

David threaded his fingers through hers. "Do you want the truth or a pretty lie to make you feel better?"

Her heart sank. Oh, no. "The truth."

"No one survived the blast."

"Oh, David." She'd hoped for a different outcome. "They didn't deserve to die because of me."

"They died in the line of duty because of a serial killer who gets a charge from hurting others. Their deaths aren't on you, Emma. Place the blame where it belongs, on the Butcher."

"I still feel guilty."

"Survivor's guilt. The best way to honor them is help us catch the killer and testify against him so he'll never have the chance to hurt anyone else again."

"Of course I will, but testifying doesn't seem like enough to honor their sacrifice."

"It's all you have to offer."

"Their poor families," she whispered. "They expect their spouse or father to come home, not see a supervisory special agent with the bedside manner of a hedgehog on their doorstep to break this horrible news."

After another hand squeeze, David made another call. A familiar voice came through the cabin's speakers.

"Heard you never came home this morning. What's up?" Elliot, David's brother, asked.

"I was called in to retrieve an HVT."

Emma frowned. HVT? What was that?

"Need help?" Elliot asked.

"Lock down the ranch and set up a perimeter watch around the house. Make sure the security system is running without glitches."

Silence, then, "ETA?"

"Ninety minutes. I'll be coming in hot."

"Copy that. We'll be ready." Elliot ended the call.

"What's an HVT?" Emma asked.

"High-value target. That's what you are."

She didn't know about high value, but she was definitely a target. "Elliot sounds good."

"He puts up a good front." David glanced at her. "Hungry or thirsty? I don't want to go into a restaurant, but we should be safe enough in a drive-through lane."

Her appetite was nonexistent. "I can't handle food right now, but I'd love some hot tea."

David smiled. "Still have that tea addiction going, huh?"

So what if she had two cabinets full of different kinds of herbal teas at her home? "Drinking tea is a sign of intelligence."

He laughed. "Keep telling yourself that. I'll take a good cup of coffee any day over your weak concoctions."

Three minutes later, he pulled into the drive-through lane of a coffee shop and ordered a large herbal tea for her and the same size of coffee for himself along with a breakfast sandwich and a scone.

"Hungry?" she teased.

"Starving. I had just finished a 20-hour workday when Jordan called me. I've been awake more than 24 hours."

Dismayed, she laid a hand on his forearm. "I'm sorry."

"Totally worth the loss of sleep to have you back in my life."

When their order was ready, David handed Emma the scone and tea. "Try to eat a little. Your body needs the fuel to keep going even if you're not hungry."

Although skeptical that she'd be able to comply, she unwrapped the scone and took a small bite. "Mmm. Cranberry and orange. This is wonderful."

"Try the tea. Hopefully, the warm liquid will soothe your stomach."

By the time they were on the interstate and heading toward home, David had polished off the sandwich.

Emma sipped her tea and took small bites of the scone until she couldn't handle any more of the breakfast bread and returned it to the bag to hold for later. Instead, she concentrated on her tea and keeping watch for trouble as they drove. Not that she'd be able to help if the Butcher came after them now. Her gun was at the FBI field office. Besides, of the two of them, David was unquestionably the better shot.

"Relax," he murmured. "Take a nap if you can."

"I want to help you keep watch."

"You're exhausted, Em. If there's trouble, I'll wake you."

"Are you sure?"

"I've got this. Rest while you have the chance."

"Wake me if you become too sleepy to drive."

"Sure."

Despite his agreement, Emma knew he wouldn't disturb her unless he had no choice. Although she doubted her ability to sleep while still on the run, she settled back in her seat and closed her eyes. Seconds later, a warm masculine hand wrapped around hers. "Thank you for coming to get me," she murmured.

"My pleasure, baby. Sleep now."

By minute degrees, tension dissipated in Emma's muscles. Between the security of being with David and no sign of a tail, she slipped into a dreamless sleep.

CHAPTER FIVE

David remained vigilant as he drove. He occasionally stole glances at the woman slumped in the seat next to him. He couldn't believe that she was alive and here with him. Even though trouble dogged her, he'd take her and the trouble over the long days and nights when he ached from her absence. Her loss had left a gaping hole in his life. Now, he felt whole again.

As the miles passed, he formulated different approaches to her problem, sifting through options and discarding those deemed too risky for the moment. The riskier options might be the only choice down the road. For now, he'd wait and watch.

One thing he did know. The Butcher would regret the day he'd laid his hands on Emma. David would see to that. If he had to turn in his badge to get the job done, he'd hand it over without hesitation. As of two months ago, he had another career option open to him, one that intrigued him.

Halfway home, Emma jerked, moaning as tears trickled down her cheeks. "No. Please, don't hurt me."

Was she remembering the Butcher's attack on her and her family? Unable to leave her in a dream world where she felt threatened, David squeezed her hand, then brushed his thumb along the underside of her wrist. "You're safe, Em," he murmured. "I'm here."

She sighed. "David."

"I've got you, baby."

"Missed you." Emma shifted until her head rested against his upper arm, then she quieted again.

His heart turned over in his chest at her words, glad the feelings growing between them before the death of her family had survived the long months of separation.

David wondered about the men in the town where she'd been living. How had they let this woman slip through their fingers? Their loss was his gain. She was back in his life, and he wasn't giving her up.

When they were close to the Morgan County line, David called Elliot. "We're twenty miles out," he said when his brother answered.

"We're ready. Owen and Caleb are waiting at the five-mile mark to escort you in. Any sign of trouble?"

"Not so far. An unfortunate diversion may have helped us escape notice for the moment."

"What diversion?"

"Long story. See you soon." He glanced at Emma to find her watching him with heavy-lidded eyes. "Have a good nap?"

"I did. I'm surprised. I haven't slept well since...."

Since her family was murdered, he guessed. No surprise. She hadn't felt safe a day since then with a serial killer searching for her. To distract Emma, he lifted their clasped hands and kissed the back of hers. "I'll take credit for providing the road noise and smooth ride to help you sleep."

"You're the reason I could rest. I feel safe with you."

"I'm glad. We're about 20 miles from the Rocking M."

"I can't believe the Butcher hasn't tried to stop us yet."

"Like I told Elliot, we might have escaped detection for the moment, but the reprieve won't last long."

"How long do we have?"

"If we're lucky, a couple of days." As soon as the Butcher learned Emma wasn't in the car, he'd resume his search. The first place he'd look was Maple Valley. David needed to have his plans in place before the serial killer came looking for her.

When he guided the SUV around a bend in the road near the five-mile mark, David spotted his brothers in one of the department SUVs. As he passed them, he noted the shocked expression on both of their faces when they saw Emma in the passenger seat.

The next few minutes would be interesting to say the least. David also needed questions answered regarding the night Emma's family was killed and how she'd escaped the same fate. That conversation would be difficult for them both. While she relived the death of her family, he'd come face-to-face with how close his girlfriend came to dying while he was in the Sandbox of the Middle East.

He still thought of Emma as his girlfriend, but was she? To this point, they'd only established that each of them hadn't dated anyone else, but that didn't mean she was wanted to continue their exclusive dating relationship. On this side of a long separation, she might have changed her mind about him or about them as a couple.

David drew in a deep breath. That was a discussion for a time when they were in a secure location and alone. He loved his brothers, but not enough to bare his soul in front of them.

Dragging his mind back on task, David pushed the SUV's speed higher, wanting Emma inside the safety of the ranch house. Even though his ride was reinforced along with bullet-resistant glass, he preferred to have a safe room close at hand because trouble was coming. The arrival time was the only question.

When the ranch came into view, two ranch hands saw the vehicles approaching and hurried to open the gate.

David slowed just enough to make the turn into the driveway and sped toward the house. He skidded to a stop and shut off the engine. "Wait for me."

He exited the vehicle and circled around the front to the passenger-side door, scanning the area as he moved into position. After his brothers were in place on either side of him, David helped Emma to the ground, tucked her against his side, and rushed her toward the porch.

Mrs. Grady opened the front door opened and waved them inside. Once the four of them cleared the threshold, she closed and locked the door. "Emma! Oh, we've missed you so much. Welcome home, child." She enfolded Emma in a hug.

When the housekeeper pulled back, she scanned Emma from head to toe, concern growing in her eyes. "You've lost weight, dear."

Emma smiled. "I missed you and your cooking, Mrs. G."

"That's easy to fix, then. We'll get you back to your fighting weight before you know it. Now, are you hungry?"

Emma winced. "Not really."

Mrs. Grady studied her a moment, then said, "I have just the thing for you." Her gaze swept over the three Montgomery brothers. "Come back to the kitchen. I have fresh coffee for you boys." She wrapped her arm around Emma's shoulders and led her away, leaving David, Caleb, and Elliot to trail after the women.

In the kitchen, she nudged Emma toward the table. "Have a seat, dear. After I pour coffee for David and the others, I'll get you fixed up."

"I'll get the coffee, Mrs. Grady." Caleb bussed her cheek. "Take care of Emma."

David sat beside Emma and took her hand again.

Elliot sat across from them, his intense gaze locked on Emma. "It's good to see you, Emma." He folded his arms across his chest. "Where have you been?"

"Several places. The last town was Rock Harbor, Kentucky."

A scowl grew on Elliot's face. "You were traveling for fun? Come on, Emma. We all thought you were dead. Eighteen months with no word from you? I never knew you could be a self-centered witch."

"Elliot." David stared at his brother. "Watch your tone and words."

"It's all right, David," Emma said. "He doesn't understand."

"Make me understand," Elliot snapped. "Because from where I'm sitting, you look like the woman who ripped my brother to shreds while you checked items off your bucket list."

"Elliot Montgomery," Mrs. Grady scolded as she placed a mug of hot tea in front of Emma and a mug of coffee in front of David. "Mind your manners."

"Well?" Elliot's eyes narrowed as he ignored Mrs. Grady's admonishment. "We're waiting for your explanation."

"If you'd shut up long enough, she'd tell you." David glared at his brother. "You're skating a thin line, bro." Much more, and David's fist would make the point.

"I was in WITSEC," Emma said. Following her words, the only sound in the large kitchen was the ticking of the clock.

Caleb set a mug of coffee in front of Elliot and dropped into the seat beside him with his own mug in hand. "Need salt for that crow you're about to eat?" he asked Elliot, his tone mild.

"Oh, my goodness," Mrs. Grady said. She laid her hand on Emma's shoulder. "That must have been so difficult for you."

"You have no idea. I was afraid every minute. I didn't talk to people much for fear that I would give myself away. The nights were the worst. Every noise jarred me awake. I was constantly on edge. I haven't slept more than an hour or two a night since...."

"I have a pretty good idea why you were in witness protection given the timing of your disappearance." Caleb sipped his coffee. "You saw the person who killed your family, didn't you?"

She nodded.

Elliot frowned. "Why were the feds involved? That should have been a local matter."

"Not when the man who killed the Tuckers is a serial killer," David said.

His brothers scowled. "Who is it?" Caleb asked.

"The feds have dubbed him the Butcher."

"Why haven't we seen a drawing of him or a mug shot?" Elliot stared at Emma with suspicion in his eyes.

"I can't remember what he looks like."

Oh, man. David freed his hand from hers and wrapped his arm around her shoulders. No wonder she'd been afraid all the time. She could have passed the Butcher on the street and not known him. "Amnesia?"

Another nod. "The doctor who treated me after I was attacked wasn't sure if the memory loss is from blunt force trauma or if it's a case of traumatic amnesia. Either way, I'm not a good witness."

"Then why did the feds have you in witness protection?"

"The killer doesn't know I have gaps in my memory. I remember a lot of things about him, just not his face. Even when I dream about that night, his face is always in shadow."

"Was it dark when he attacked you and your family?" David asked.

She shook her head. "Mom needed ingredients to finish dinner, so I had driven to the grocery store while she finished icing cupcakes. The sun was still out when I returned."

"Sounds like traumatic amnesia since you remember that much," Caleb murmured.

David kissed Emma's temple. "The Marshals wouldn't let Emma call me."

"I begged them to let me talk to you for just a minute, but they refused, insisting I would endanger you and everyone you cared about if I broke the rules," Emma said to David. "I had already lost my family. I couldn't stand the thought of losing you and your family, too."

"So, how do things stand now? Why are you here? Are you out of WITSEC?" Caleb asked. "Did the feds finally catch the killer?"

"The Butcher keeps finding me," Emma said. "I haven't broken any rules from the day the FBI came to my hospital room to talk to me and offer their protection, yet he still learns my new identity and locates my new safe house. The longest I've gone without a security breach is six months."

David hugged her tighter when she shuddered. "Tell them about last night." When she did, he realized how close he'd come to losing her for good.

After she fell silent, Elliot dragged a hand down his face. "We need to tell Levi and Owen."

"I'll fill them in later." David glanced at Caleb. "I want six ranch hands on perimeter watch around the house. The five of us will split bodyguard watch inside. At no time is Emma to be alone."

"How long do we have?" Elliot said.

"No more than 48 hours, probably less."

"Why does the killer want you, Emma?" Caleb asked.

She stared. "You know why."

"Do I? Are you sure being a witness is the only reason?"

"What other reason could there be?"

"What's your point?" David glared at his brother.

Caleb held up a hand. "Hear me out before you tear off my head. Even though she's the only witness, he must realize something is wrong because his picture hasn't hit the media. So, what's driving him to come after her?"

David shifted his gaze to Emma for a moment before he refocused on his brothers. "Special Agent Jordan said Emma was the Butcher's only victim to survive and he'll keep coming after her until he corrects his mistake."

Caleb and Elliot grimaced. "You're talking about Craig Jordan?" Elliot asked.

"Unfortunately."

Caleb groaned. "This will be a disaster of the highest order. Every op he touches gets screwed up."

"That's why I'm counting on you."

A slow nod from each of his brothers. "We won't let you down," Elliot said. His gaze shifted to Emma. "Either of you."

CHAPTER SIX

Emma stood in the center of the room Mrs. Grady had prepared for her. The room was beautiful, perfect in fact, yet she dreaded staying here. In a large, well-fortified house with armed guards close at hand, she should feel safe and protected. She didn't. She felt more vulnerable than ever. Unless David had changed rooms after his father died and he'd mustered out of the Navy, his bedroom was in another wing of the house. Too far away for her peace of mind. She only felt safe with David near at hand.

She frowned. Having survived interminable months without a big, bad Navy SEAL to protect her from a deranged serial killer tracking her around the country, she should be used to protecting herself by now. When had she become a coward?

Her skin prickled with awareness. Although she didn't hear anything, Emma sensed that David had entered the room. She waited for him to speak.

"Emma?" He came to her, concern in his gaze. "Is something wrong with the room?"

She hesitated, then shook her head.

His lips twitched. "You'll have to try harder to convince me. What's going on?"

"Are you still sleeping in the same room?"

Understanding dawned in his eyes. David intertwined their fingers. "This is a suite. At night, I'll sleep in the sitting area on the couch when I'm not on watch. If I'm working, one of my brothers will be close. You will always be protected."

Relief overwhelmed her at his words. "I should tell you to go on to your own room so you'll be comfortable while you sleep." She needed him. In more ways than just as a bodyguard. Man, she had it bad for this handsome SEAL. Lawman, she silently corrected herself.

"I'd sleep on the floor without a second thought to ensure your safety." He squeezed her hand. "I wasn't kidding when I said I wasn't letting you out of my sight. I spent too many gut-wrenching months mourning your loss. I won't leave you alone and vulnerable."

Emma's vision blurred. "Thank you."

"Hey, no tears. You know I can't handle them."

She smiled. "You never could. For a battle-hardened Navy SEAL, you have a serious chink in your armor."

"Only your tears bother me."

"Why?"

"Because you matter to me. You always have." He bent his head and kissed her. "We need to talk, but now is not the time. We're both tired, and I know from experience that speaking of real-life nightmares brings on the kind that invade your sleep. Rest for a while. Elliot and Caleb have the watch. I'll be on the couch in the next room. You're safe, Emma. We'll talk after you wake."

Safe. Such a beautiful word, but the reality was a mist. Experience was a hard teacher, but she'd learned her lesson well. While she might not sleep, David needed to. "I'll be fine. Go. Sleep."

After a long look at her, David gave a short nod and went to the sitting room. Emma toed off her shoes and stretched out on the bed, not holding out much hope of actually sleeping. Too many fears, what-ifs, and worry filled her mind.

She spread a blanket over herself and closed her eyes. She'd rest a few minutes to ensure David was out, then go to the kitchen to help Mrs. Grady with dinner preparations.

When Emma woke sometime later and glanced at the clock, her eyes widened. Good grief. She'd been asleep for four hours, more than she averaged each night. Perhaps David was right. All she'd needed to rest was the assurance of safety.

No. The truth was that she needed David to feel safe enough to rest. What would she do if she had to go back into hiding? He couldn't go with her.

Shoving that worry aside, Emma sat up, swinging her legs over the side of the bed. Hopefully, David was still asleep. Deciding to peek in on him, she slipped on her shoes and walked to the sitting room. The sofa was empty.

Dismay coiled in her gut. Did he sleep at all? She wouldn't be surprised to learn he'd waited for her to fall asleep, then resumed his bodyguard duties. He had always taken care of her first no matter the cost to himself.

She walked downstairs toward the kitchen. The murmur of male voices made her pause. Was it the Montgomery brothers or a few ranch hands? The hands were in and out of the kitchen at various times throughout the day. Although the killer would find her eventually, Emma didn't want to make his job easier by appearing in public.

She eased closer and listened. David, Caleb, and Elliot. Breathing easier, she walked into the kitchen. Conversation ceased.

David came to her and cupped her cheek. "Feel better?" he murmured.

She nodded. "Did you sleep at all?"

"Enough."

Her eyes narrowed. What did that mean? "David."

"I'm fine, Em."

"Are you hungry, dear?" Mrs. Grady asked her. "I have chicken salad and croissants, or I can make something else if you prefer."

She hugged the housekeeper. "Chicken salad sounds great. Thanks, Mrs. Grady."

"Iced tea all right?"

"Yes, ma'am. I can fix my lunch. You don't need to go to any trouble for me."

"Have a seat, dear." She waved her toward the table. "Preparing your plate will only take a minute."

David seated Emma, something that she'd missed over these long months. The Montgomery boys knew how to treat their women. She's been honored to count herself among that small, privileged number. Did David still place her in that elite category?

A moment later, Mrs. Grady set a plate in front of Emma that also contained a small bowl of fruit salad.

The housekeeper eyed Caleb and Elliot. "Don't you boys have something else to do?"

Caleb grinned. "Trying to get rid of us?"

"Yes. I think David and Emma need some time to themselves."

The two men placed their dishes in the dishwasher and made themselves scarce without argument. Emma knew they wouldn't be far away.

Mrs. Grady retrieved a bottle of water from the refrigerator and walked toward the back door. "I feel a need to work in my garden for the next hour or so." She closed the door behind herself.

Emma's lips curved. "Wow. I can clear a room in no time."

David chuckled.

After she took a bite of the croissant, he began to tell her about the calves and foals born in the past few weeks along with suggestions for their names, each one worse than the last. "You can't call a colt Spot," she protested. "That's a dog's name."

"It fits. He has spots." Humor gleamed in his eyes.

"You're just trying to rile me."

"Maybe."

Definitely. She was onto his game, especially when she looked down at her plate and realized her food was gone. He'd deliberately distracted her, and Emma had consumed every bite while he regaled her with ranch tales. "What about Spirit? You said he has a lot of spirit. The name seems appropriate."

"I'll think about it. What about the filly? She's beautiful and has delicate features." He winked at her. "Like you."

She was in so much trouble. David Montgomery was a charmer. "Eve."

"Perfect. I'll pass the names along to the ranch foreman and my brothers. Thanks for the suggestions." He stood and held out his hand. "Come with me. I have something to show you."

Curious, she followed him from the kitchen. "Are we going outside?" She was tired of being indoors. She'd been afraid of spending much time in the different communities the past few months. Everyone had cell phones, and Emma couldn't afford to have her face on social media.

"I have the next best thing in mind." Soon, he opened a door and stepped back to allow her to enter first.

Emma's breath caught in wonder at the transformation in front of her. What used to be his father's study was now a glassed-in wonderland of plants. "A solarium! When did you and your brothers install this?"

"The contractor started on it when we were deployed the last time."

About the time she'd been attacked and ended up in WITSEC. Sadness filled her at the changes she'd missed. This must be only one of many here and in town. While she'd remained in stasis, the world had moved on. "Did you have this done for Mrs. Grady?" The housekeeper, who was more of a surrogate mother to David and his brothers, loved plunging her hands into dirt and coaxing plants to grow.

Before answering, he led her to a bench in a small sitting area hidden from sight by the lush foliage. David wrapped his arm around her shoulders and relaxed against the back of the bench. "Mrs. Grady appreciates it, but she's not the reason we had the solarium installed."

"What is?"

"Not what. Who." He turned to her. "You're the reason I pushed the others to build this room."

"Why?" She drew in a deep breath, the scents reminding her of the hours she had enjoyed working in the yard and gardens at the Rocking M. David had built this beautiful haven for her? She was having a difficult time wrapping her mind around that knowledge. Why would he do this for her?

"You fell in love with the solarium design at the Lawn and Garden Show in Nashville. Remember?"

She glanced around the room, only now realizing that this solarium was exactly like the one she'd admired at that show. "Yes, of course. Why build this for me?"

He kissed her, the touch gentle yet thorough. When he drew back, he said, "I wanted you to have a sanctuary while I was deployed, a place to remind you of me and how much I care for you."

Her breath caught. "You created a safe haven for me."

"I didn't know another way to help you cope with pressure from your parents. I would have asked one of my brothers to watch over and protect you, but at the time, that wasn't possible."

No, they had also been deployed. She hugged him. "Thank you for the gift. I hope this indoor garden brought you peace when you left the military."

He remained silent.

When she leaned back to look into his eyes, her heart sank. "David?"

"I haven't been inside this room since it was completed," he admitted. "I had the solarium created for you. When I thought I lost you, I hurt too much to step inside. Every plant, every leaf, even the soil reminded me of you. Mrs. Grady refused to believe you were dead. She maintained everything until you returned."

Unable to help herself, Emma captured his mouth and set about showing him how much his gift meant to her. Several long minutes later, she broke the kiss and just held him. Her heart ached with the knowledge of how much he'd suffered. "I'm sorry I hurt you. I should have stood up to the Marshals and insisted on getting word to you. Please, forgive me."

"There's nothing to forgive, baby." David trailed his fingers down her cheek in a gentle caress. "The Marshals didn't give you a choice. They have rules in place for a reason. I'm grateful I have a second chance with you." His gaze searched hers. "If you still want to be with me." Uncertainty filled his eyes.

This was the discussion she'd been dreading. The women in Maple Valley thought the Montgomery boys were prime husband material. She couldn't imagine them letting David sit on the sidelines for more than a few months without trying to take her place in his life. Although he hadn't dated anyone since she disappeared, that didn't prevent his interest in another woman. David was honorable to the core. Emma didn't want him to resume their relationship because of an old promise between them. "Do you still want an exclusive dating relationship with me?"

"Yes." No hesitation.

"The women in Maple Valley must have pursued you while I was gone."

He snorted. "Is the sky blue? I felt like I had a target on my back. Every time I showed my face in public, at least one woman made it a point to extend an invitation for a meal or coffee. The interest was one-sided, Emma. I never considered accepting an invitation. I wasn't interested and didn't think it fair to lead them on when I knew the relationship would never go anywhere. What about you? Are you interested in an exclusive dating relationship with me after all these months?"

She smiled, the knots in her stomach unraveling. "Nothing would make me happier."

David relaxed. "Excellent. Now that you've returned to my life, I'm not letting you go. We stick together, no matter what."

Emma blinked. He couldn't mean that like it sounded. "What if I have to return to witness protection?"

"I'll go with you."

Stunned, she shook her head. "You can't. Your brothers and the citizens of Morgan County need you."

"My brothers are grown men who can take care of themselves and the county's needs. You're my priority."

"If I have to stay in protection, you can't see your brothers. I won't ask you to make that sacrifice."

"You're not asking. I'm telling you what I want. As for not seeing my family, all of us are Special Forces. We'll find a way to see each other." He started to say more, but his cell phone rang.

David glanced at the screen and scowled. He swiped his thumb across the surface and tapped the speaker button. "Yeah, Montgomery. You're on speaker."

"Where's Ms. Tucker?" Craig Jordan demanded.

"I'm here," Emma said. Agent Jordan didn't sound happy.

"The Butcher made contact. He sent you a message."

CHAPTER SEVEN

David's hand tightened around his cell phone until the plastic groaned. "When?"

"Not sure. The timeline is murky. Sometime after she escaped from her safe house."

Murky? David scowled. He had to be kidding. Jordan was a senior agent with the FBI. Their pockets were much deeper than David's county budget. How could they not be able to nail down a timeline?

"What did he say?" Emma asked, voice shaky.

He wrapped his arm around her and tucked her closer to his side. If he could, he'd shield her from this latest move in the game. Since that wasn't possible, all he could do at the moment was offer support.

The sound of paper shuffling came through the speaker. "He said, 'No more playing nice. Next time I won't miss.'"

David's jaw tightened. "You checked traffic and security cams in the area?"

"Waiting on a warrant."

Emma didn't have time to wait for the feds to wade through red tape. The Butcher was a threat to Emma's safety as well as anyone around her. David knew he'd have a battle on his hands to stay with her. His girlfriend would sacrifice herself to keep him and those he loved safe. She'd already given up more than a year of her life for that reason. He wouldn't let her give more. He needed the information now. "I might be able to find the information we need."

"Legally?"

"You sure you want me to answer that question?"

A growl. "I have to be able to use information we gain in court, as you well know."

"Keep pushing for the warrant. I'll see what I can find out on my end." He paused, then asked the question he knew Emma wanted answered. "Any survivors this morning?"

"You know the answer to that question. We lost four good men today. Tell me what happened again. We need a lead to help us bring closure to their families."

Although skeptical, David complied with the request, repeating the sequence of events along with his observations.

Jordan sighed. "Ms. Tucker, what did you see?"

"Nothing."

A pause. "What do you mean, nothing? The vehicle exploded in your line of sight."

"In David's line of sight, not mine. He asked me to sit on the floor until we were out of the city. My view this morning consisted of carpet and a very handsome driver."

"Please," the agent muttered. "That's just embarrassing."

She smiled. "Which part? The carpet or the driver description?"

David chuckled.

"Now you're just messing with me," Jordan complained. "All right, Montgomery. I'll push for a warrant. Troll your sources for information. If you find something, I need a trail to follow that will hold up in court. Understand?"

"Copy that." David ended the call. "You okay?" he asked the woman in his arms.

She shook her head. "The Marshals died to keep me safe. I feel so bad for their families."

He tightened his arms. "They were doing their jobs."

"They paid dearly for it, and now, so will their wives, children, parents, and siblings. I can't believe someone hates me enough to want me dead."

"Hate's the wrong word. He's afraid of you and what you might remember. Because of the fear, he wants to eliminate the threat that you might talk."

"But I didn't see enough."

"You saw more than you remember, and your subconscious is protecting you until you're ready to deal with the truth. That's one reason he wants you dead."

"There are more reasons?"

Yeah, there was at least one more, a reason Emma wasn't ready to hear. Soon, though. "Perhaps."

She stared. "If your intention was to make me feel better, you failed. So, what sources do you plan to tap for information?"

"I know two men who might be able to get what we need."

"Call them."

"The information won't be obtained through legal channels," he warned. He should feel guilty about that since he was in law enforcement. He didn't. Jordan could have the collar. All David wanted was Emma's safety.

"I don't consider that a problem," she said, "but you and Agent Jordan will. I want this man stopped so no other innocents are murdered. I want to go to the movies with you, take walks in the rain, and talk on the phone with you overnight when you're running patrols." She rested her head against his chest. "I don't want to be afraid anymore,

David. I don't know what it means to sleep the whole night now. Every unexplained noise has me reaching for my Go bag, ready to dive out a window or into an escape tunnel. That's no way to truly live."

"We'll get there." He watched her a moment, hating what he'd have to put her through in the next few minutes. If it wasn't necessary, he would find another way to obtain the information he needed. He'd already studied the police report on the Tuckers' deaths. Local law enforcement had conveniently neglected to mention the woman who lived to tell the tale, no doubt a favor to the FBI to protect their only surviving witness. Delaying the inevitable, however, wouldn't aid either of them. "Tell me about the day the Butcher attacked you and your family."

She flinched. "Why?"

"I have questions only you can answer."

"Some witness I am. I can't remember the critical piece of information that would set me free and lead to the capture of a demented killer."

He captured her lips in a soft kiss. "Please, tell me what happened."

Emma sighed. "Where do I start?"

"When you first woke up that morning. Run me through your day. I'll stop you when I need clarification." Knowing she would need the beauty surrounding her to get through her recitation of events, David gently turned Emma at an angle so she faced the foliage while her back rested against his chest. He wrapped his arms around her waist. "Is this okay?"

She nodded and relaxed against him.

"Did you sleep in that morning?" he prompted to get her started.

A short laugh escaped. "Fat chance of that. Dad wouldn't allow any of us to sleep later than six and insisted that we eat breakfast promptly at 6:30. I didn't miss that when I moved into my apartment."

David kissed the side of her neck, offering silent comfort at the difficult memories. James Tucker had been a hard taskmaster. Even when Emma moved out on her own after she graduated from college, her father still treated her as though she lived under his roof, expecting her to toe the line any time he demanded. She would have blown him off if it hadn't been for her younger sister. Born twelve years after Emma, her sister had graduated from high school weeks before she died. Anne had begged Emma to go on the family vacation to the beach, probably as a buffer between her and James. Anne and her father hadn't gotten along. And Marian Tucker, Emma's mother, hadn't been strong enough to stand against her husband's wishes or his fists. "I'm sorry. Doesn't sound like much fun. Vacations are supposed to be a change of pace from the norm."

"Not in my father's eyes. I would have been awake early that morning anyway. Seagull Island was hosting a festival that day, and Anne wanted an early start to see all the offerings from the vendors. The booths were up and running by 9:00 a.m. She and I had planned to purchase breakfast from the vendors, but Dad vetoed that plan."

"Let me guess. He said it was a waste of money."

Emma sighed. "Everything was a waste of his money except for what he wanted. Anne and I decided to eat enough to satisfy him, then I would purchase our food from the street vendors while we were at the festival."

"Smart. You got him off your backs and still let Anne sample food." He kissed the side of her neck, smiling when she shivered in his arms. "Any problems before you left for the festival?" When she stiffened, David waited her out in silence.

"How did you know?"

"I knew your dad." He tightened his hold. "Did he hurt you?"

She shook her head.

Even though she described events that took place more than a year earlier, David breathed easier. "You can tell me the truth, Em." Her father was out of his reach.

"I am. Dad was afraid to lay a hand on me after your confrontation with him before your last deployment."

Excellent news. When he'd been home on leave, David had gotten into James's face after he'd discovered the bruise on Emma's side. She'd stretched to reach a bowl on a high shelf, causing her shirt to ride up and revealing the injury. After much persuasion, she had admitted to stepping between her father and Anne when he'd gone after the younger girl. Since James hadn't touched Emma the last morning of his life, that left either her mother, Marian, or Anne. "Who did he hit?"

A soft sigh. "Mom. The coffee wasn't to his liking."

"How did you stop him?" Once James started beating on his wife or daughters, he couldn't stop.

"Threatened to call the police and leak his arrest to the Maple Valley gossips."

"How did he take it?"

"About like you'd expect. He threatened to throw me out of the beach house if I interfered with him disciplining his family again. The threat was without teeth, though. He knew I would follow through on my threat."

That didn't sound like enough of a deterrent to force James to back off. "What else did you threaten him with?"

She gave a short laugh. "The only person he was afraid of. You. I told him if he didn't stop, you would have another conversation with him and this time, he'd be the one with bruises and cracked ribs."

Satisfaction flooded him. "I would have done more than that, and your father knew it."

"What did you tell Dad when you talked to him? He wouldn't even tell Mom what you said."

He hesitated, concerned about how she'd react. But if their relationship was going to last for the long haul, she needed to understand and accept the lengths he would go to in protecting her. "I told him that if he ever laid a hand on you in anger again, I would kill him and bury the body where no one would ever find it."

She was silent for a long moment, motionless. "Did you mean what you said?"

"Given how I feel about you, do you need me to answer that question?"

Emma tilted her head to lean against his. "He must have believed you because he didn't touch me after you talked to him."

"I'm sorry I wasn't able to protect you more, Emma. I should have been here for you." He'd spent years protecting his country, yet he'd failed to safeguard one of the most important people in his life.

"Don't, David. None of that was on you. I should have found the courage to speak up before and stop him."

"You moved out to protect yourself and did your best to protect Anne, offering her shelter whenever James was on a rampage. Your sister wouldn't let you call the police, would she?"

"She didn't want people in town or her friends to find out. She begged me not to tell. That's why Anne spent so much time at the homes of her friends or my apartment."

"You made her life more bearable and provided her with a safe haven. So, James went after Marian that last morning. You threatened him with the police and me, and he backed down. What happened after that?"

"Anne and I left the beach house and walked to the middle of town where the festivities were taking place."

"What time did you arrive?"

"Does it matter?"

"I'm gathering facts. I don't know what's important and what's not. Details add to the total picture and might help us break the case wide open."

"We helped Mom clean the kitchen and make a fresh pot of coffee, then left. We walked about an hour so I think we arrived in Seagull around 10:00. I didn't look at the time."

She and her sister had walked for an hour? He scowled, thinking about the risk to their safety. "Why didn't you drive?"

"Dad wouldn't let us use the car."

Of course he wouldn't. James would drive himself wherever he wanted to go, but wouldn't think twice about inconveniencing his family or putting them in danger. David had seen the same behavior when he and Emma were in school together. At the time, he'd assumed her dad was tightfisted with money. When he figured out what was happening inside that house, David recognized the behavior as a control mechanism. He wanted his wife and daughters to feel helpless.

He nuzzled Emma's neck. Instead of feeling cowed, his girl had used that frustration to fuel her plans to escape her father's tyranny. "Go on," he murmured, his lips brushing her petal-soft skin.

Emma drew in a sharp breath. "You're distracting me."

"Am I?" Another kiss. "What did you and your sister do when you arrived in Seagull?"

"Visited every booth. Anne enjoyed herself. She bought inexpensive gifts for her friends and one for herself to remind her of the trip."

"Where did she get the money?" He had a pretty good idea. James wouldn't hand over money for souvenirs.

"I gave her money as a graduation gift. We took our time visiting all the booths and food vendors." She gave a soft laugh. "By the time we left, both of us were ready to pop we'd eaten so much."

"Sounds like a fun day. What time did you leave the festival?"

"Five. Dad decided that we were having dinner at 8:00 that night. I thought it would be plenty of time to get back and help Mom with food preparation."

"You must have arrived at the beach house around 6:00. Did anything catch your attention when you were walking back?"

Emma glanced at him, a puzzled expression on her face. "How did you know?"

"A lucky guess." The serial killer must have locked onto Emma while she and Anne walked around Seagull.

"A car seemed to be keeping pace with us until I looked back. The vehicle turned off onto another road a block later."

"Did you see it again?"

"I think so, but I convinced myself that it was a coincidence. You wouldn't believe how many black cars I saw on Seagull Island." She looked at David. "Was the driver the serial killer?"

"It's possible. Then again, black cars abound in the US. You might have been right to think it was a coincidence." He didn't think that was the case, though.

More important, if he was very lucky, his computer friends might be able to locate traffic cam footage showing the vehicle that trailed Emma and Anne. If he was right, the killer had stalked Emma, trailing her to the beach house and her family.

CHAPTER EIGHT

"What happened when you arrived at the beach house?" David asked. He tucked Emma closer to his chest when she started to tremble.

"Mom was in the kitchen, peeling potatoes. Cupcakes were in the oven, and a roast simmered in the crockpot. I remember thinking the food smelled terrific."

"Where was James?"

"Asleep in front of the television while Mom worked on dinner."

"Typical," he murmured. James also hated to repair anything around the house. When David began dating Emma, he had completed repairs at the Tucker house when he was home on leave.

"Dad wanted cupcakes for dessert, not the lemon pound cake Anne requested for her birthday dinner. Mom didn't have all the ingredients to make the icing Dad preferred."

Since Marian didn't know how to drive and James wouldn't go to town unless he wanted something for himself, Emma must have gone back to Seagull. She wouldn't have wanted Anne to risk her father's anger by leaving the house without his permission. "James wasn't satisfied with store-bought icing?"

She shook her head. "He told Mom frequently that her only talents were cooking and cleaning, so she worked hard to keep the house perfect and provide meals that rivaled a professional chef's."

Hearing that stoked David's anger at her father. His own father had treated his mother like a princess. Although David was young when his mother died, he remembered the deep love and respect his parents had for each other. After she was gone, his father continued to speak of David's mother the same way, sharing stories and teaching his sons how to treat their own wives if they married one day.

"I didn't want Mom or Anne to have another run-in with Dad, so I volunteered to go back to town for the ingredients Mom needed. I drove the car. If I walked, I wouldn't have made it back in time for Mom to finish dinner on time. I hoped Dad would be too afraid I'd follow through on my threat if he hit Anne and Mom while I was gone."

"Did anything catch your attention when you drove to town, like the black car showing up again?"

"I didn't notice anything."

Perhaps the killer parked a short distance away from the Tucker beach house and missed Emma driving to town. "No problems on the way back?"

Another head shake. She fell silent.

He gave her a minute, then said softly, "Finish it, Em."

"There's not much more I can tell you."

"When you parked in the driveway, did you notice anything off? A car that didn't belong in the neighborhood or someone watching the house?"

"I didn't pay attention. I wanted Mom to have the ingredients she needed so Dad wouldn't go ballistic."

"Close your eyes."

"Why?"

"Trust me."

After a quick glance at him, Emma turned around again and complied. "Now what?"

"Let your mind drift back to that afternoon. Let the memories surface naturally. What did you think about on the return trip to the beach house?"

"I needed to be back before Dad woke up and realized I'd taken the car. He would have been furious with me and even more angry at Mom for allowing me to do it."

"What else?"

She pressed her back tighter to his chest. "You."

David smiled. "Good thoughts, I hope."

"I remember thinking how much I missed you, that you would have been right at home on the beach and manning the grill for dinners instead of Mom and I doing all the cooking. You had only been gone for a month, but it felt like a lifetime since I'd seen you. I had 42 days left until my flight to San Diego."

He kissed the rim of her ear. "I was counting down the days, too. What happened once you arrived at the beach house?"

"I climbed the stairs to the beach house." Her muscles tightened.

"Describe the house." If he didn't distract her, she'd freeze up and give him what she told the feds. He needed more.

She relaxed again. "The house was three stories. Dad didn't want his bedroom on the same level as mine and Anne's. The house's exterior was mint green, a color Dad despised, but no other rental was available at the same price. A balcony circled the house, connecting to the deck at the back. Stairs led from the deck to the sand."

"You had a beachfront house."

"It was beautiful. I walked the beach every morning and evening, wishing you were with me to enjoy the beauty and peace."

"I'd have enjoyed being anywhere with you. Instead, I was stuck in the Sand Box where the temperature hit 120 on a cool day. So, you climbed the stairs. At the top, what did you do?"

"Opened the door. The lights were out, and the house smelled like Mom burned the cupcakes. I remember thinking the house was as silent as a tomb. Turned out I was right."

"What else?"

"Something smelled really bad, and a copper scent filled the air. I was too slow to catch on to the truth, but I was concerned with checking the cupcakes and wondering if a return trip to the store was coming. I set the bag on the counter and checked the cupcakes. They were black when I pulled them from the oven. Since Dad wasn't shouting at Mom, I assumed he was still asleep."

Would have been unusual if he'd slept through that. James had been passionate about food.

"I looked for Mom, wondering if she fell asleep or stepped out on the deck and lost track of time."

When she didn't continue, he said, "You found her."

Emma's breath hitched. "She was in the bedroom. Blood was everywhere."

He turned Emma and urged her to rest her head against his shoulder. "Shh. Take a break. While we've been separated, did you sail or surf?"

Emma pressed her damp face against his neck. "I didn't want to do either without you."

"When this is over, we'll plan a vacation where we can surf and sail."

"Scuba diving, too?"

He smiled. "We'll have to do a few diving lessons first."

"Sounds like fun."

"It is." Under the right circumstances. When he'd been an active-duty SEAL, his underwater swims were completed at night. Stateside, he dived as much as possible and loved it. Sharing one of his favorite pastimes with Emma would be a treat. "I think you'll like it."

"I'm not a good swimmer, David."

"I remember. I'll be with you the entire time." He fell silent, holding Emma until her trembling ceased. After giving her a few more minutes of peace, he kissed her temple. "Ready to continue?"

A slight nod.

"You found your Mom. What did you do?"

"I checked for a pulse, but didn't find one. I thought Dad killed her. Then I started to worry about Anne and hoped she had escaped Dad's rampage and gone for help."

"You didn't believe that."

She sighed. "No. If Dad had attacked Mom that viciously, Anne would have tried to stop him."

"You looked for her next?"

"We had two bedrooms connected by a bathroom. I found her in the bathroom. Anne tried to run from the killer into my room, but he caught her before she escaped."

He thought about that a minute. "Was there an exit to the outside from your room?"

A nod. "She was fifteen feet from freedom and safety."

"What did you do next?"

"Grabbed my cell phone and called the police." Her arms tightened around his waist. "My first instinct was to call you."

Man, that hurt. Regret filled him. "I'm sorry, baby. I should have been there for you."

"In a way, you were."

"How do you figure that?"

"The only way I could function was to ask myself what you would do. Anyway, the dispatcher told me to get out of the house." She stopped again.

"Did you?"

The trembling resumed. "I heard a noise. I started to turn, and someone hit me. The blow knocked me to the ground. A baseball bat landed on the ground beside me. I looked up and saw a man dressed in black, a bloody knife in his hand. I must have passed out because the next thing I remember was waking up in the ER with a medical team working on me."

"Are you still seeing a black circle where his face is supposed to be?"

She nodded. "I'm sorry."

"You're doing great, Em. Ignore his face. Close your eyes, and focus on his hands. What do you see besides the knife? What color is his skin?"

"He was Caucasian. He had a scar on the webbing between the thumb and forefinger of his right hand and a tattoo."

David frowned and pulled his phone from his pocket. He did a quick search and showed her the screen. "Did you see something like this?"

She shifted. A second later, she gasped. "That's it. How does the killer have the same scar?"

He urged her to lay her head against his shoulder again. "It's called a shark bite, an injury that occurs when people hold a pistol improperly, and the slide catches the webbing on the recoil. If the cut is deep enough, it leaves a scar like that one."

"Great. He's handy with guns as well as baseball bats and knives."

David slid his phone away, then trailed his hand up and down her back. "Was your head wound bad?"

"Not really. I lost a lot of blood from the knife wounds."

He stilled. "The killer stabbed you?"

"Twice."

"Where?"

"My left side and just below my collar bone. According to Agent Jordan, the Butcher was just getting started when he was scared off by the police sirens."

Oh, man. He'd come close to losing her forever that night. David tightened his hold on Emma. "Thank God they arrived in time."

"When I woke up in the ER, I couldn't remember anything that happened. The pain in my head was horrible, and I kept throwing up. The next few hours are a blur. Sometime during the night, the doctor allowed the police to question me. The police detective told me that Dad was dead, too, and the FBI were sending agents to talk to me. I was so sick and weak I didn't understand half of what he told me. After the doctor asked the detective to leave, he gave me pain medicine."

"I'm so sorry you went through that alone, Emma."

She swiped at her tears. "The FBI should have caught this man before that night. If they had, I'd still have my sister and parents."

"The killer will pay for what he did. When did the feds arrive?"

"Sunrise. I remember wishing that Anne could see the beautiful start to another day at the beach. It would have been our last full day. We were scheduled to return to Maple Valley the following day."

"Do you remember which agents came to see you?"

"Agent Jordan and another man. I don't remember his name. He was nice to me, though."

"Is that when you heard about the serial killer?"

She nodded. "Agent Jordan said I needed to go to a safe house because the killer would be furious I was still alive. I had never heard of the Butcher."

"The feds have kept him out of the news cycles." They might receive tips from the public if they spread the word.

"How long were you in the hospital?"

"Three days. The FBI wanted to move me sooner, but the doctor wouldn't release me. While I was there, Jordan assigned two agents for guard duty, one in my room and one in the hall."

He'd have done the same in Jordan's place. If David had been stateside, he would have been in the room with Emma.

"Having an agent inside my room was uncomfortable. I had trouble sleeping and woke up screaming more than once."

Oh, man. "Nightmares or memories?"

"Both, I think. I repeatedly dreamed that a man dressed in black was coming for me, but his face was always in shadow."

"You said the killer had a tattoo."

"The design was on his forearm. I've tried to remember what it was, but I can't. It's a blank. I just know he had one."

"They're pretty common. Many people have body art these days."

"Do you?"

He snorted. "Are you kidding? Mrs. G would have my hide."

"A lot of military personnel have them."

"Wearing a tattoo wouldn't have been wise while I was on the Teams. A tattoo could have identified me as American, and we spent a lot of time in countries that didn't appreciate American efforts to fight terrorism."

"After you left the military, you came home."

"Where Mrs. G waited for me. I didn't want to upset her, and you know I'm not a fan of needles." He threaded the fingers of one hand through her hair. "I also didn't know if you liked tattoos. I respected your opinion enough to ask before I did something that couldn't be undone."

"I'm a blessed woman."

David kissed her temple. "I'm the most blessed man on the planet to have you in my life. Did the man who attacked you say anything?"

Emma hesitated. "He did, but I couldn't focus. I can almost hear his words when I dream about the attack."

"Your brain is trying to untangle the garbled words. Pushing to remember won't help."

She sighed. "Easy for you to say. You don't know how frustrating this is. I want to help Agent Jordan so I can get my life back."

"We'll help Jordan find the killer." He grimaced.

Emma laughed. "Bet that hurt, didn't it?"

"You have no idea. Special Agent in Charge Craig Jordan is my least favorite fed."

At that moment, Caleb called out from the doorway, "David, you in here?"

"What do you need?"

"We have a problem."

CHAPTER NINE

Emma straightened. Caleb's voice indicated a serious issue. Was the problem related to David's job as sheriff or her stalker?

David stood and tugged Emma to her feet. They walked hand-in-hand to the door.

Caleb's eyebrows soared when he saw their clasped hands. David's brother wouldn't be the only person to express surprise when that she and David still felt the same about each other.

In truth, her feelings were stronger and prayed the serial killer wouldn't be the cause of another separation. Emma didn't want to be apart from David again.

"Sit rep," David ordered.

"The gate guard reported that a delivery service dropped off a package at the guard house." He inclined his head toward Emma. "The package is addressed to Em." Caleb held up his hand. "I already warned Rex to keep his mouth shut. He swore he'd keep quiet."

"Do you trust him?" Emma asked. The last thing she wanted was to endanger Mrs. G and the Montgomery brothers. If word spread that she was here, she would draw the killer to the Rocking M. Her stomach knotted. Someone knew she was here. Was that someone the killer?

David squeezed her hand. "He's loyal to the family."

"News of Emma's return will spread eventually," Caleb said.

"I know. Obviously, someone knows or suspects she's here."

"The question is, who? The feds or the killer?"

Emma shuddered. "I hope it's Agent Jordan."

David looked at her. "I'm not betting on it. Although my opinion of Jordan isn't high, I can't imagine him being stupid enough to send a package addressed to you to the ranch."

"What's in the package?" she asked Caleb.

"Haven't opened it yet." A wry smile formed. "The sheriff is a control freak. You should know that if you plan to date him."

David scowled at his brother.

Although Emma appreciated their attempt to lighten the mood, the need to see what was in the package for herself rode her hard. "Let's go."

They followed Caleb to the kitchen where Elliot waited. Mrs. Grady wasn't in the room. Elliot had probably sent the housekeeper to a different part of the house to protect her.

David stopped Emma before she walked into the kitchen. "I need you to wait in the living room until I'm sure it's safe."

Her gaze shifted to the package on the table. "You think there's a bomb inside?"

"I don't know. No one should know you're here except Jordan. That only leaves one other person who would suspect I brought you here."

She gripped his forearm. "Don't open it. Call the bomb squad."

He smiled. "My brothers and I are the closest thing to a bomb squad in this county." David bent and brushed her lips with his. "Don't worry. We all have some EOD training."

Some? Emma preferred to have the best bomb experts to handle the package instead of David and his brothers.

"I'll see what we have," David continued. "If we can't defuse the bomb, we'll move to Plan B."

"Do you have a Plan B?"

Caleb snorted. "We always have more than one plan."

David cupped her cheek. "Please, stay here."

"Be careful."

"Always." He trailed his thumb over her bottom lip. "I'm not giving up more time with you. The Butcher stole too much from us. He can't have more." David nudged her toward the living room. "I won't be long."

Emma retreated to the couch and perched on the edge of the seat, unable to relax while David was in harm's way on her account. Although she longed to see the contents of the package, she didn't want David or his brothers distracted at a crucial moment.

She considered who knew her location. David was right. Even Gigi, her best friend, still didn't know. That left the FBI, and the killer. The Butcher would look for her in Maple Valley. Since David and his brothers were law enforcement and trained by the military, Emma would turn to these men for help first.

She didn't trust Agent Jordan to maintain silence since keeping his team of agents in the loop meant sharing her location. Emma frowned. If Agent Jordan knew she was here. How would the agent know that information? David could have taken her somewhere off the grid.

Were they followed to the ranch? No, she decided. David would have noticed.

Finally, David returned, his expression grim.

Emma jumped to her feet. "Is there a bomb?"

"Come with me." He held out his hand and led her to the kitchen table. His brothers had similar expressions on their faces.

David wrapped his arm around her shoulders. "Don't touch anything. Although I doubt we'll find prints, we'll check anyway."

She glanced at the contents scattered on the table. No wires, cell phone, dynamite or other material a bomber might use. Only photos and a note typed in large font on plain white paper.

"Read the note first, then we'll examine the photos together." David seated her, then sat in the chair beside hers.

With a gloved hand, Elliot nudged the note toward her. Emma read the short message, her eyes widening. "I'm coming for you, little mouse. You won't escape," she read aloud. "Not very original, is he?"

"Does the name 'little mouse' mean anything to you?" David asked.

"It's an insult."

"Calling you 'little mouse' is a reminder that he's the hunter and you're his prey," Elliot said.

"I prefer my explanation."

A spark of humor lit his eyes. "I don't see you as a mouse, Emma. You're a survivor. Kudos to you for that."

"Thanks."

He nodded and slid the note into a plastic bag to protect it.

"Photos next, Em." David motioned to the first of four photos Caleb pushed toward her.

Emma clamped a hand over her mouth, shock and a hefty dose of fear rolling through her body. How had the killer slipped into her bedroom while she slept or took a picture without her being aware of it? She'd followed the Marshals' rules and kept the curtains closed at the safe houses.

"Where was this taken?" David prompted.

"My first safe house. I recognize the lamp on the nightstand." She turned to David. "How did he get this picture? The marshals were with me, and I didn't open the curtains."

"What about the next picture?"

"The second safe house. I hated that wall clock. The constant ticking noise drove me crazy and made it almost impossible to fall asleep every night. I took the clock down a few days before the marshals moved me."

"And the third?"

"Every photo was taken at a different safe house. I don't understand, David. He found me and took pictures of me sleeping. Why didn't he kill me?" Emma shuddered again.

He drew her against his side. "An excellent question I intend to ask Jordan."

She stared at the photos again. "If the killer wanted to toy with me, why didn't he send me the pictures in the mail at the safe houses? I was with the marshals at the first house. After that, they gave me new identities and took me to the new place overnight. They were careful not to be followed."

"Not careful enough," Elliot said. He inclined his head toward the photos. "There's the evidence."

David frowned, but didn't dispute his brother's comment. "Bag and tag the evidence. I want these processed as soon as possible."

Caleb's lips curved. "Before we turn it over to Jordan?"

"Of course."

"He won't be happy."

"Do I look like I care?'

His brothers chuckled.

"I need to update Jordan, then call a friend to request technical help with security and traffic cam footage. Get going. I have the watch."

"I'll go." Caleb pushed back from the table and stood. "Elliot will stay. You need one of us here for backup." He gathered the bagged evidence and left.

Elliot rose. "I'll be in the security room, watching the monitors." After a glance at Emma, he left the room.

"Mrs. Grady is in her apartment," David said. "If you tell her your sizes, she'll be glad to pick up clothes for you."

"I'd appreciate that." She desperately wanted to change into fresh clothes. "Would she mind buying basic toiletries, too?"

"I doubt it, but we'll ask." He knocked on Mrs. Grady's door.

When she opened it, she asked, "Everything all right out there?"

"Nothing dangerous. A note and pictures. Do you have time to do Emma a favor?"

"Of course. What do you need, dear?"

"A few changes of clothes and basic toiletries. I hate to ask, but I had to leave everything behind."

The older woman grabbed a notepad and pen. "Write down your sizes and what you need. I'll take care of it for you."

Emma completed the list and handed it to Mrs. Grady with a hug. "Thank you. I have money to pay for everything."

David trailed his hand down Emma's back. "I have it covered. Use the ranch credit card, Mrs. G."

"I'll be back soon." Mrs. Grady grabbed her handbag.

"We'll be in the solarium. If we have to relocate before you return, I'll tell you where to meet us."

Relocate? Emma's heart sank. Would she have to go on the run again?

CHAPTER TEN

David hated the expression of fear on Emma's face. He knew the killer would find them, but this fast? Either Jordan had a leak in his unit or the Marshals had loose lips. Either way, he intended to locate and plug the leak.

He dropped a light kiss on Emma's mouth. "Come on. We have calls to make."

With his hand pressed against her lower back, David guided Emma to the solarium. When they returned to the bench, he contacted Craig Jordan, placing the call on speaker.

"Yeah, Jordan." The FBI agent sounded distracted.

"It's Montgomery. Can you talk?"

"Hold." The agent's voice became muffled as he spoke to someone nearby. After a moment, he returned. "Go."

"We have a problem."

"Is she safe?"

"Yes."

"What happened?"

"A package was delivered, addressed to your witness." While David's phone was encrypted, he didn't know what safety measure Jordan had on his own cell phone. He refused to confirm Emma's whereabouts with a careless word.

Jordan swore.

David scowled. "Watch your language. You're on speaker."

"Sorry," the other man muttered, sounding insincere. "I'll leave Nashville as soon as I can. Don't touch the package."

David rolled his eyes. "Get real, Jordan. I'm a cop. I'm not leaving a suspicious package sit unopened in my house."

"Are you out of your mind? A bomb could be in there."

"Could have been, but wasn't. And before you ask, I took precautions not to contaminate evidence. The killer sent a note and photos. I'll send you copies." He expected a verbal explosion and wasn't disappointed. More ripe cursing from the special agent. "Last warning, Jordan. Control your mouth or this call ends, and I'll be less cooperative with the next piece of information."

"Fine," he snapped. "Don't send me copies of anything, Montgomery. I'm coming to examine the evidence and send it to the FBI lab for analysis. Don't mess with the evidence. Don't breathe on it or touch it. Am I clear?"

"Crystal."

"Where are you?"

"The ranch."

A loud groan from the fed. "I can't believe you took my witness there. That's the first place the killer would look for her, obviously."

"And yet he didn't touch her, did he?"

"You should have chosen a place off the grid."

"That plan didn't work well for you and the Marshals."

"What does that mean?"

"Do you need me to spell it out for you?"

A growl. "I should take my witness into protective custody."

"Try it." Although soft, David's voice held an underlying layer of steel. "You'll regret it."

"Are you threatening me, Montgomery?"

"I'm explaining the facts. You aren't taking her." Not without him. "If you want the evidence, you better hurry. Otherwise, it might end up in a private lab."

More swearing as the call ended.

Emma leaned her head against David's shoulder. "Agent Jordan is furious." She sounded worried.

"I meant what I said, baby. He's not taking you."

"Will he cause you trouble?"

"He'll try. Your safety is my first priority. It should be his."

"Maybe I should return to witness protection."

"After seeing the pictures the killer sent, it's obvious you aren't safe in WITSEC."

"What should we do?"

"We have two options. Run and hide, or stand and fight."

"I can guess, but tell me your choice."

"Stand and fight. I may have to choose a different battlefield to protect our employees, but we should stand and fight." He cupped her cheek. "I can and will protect you, Emma. If you trust me, I won't let you down."

"I do trust you, but don't destroy your law enforcement career to stand against Agent Jordan. There's animosity between you two."

Understatement, that. "That won't end soon. Our focus is on catching the Butcher instead of catering to Jordan." David wanted Emma safe, no matter what path that took.

"How long before the FBI arrives?"

"Depends on whether Jordan follows the posted speed limit. Ninety minutes or less."

"Will he come alone?"

"Not a chance. Jordan always travels with at least one other agent." David searched his contact list and called the man he hadn't expected to talk to this soon.

A moment later, a deep voice said, "Maddox."

"It's David Montgomery, sir."

A slight pause. "Changed your mind about working for me?"

Emma's eyes widened.

David stroked her hair. "You're on speaker. I haven't made a decision yet."

"I'll wear you down. I need you and your brothers, and I'll make it worth your while. You have skills Fortress needs. We could call you the M team."

David chuckled. "Nice. I'll keep that in mind."

"What do you need, David?"

"Tech help."

"Talk to me."

He summarized what he needed and why. "Would one of your techs have time to conduct an online search?"

"I'll have someone contact you soon. Anything else?"

Although he hated to ask, David swallowed his pride and requested the help he needed to take care of his woman. "I need help protecting Emma. My brothers will back me up, but the citizens of Morgan County count on us to protect them, too. I can't leave them without enough law enforcement coverage. We can juggle job responsibilities and Emma's protection detail, but aside from my brothers, the deputies aren't trained to deal with a serial killer."

"I understand. Expect a Fortress team soon."

Tension leached from his muscles. Maddox never broke a promise. "Thanks. I only need two operatives to relieve so I can sleep or cover a work shift."

"A team will contact you soon. Anything else?"

"No, sir. Thanks for the assistance."

"I still owe you for your help two months ago, and I pay my debts. Think about working for me part-time. I'll work it so your team is deployed a few days a month." David's mouth curved. "Yes, sir."

"I expect an answer after you take down your man. Later." Maddox ended the call.

"Who is Maddox?" Emma asked.

"Brent Maddox is the CEO of Fortress Security, an elite black ops firm specializing in hostage rescue and counter-terrorism. Fortress also has a bodyguard training school, and sells and installs security systems."

Emma frowned. "I've never heard of it."

"Not surprising. They don't advertise."

"How does the company survive without advertising?"

"Word of mouth recommendations only. Maddox's teams are the best in the black ops community and in high demand. They don't need to advertise."

"How did you hear about them?"

"Maddox is a SEAL, and the spec ops community is close knit. I heard about Maddox and his company before I left the Navy."

"Did you apply for a job with Fortress when you came home?"

He smiled. "Maddox doesn't accept applications. The only way into Fortress is for Maddox to ask you to come in for an interview."

"And he wants you and your brothers to interview with him. Will you do it?"

"I'm busy at the moment." He sent her a meaningful glance. He'd missed so much time with Emma, and he wouldn't leave her until she was safe.

"You won't always be distracted with my situation. Do you want to work for Fortress?"

His smile faded. The idea would be a dream come true except for two things. One, he loved his job as sheriff. Keeping Morgan County citizens safe was a high honor.

Two, he didn't want to cause Emma undue stress with his absences. As a Fortress employee, he'd spend more time away from Emma. His responsibilities as sheriff didn't fit into traditional office hours. He'd lost count of the number of nights he got off shift late because of a crisis or paperwork. "Would it bother you if I accepted the job?"

"I want you to be happy, David. If working for Fortress is what you want, go for it."

"I'll be gone for a few days each month."

"If the Butcher is behind bars, I'll be safe. If he's still loose, you can arrange protection for me while you're gone."

If the Butcher was still free and looking for Emma, David wouldn't accept Fortress missions. Trusting her safety to someone else wasn't happening.

He couldn't make the decision now. Other factors were at play along with other people to consult before he could decide.

David wouldn't let Emma slip from his life again. If him doing black ops work a few days a month distressed her, he'd refuse the offer.

Another factor in accepting the offer was his brothers' agreement to join him. The Montgomerys were a team. He trusted them to have his back just as he would have theirs. If his brothers refused the offer, so would David. "I haven't decided yet, but if you don't want me to take the job, I'll refuse the offer without discussing the option with my brothers."

She brushed her lips over his. "I handled your deployments for months at a time as a SEAL. I'll deal with absences for a few days a month. The only thing I want is for you to be happy."

"You make me happy," he murmured, and captured her mouth in a series of long, deep, drugging kisses. His hand cradled the back of her head. Man, he adored this woman.

When he lifted his head, Emma moaned. "No, not yet."

He started to lower his head for more pulse-pounding kisses when his phone rang. He sighed. Lousy timing.

David checked the readout on his screen. A blocked number. Had to be someone from Fortress. He swiped his thumb across the screen and hit the speaker button. "Montgomery."

"Zane Murphy. Maddox asked me to help with online searches, Sheriff."

"It's David, and you're on speaker with Emma."

"Hello, Emma."

"Hi, Zane. Thanks for helping us."

"Glad to do it. The boss tells me you're a tough lady."

She drew in a sharp breath. "Really?"

"He says exactly what he means, Emma. David, how can I help?"

David summarized what had happened since Emma's family was attacked at the beach. "This guy keeps finding Emma even when the Marshals gave her a new identity and moved her to another location. I need to capture the killer before he finishes this sick game or crawls into a hole so deep I won't find him until he strikes at us or another innocent person. How much of a rule follower are you?"

A short laugh. "I was a SEAL, like you. We get the job done however we have to. I'll never admit that I enjoy beating the feds' online security, but if you want me to hack their databases, I'm in."

David smiled. "Good. I need everything the FBI has on the Butcher. SAC Jordan isn't sharing intel. His version of sharing is a one-way street."

"Craig Jordan?"

"Yeah. You know him?"

Murphy groaned. "Unfortunately. I'll be happy to copy his files on the Butcher. Tell me your email address." When David complied, the Fortress tech said, "I'll send everything to your email. What else do you need?"

He listed the addresses of Emma's safe houses. "Look for security or traffic cam footage at the safe houses and the beach house the Tuckers rented."

"I'm not sure I'll have much success with the beach house, but I'll try." Zane spouted off his phone number. "Add my number in your contact list. Text me if you think of anything else."

"Thanks."

"Yep. Later, David and Emma." He ended the call.

"Maddox doesn't mess around, does he?" Emma said. "Your call with him ended five minutes ago, but you already have tech help."

"He only hires the best." But was Zane the man for this job?

David's cell phone rang again. He frowned, glancing at the readout. Answering the call, he said, "Jon, how are you?"

"That's what I called to ask you. The boss said you needed help with a problem. What's going on?"

Relief flooded him. Maddox must have assigned Wolf Pack to help him protect Emma. "First, you're on speaker with Emma, my girlfriend." He explained what he needed and why.

A soft whistle. "Wolf Pack will be in Maple Valley in three hours unless you need us sooner."

"That's great. Thanks, Jon."

"I'll touch base with Zane before we load up and see if he needs a hand."

"You know him well?" He needed the best tech help available. The odds of Zane finding useful footage was slim. As for the FBI's information on the Butcher, if Zane wasn't able to find it, Jon could unearth the information for him.

"Oh, yeah. Zane has saved our hides more times than we can count. He's a tech and communication wizard. You're in great hands, but Z is in high demand by our teams. If a team is in a hot zone, he'll shift priorities and shuffle your search requests down the list. If I help with your research, we'll obtain results sooner. See you soon."

David sat back and hugged Emma. "Fast work, indeed."

"Who is Jon?"

"A fellow SEAL, legendary sniper, and skilled interrogator."

"He works for Fortress?"

He nodded. "Jon is a member of Wolf Pack, a team of SEALs. His team was in Maple Valley two months ago, and used a home nearby for a safe house. I'd trust those boys with my life and yours."

She smiled. "And you want to do what they do."

"Who wouldn't want the freedom to right a wrong or protect an innocent using skills the military taught us?" He stood and held out his hand. "Come with me."

"Where are we going?"

"For a short walk. It's a beautiful day, and I want to show you something you'll like."

"I thought you didn't want me to be seen around the ranch."

He nudged her toward the solarium's door leading to the backyard. "Apparently, the Butcher already knows. Besides, where I'm taking you, we're unlikely to run across anyone this time of day."

David escorted her to the closest barn. The hands were scattered around different parts of the ranch at the moment, leaving this barn empty. As they approached the door, soft whines and yips filled the air.

A smile curved his lips when he opened the door and ushered Emma inside the cavernous interior. The yips and whines grew louder.

"Puppies?"

He drew her with him to a stall where Daisy, one of their Blue Heelers, kept a close watch on her pups.

Emma grinned. "They're adorable. How old are they?"

"Seven weeks. You can have first pick of the litter." Two neighbors each wanted two dogs and didn't care which ones they received. That left the fifth pup for Emma.

Her face lit. "I always wanted a dog, but Dad wouldn't allow us to have pets. He said they were too expensive and too messy."

"They can be," he admitted. "Around a farm, though, working dogs are worth their weight in gold. Daisy is a skilled worker. She's about ready to return to the fields."

David sat on the floor with Emma and enjoyed watching her play with the puppies and cuddle them. After a long while, he asked, "Have you decided which dog you want?"

She nodded and picked up a puppy. "This sweet girl."

He snapped a picture of her with his phone. "Excellent choice. She's smart and has a good personality. She'll be good with kids, too. Do you have a name for her?"

"Not yet."

"Think about it and let me know your choice."

Emma gave him a sideways glance, eyes twinkling. "You'll let me name her?"

"She's yours. Why wouldn't I?"

"You don't know what name I'll choose. What if I pick something like Fluffy or Venus?"

He flinched. "Be a shame to saddle a great dog with a lame name."

She burst into laughter. "Very diplomatic, Sheriff Montgomery. Never fear. I promise to give this sweetheart a name worthy of her character."

He scratched the pup behind one ear. "I have another surprise for you."

Emma looked up. "What is it?"

David rose and tugged Emma to her feet. He led her to the back of the barn and opened the door to the fenced field. While he didn't want her out in the open, she wouldn't need to be exposed to see what he had for her. He'd prayed she was alive through those long, dark months. When her grandfather was murdered, David had nurtured her legacy.

From the barn doorway, Emma stared into the distance. Her eyes widened when she heard the soft bleating of sheep. Her eyes widened. "Sheep?" She spun. "Are those my sheep?"

He cupped her cheek. "I couldn't let your dream die." Even though every indication pointed to Emma's death, he'd refused to give up hope.

Emma threw her arms around his neck. "Thank you. You don't know how much I've missed working with my sheep and their wool." After a lengthy, deep kiss, she pulled back. "What about my equipment?"

"In storage. Your carding machine and spinning wheel are safe along with the table you used plus your washing set up."

Her eyes glazed with tears. "I don't know what to say," she choked out. "You had no reason to hold onto my equipment. I thought I would have to purchase new equipment when the FBI arrested the Butcher."

"When your grandfather died, I brought the sheep and equipment here for safekeeping."

"But everyone must have thought I was dead."

"Mr. Watts didn't, and until I found your body, I refused to believe it. Your grandfather left his house to you. My brothers and I made sure everything was kept up." He brushed his thumb over her bottom lip. "I had a professional cleaning company take care of the crime scene. You can visit the house when you're ready."

She pressed a gentle kiss to his mouth, sending his heart into overdrive. "I'm so blessed to have you in my life."

Before he could respond, his cell phone signaled an incoming message. David glanced at his screen and grimaced. "Time to face the music. The feds are here."

CHAPTER ELEVEN

David led Emma to the solarium entrance and locked the door behind them. He faced Emma. "You can rest for a while or just hide out for a while." He smiled. "I'm the one in trouble with the big, bad FBI agent, not you."

"Ha. Agent Jordan will want to see for himself that I'm alive and unhurt."

He would pressure Emma to go back into WITSEC. With the feds' lousy track record of safety breaches, that option wasn't one David would let her choose without him by her side. She would never be that vulnerable again. "If you don't want to see him, I won't let him near you."

"I'll be fine." She laid her hand on his chest. "I'm not made of spun glass. You don't have to protect me from Agent Jordan."

He kissed her gently. "You've never been fragile, baby. Otherwise, your home life would have broken you. Instead, you survived an abusive childhood as strong as steel. I want to protect you from unnecessary unpleasantness."

"We'll deal with Agent Jordan together."

After a lingering tender kiss, David escorted Emma to the kitchen where his brothers stood guard in front of the counter with the bagged contents of the package, barring Jordan and two other agents from confiscating the evidence without David's consent.

Fast work on Caleb's part to return to the ranch with the processed evidence. He gave a nod of appreciation to his brother who saluted. David's cop shop might not have the bottomless budget of the FBI, but they could hold their own with standard evidence processing. Anything more extensive would have to go to the state crime lab.

The three agents glared at David and Emma. "Who are these two idiots?" Jordan snapped. "I should arrest them for impeding my investigation."

"Meet two of my brothers, Caleb and Elliot. They're law enforcement as well." He waited a beat, then said, "Are you planning to introduce your cohorts?"

"Justin Wells and Phil Jones." He motioned to each man as he spat out the name. "Is this all of your siblings or should I expect more Montgomery brothers?" His tone was sour.

What game was he playing? Jordan must have run a background check on him when Emma joined WITSEC. Although he wouldn't have learned much about him, the FBI agent would know about his family. "Two more."

Jordan scowled, then inclined his head toward the evidence. "Is that everything?"

David's eyebrow rose. "Why would we withhold evidence? We're on the same team."

"Power play. Locals often throw their weight around and engage in a futile turf war."

Elliot snorted. "That's your game, not ours. Our mission is to protect Emma since you and your buddies can't seem to do the job."

"Explain that," Jordan snapped.

"Got you where it hurt, didn't he?" Caleb folded his arms.

"We have more experience than you do," Wells gritted out.

"Maybe in law enforcement."

He narrowed his eyes. "You're former military?"

"No such thing as former military."

"Let me guess. A jet jockey?"

The sneer in the agent's voice made the Montgomerys stiffen. "All of us were spec ops," Elliot said.

"Army grunts, I'll bet. All brawn, no brains."

Enough. David refused to discuss the details of their backgrounds. Jordan and his buddies would dig into their backgrounds before sunset. The feds wouldn't learn much, only enough to prove they were skilled warriors. Their missions were classified, most not even named.

Jordan scowled at David, then Emma. "These cowboys can't protect you. Only someone incompetent would hide you in the place a killer would search for you. I can protect you. If you stay with Montgomery, you'll play into the Butcher's hands."

"I'm not returning to WITSEC," Emma said. "I trust David with everything, including my life."

David sucked in a breath. Everything? Did that mean she trusted him with her heart? He hoped so because he was head-over-heels in love with her.

Jordan flicked an angry glance David's way. "He hasn't made good decisions so far. The stupid stunt he pulled is why I wouldn't allow you to contact him. He doesn't know what he's doing. Men like him are all swagger and no substance. No matter what he said, he can't do what we can."

"Listen to him," Jones urged. "Between the three of us, we have more than 25 years of experience in law enforcement. Do you want to trust your life to an Army grunt who doesn't understand the mind of a criminal? Do you want to trust your life to a man distracted by his emotions?"

"Jones is right," Wells said. "Your boyfriend can't protect you when he's more focused on you than on potential threats. Are you willing to bet your lives on his ability to compartmentalize? If you trust me with your life, I'll make sure no one finds you who shouldn't. I'll keep you safe."

"How do you know Montgomery isn't responsible for your problems?" Jones added. "You only have his word that he was overseas at the time of the attack in Seagull. He could have lied. What if he's the one who hurt you and murdered your family?"

Where was this garbage coming from? David had been overseas on a mission when Emma and her family were attacked. He didn't murder his girlfriend's family and would never lay a hand on Emma in anger.

Why were the feds desperate to have Emma at their beck and call? She had promised to testify in a trial. What more did they want? "She made her choice. If you continue to badger her, I'll boot you out the door and off our property. Am I making myself clear?" David glared at the three agents. They'd be wise to heed his warning because he wouldn't hesitate to kick the feds off Montgomery land. By the time they returned with legal documents, he and Emma would be long gone.

"Ms. Tucker?" Wells pressed. "Please, reconsider my offer. I'd hate for you to be hurt or killed because of Montgomery's incompetence. I swear on my life that I'll take care of you. No one will slip past me."

David flicked a glance at Caleb, who turned, grabbed the bags of evidence, and handed them to Jordan.

"Take it and go." David wrapped his arm around Emma's waist. "I expect a copy of the report. If I don't receive one, I'll go above your head to your supervisor. Since local and federal law enforcement agencies are supposed to work together, your boss won't appreciate a complaint about a lack of cooperation."

Jordan's jaw clenched. "If you involve Whitehead, he'll insist the FBI take over the case. The Butcher crossed state lines. That makes this our jurisdiction and our case."

"Darren Whitehead?"

The agent stared. "Yeah. You know him?"

"His son was in my military unit." He was David's best friend. That meant David had leverage to get Jordan off his back or to stop pressuring Emma to rejoin WITSEC.

More staring. "His son was a SEAL."

"So was I."

Wells muttered a soft curse. Jones whistled. "So, you might know your way around a weapon," Wells said with a sneer. "That doesn't mean you know squat about catching a serial killer. They're wily, determined, and scary smart. They don't know the meaning of the word quit."

Neither did SEALs, and they, too, were wily, determined, and smart. "Why are you singing this guy's praises?"

"Underestimating him will be dangerous to you and your girlfriend. I'm trying to protect both of you."

Elliot snorted, earning him a glare from the FBI agents.

"You're wrong," Emma said, voice soft.

"About what, ma'am?" Wells asked.

"The Butcher should be afraid of David and his brothers. He thinks he knows who and what he's tangling with. Whatever he thinks, he's wrong. I won't run and hide again, Agent Wells. I won't hide in WITSEC. He doesn't get to live his life however he wants while he forces me into a box because I'm afraid. No more. I'm finished running."

"He'll keep coming after you until you're dead."

"If he comes after her again, he'll be the one who dies," David said. "No one is going to take her away from me again, not even the FBI."

"Even if it's the best thing for her, the safest thing?" Jones snapped.

"I wouldn't call breaches in security at every safe house something to brag about, would you?"

Wells' face darkened. "The breaches aren't on us when the witness doesn't follow the rules."

Of course the feds would blame Emma. He tightened his grip on her in silent warning. "Take the evidence," he said to Jordan. "I expect a copy of the report within 24 hours."

The agent scowled. "I can't guarantee the results will be in."

Elliot snorted again. "So much for cooperation," he muttered.

"You lost four agents this morning," David said. "You expect me to believe that any evidence linked to the Butcher won't have top priority? Twenty-four hours, Jordan."

With a ripe, low-voiced curse, the special agent in charge stalked from the room with his two cohorts trailing behind.

As Wells reached the kitchen threshold, he paused with his hand on the doorjamb and glanced back at Emma. "Think about what I said. You deserve peace. Montgomery can't provide that, but I can. Please, let me help you." With that parting shot, he hurried to catch up with his co-workers.

No one moved until the front door closed behind the agents, then Caleb said, "Can you believe that garbage? They act like we're rednecks with peashooters instead of men trained by the greatest military in the world to take on the most heinous terrorists in existence."

"Their opinions don't matter." David turned and cupped Emma's face between his palms. "If you change your mind at any point and want FBI protection, tell me and I'll arrange it. The same condition applies, though. If you go into WITSEC, I'm going with you. We're a team.

Teams stick together through good times and bad. I'm not leaving your side, Emma."

Out of the corner of his eye, David saw his brothers glance at each other, but neither made a comment. Good. He wanted their support, but he'd go into WITSEC without it because the alternative was leaving Emma vulnerable. That was never happening again.

He looked at Caleb. "When are Levi and Owen off shift?"

"Fifteen minutes ago. They should be here any minute."

"Good. Brew a pot of coffee. As soon as they arrive, we'll talk."

As the coffeemaker finished the brew cycle, David's remaining two brothers walked into the kitchen and came to a sudden stop when they saw Emma.

"Em!" Levi hugged her. "I'm glad to see you. Where have you been?"

"It's a long story."

"Have a seat." David grabbed mugs and poured coffee for his brothers. "We'll have company soon."

"Who?" Owen asked as he took a seat across from Emma. He watched her, wariness and unasked questions in his eyes.

"Wolf Pack."

The brothers exchanged glances. "Do they need to use the house again for a principal?" Elliot asked.

"They're here to help with Emma's protection."

Levi and Owen looked at her. "Sounds like you've been busy while everyone thought you were dead," Owen said.

"Owen." David stared at his brother. "You're digging yourself a hole, bro. Listen to her explanation before you dig the hole too deep."

"I want to know why one of you didn't tell us that Emma was back." Levi folded his arms. "Since you're obviously not dead, Em, how about telling us why you disappeared from David's life for over a year and left him to grieve your loss."

"I was in witness protection," Emma said.

Owen and Levi were silent a few seconds, then Levi blew out a breath and said, "This relates to your family's murder. Tell us what happened, Em."

She launched into her explanation as David set a mug of tea in front of Emma, then sat in the chair beside hers. He rested his arm across the back of her chair and watched the play of emotions on his brothers' faces. As she spoke, his brothers' expressions morphed from disbelief to anger on her behalf.

When she lapsed into silence, Owen dragged a hand down his face. "I'm sorry you went through all that." He frowned. "Why didn't you call us, Emma. We would have helped you."

"I didn't know you were out of the military, or I might have been tempted to do just that despite Agent Jordan's warning. Believe me, I wanted to contact David." Her voice thickened. "I hated hurting him."

"You should have heard the feds trying to convince Emma to return to WITSEC," Caleb said. "They're desperate to have her back in protective custody."

"She's the only witness to survive the Butcher," David said.

"Some witness." Emma sipped her tea. "I can't remember the killer's face."

Owen leaned forward. "You saw him?"

She nodded. "Even in my dreams, his face is in shadow. Believe me, I would give anything if I could remember because this nightmare would be over sooner. I don't want David hurt because of me."

He kissed her temple. "I'll be fine, baby. As for not remembering things, you're already recalling more details than you did when you first woke in the hospital and gave your statement to the feds."

"Safety," Elliot said. "She feels safe with you, David. That's turning a key in her mind to unlock the memories."

"It's not enough," Emma said. "How many people has the Butcher killed while my brain protected me because I was afraid?"

"That's on the FBI," Caleb said. "They could have arranged for you and David to meet, but they wanted to keep the upper hand."

David shoved aside his empty mug. "We need to focus on the present and how we'll protect Emma from this serial killer."

"We do whatever is necessary." Elliot's expression darkened. "No matter what, the Butcher is going down. His killing spree stops here."

"You heard Agent Wells," Emma said. "The Butcher is crazy smart. Agent Jordan told me he hasn't made any mistakes. That's why they haven't been able to catch him."

Levi snorted. "You got one part right. The Butcher is crazy. No one is perfect, though. He'll make a mistake."

"He already has made one," David said, voice soft. "He hurt my woman and killed her family. He picked the wrong woman to terrorize. I'll make him pay."

"We'll make him pay," Owen corrected. "We're a family team. We do the job together. Emma is family. Anything that hurts Emma hurts all of us."

"You don't know how much that means to me," she said, voice soft. "Or how much you all mean to me."

"Enough to keep yourself in exile to protect us?" Levi asked. When she didn't reply, his lips curved slightly. "Figured as much. Nothing else would have kept you away from David this long."

"My months of exile prevented me from seeing my grandfather the last months of his life." Her voice hardened. "I will never forgive the Butcher for what he did."

He might have done more than Emma realized. Although the MO wasn't exactly the same in Mr. Watt's death, David was beginning to piece a few things together and he didn't like the picture forming in his mind.

His cell phone rang. David glanced at his screen and swiped his thumb across the surface. "Yeah, Kip?"

"The Fortress team is here, sir."

"Let them through."

"Yes, sir."

Time to make plans to end the Butcher's reign of terror.

CHAPTER TWELVE

Emma stared at the five tall, muscle-bound men who walked into the kitchen with silent treads. Talk about intimidating. They also looked like they could go toe-to-toe with the worst criminals the world had ever seen without batting an eyelash. The newcomers reminded Emma of David and his brothers.

The Montgomery brothers greeted the men with handshakes all around and a few shoulder claps. The team of five must have made quite an impression on the Montgomerys. She trusted David's judgment. If he trusted them, she could trust her life to them as well.

"Welcome back to Maple Valley and the Rocking M," David said. "Want coffee? We just made a fresh pot."

"I'm in," one of the men said. "Who's the pretty lady, David?"

"This is my girlfriend, Emma Tucker. Emma, meet Eli, Jon, Cal, Rafe, and Jackson. These men are members of a Fortress black ops team."

"The best one," Eli said with a slight Southern drawl. "We also have the best name." His eyes twinkled as he glanced at his teammates.

His dark-haired, intense companion rolled his eyes. "I still say the name is lame."

"You, my friend, have no taste." Eli turned his charming smile on Emma. "Ignore Jon, ma'am. He's griping because my last name is Wolfe and our team is named Wolf Pack."

"You're the only one who loves the name, buddy," Cal said. "The other teams are shaking their heads, snickering behind our backs. That should tell you something."

"How is Rachelle?" David asked Cal.

He grinned. "She's great. Beautiful and perfect, too. Thanks for asking."

"Ask him how many days until he marries the lovely Rachelle," Rafe said.

"Well?" David asked.

"One hundred and twenty days and," he glanced at his watch, "seven hours."

"But who's counting," Jackson said as he dropped into the nearest chair at the kitchen table.

Cal squeezed his shoulder before taking the seat beside him. "You're just envious, buddy."

"Yeah," the man admitted. "I am. If you're dumb enough to let Rachelle slip through your fingers, I have first dibs on asking her out."

A snort. "Don't hold your breath."

Caleb pushed back from the table and walked to the cabinet with coffee mugs. "Need cream or sugar?" he asked the visitors.

Each member of Wolf Pack shook his head.

Of course they didn't doctor their coffee. They most likely drank it black and strong enough to peel paint from the walls like David and his brothers did.

When David seated Emma at the table and sat beside her, the rest of the men joined them.

Eli said, "Jon updated us on the drive from Nashville. How can we help, David?"

"I didn't ask for a full team. I requested an operative or two so I could sleep. My brothers and I have a responsibility to protect the citizens of Morgan County along with Emma. Although I appreciate the help, I don't understand why Maddox sent five operatives."

"Cal was a Metro Nashville homicide detective and Rafe was FBI," Eli said. "They can help patrol the county while the rest of us protect Emma and hunt for the Butcher."

"I can handle my job and the protection detail," David said.

"Your attention will be focused on Emma, not your job. Inattention on the job can be deadly."

"He's right," Elliot said. "You won't want to be separated from Emma. You'll focus better if you're working from home or wherever your base happens to be."

David looked surprised.

His brother folded his arms. "Did you think we wouldn't know how scattered your focus is right now? Sorry, bro, but you weren't worth much after you returned from that last deployment and began the hunt for Emma. Yeah, you pulled yourself together, but not right away."

"We also know you want to move Emma from the Rocking M, especially since the Butcher suspects she's here," Owen added. "We need to find a place to hole up that we know well. If we can't use home turf, we need a safe house close by so we can provide backup when it's needed."

When, not if. Emma shuddered. The brothers were correct. The Butcher would come after her sooner or later. When he did, they'd need every advantage to defeat him. Agent Wells' offer of protection drifted through her mind again. She rejected it, her stomach twisting into a knot. Although she couldn't put her finger on why, but she would rather choose Craig Jordan than Wells if the Fortress team and the Montgomery brothers couldn't watch over her.

Emma's lips curved. A true testament of how uncomfortable she was with Wells because she trusted Jordan about as far as she could throw him. In other words, not at all.

"A safe house is best," Jon murmured. "We don't want Mrs. Grady in the line of fire again."

Again? Brows knitted, Emma looked at David for an explanation but it was Cal who explained.

"Mrs. Grady was injured when gunmen came after Rachelle when she was here." He grimaced. "Our team was drawn away, leaving Rachelle and the housekeeper vulnerable. I won't take that risk a second time."

"Where is the safe house?" she asked David. From the corner of her eye, she noted the exchanged looks between his brothers.

"You didn't tell her?" Levi's eyebrows rose.

"When have I had time?" David countered, never taking his gaze from hers.

"Tell me what?"

"The safe house is one you're very familiar with." He captured her hand and pressed a kiss to her knuckles. "After your family died, your grandfather put the family home up for sale."

Emma stared at him as the truth dawned on her. "You bought it."

He gave a slight nod. "I didn't know if you wanted it or not. Since your grandfather couldn't make the payments on your family home as well as his own, I bought and remodeled the house. New furniture, new decorations. I stored everything inside for you to look through when you're ready."

Because he knew the house brought back memories of abuse from her father.

"Remodeled is a mild word for gutted," Owen chimed in. "You won't recognize the place."

"He also added several new security features," Caleb said. "You'll be safe there, Em."

He'd spent a ton of money on her family home in the hope that she was still alive and would return to him one day. If she wasn't already in love with him, that gift alone would have tipped her over the edge. Emma kissed him lightly, well aware of their audience. "Thank you," she whispered. "What about my belongings at my apartment?"

"I let the apartment go, but I moved everything into storage along with your equipment."

"When do you want to shift locations?" Eli asked.

"Tomorrow night at the latest. We'll go after darkness falls," David answered. "I'd rather not advertise what we're doing."

"In a town this size, won't take long for folks to figure out where you are," Elliot warned.

A slight nod. "I'm aware. I'm only planning to stay at the safe house long enough for the Butcher to learn Emma is no longer at the Rocking M."

"And then what will we do?" she asked.

"Find another place with tight security."

"What's the point? He always finds me, no matter where I go." The Butcher was the source of her worst nightmares.

What if he hurt David? She dragged in a ragged breath. No. She couldn't dwell on that. David was a Navy SEAL, one the deadliest warriors on the planet. If he couldn't protect himself, no one could.

"Hey." The warrior in question cupped her chin and turned her face toward his. "You're not in this alone any longer. You have me, my brothers, and an entire black ops team at your back. We'll turn the tables on this guy and track him down. By the time we're finished with him, he won't be a threat to you or anyone else again."

She stared. "You're going to kill him?"

"If he gives me no other option, I won't hesitate to take him down. I want you safe, baby. I'll do my best to take him alive so he can stand trial, but I won't feel one ounce of remorse if I have to kill him to protect you." His thumb brushed along her jaw line. "He made his own choices. Whatever happens to him is not on you."

"He'll hurt you, maybe kill you." Emma's voice broke. "I can't live with that."

A soft whistle from Levi. "Ouch, bro. She hit you where it hurt."

David ignored him. "He'll try and fail." Another stroke of his thumb. "I have a very good reason to stay alive. I'm not letting our second chance slip through my fingers by doing something stupid and giving this guy the upper hand."

A second chance. Emma wrapped her arms around his neck, unable to resist despite their audience.

"Are we on the same page, Em?" he murmured against her ear.

She nodded. "Why are we waiting until tomorrow night to move to my childhood home?"

"If the Butcher is watching, and we have to assume he is, he'll expect us to run in a panic because he found you again. We're not playing into his hands. Besides, we set up security measures around the ranch and inside the house. We'll know if he makes a move this direction. He won't walk onto the grounds or into the house without us knowing. If he does come for you, we'll stash you in a safe place while we go after him."

"No place has been safe so far." She ought to know. The Butcher had almost caught her the last time she had to run. So close. She shuddered.

"We have a safe room. He can't get to you in there. All you have to do is trust me, and we'll get through this together. At the end of this mission, the Butcher will be out of your life for good." He eased back and cupped her face between his palms. "I will see you through this, Emma."

The utter confidence in his voice and the blazing hot intensity of his gaze made her entire body relax for the first time in months. He meant every word. She didn't have to carry this burden alone anymore. And, thank goodness, she didn't have to depend on the FBI to keep her safe any longer. David was right not to trust the feds. Their protective measures hadn't inspired confidence.

Knowing all those things gave her the confidence to take that last leap of faith into David's arms. Her SEAL wouldn't let her down no matter how difficult the fight with the Butcher. "I believe you," she murmured. "So, the hunter is going to become the hunted?"

Satisfaction gleamed in his eyes. "Oh, yeah. We're going to run this man to ground and make sure he never hurts anyone else again."

CHAPTER THIRTEEN

David pushed his coffee mug aside, his gaze sweeping over the black ops team seated around the table. "Time for the next watch shift. Who's up?"

"That would be me and Jon," Eli said as he stood. "You and Elliot have the watch in four hours. Are you bunking in the same place as two months ago?"

"The sofa in Emma's suite. I don't want to be far from her. When I'm on duty at night, one of my brothers will be there." He trusted Wolf Pack, but with Emma's safety at risk, David wanted one of his brothers protecting her.

"Although I don't blame you, we have your back and Emma's. If a problem arises, I'll let you know."

David headed toward the stairs as his need to check on Emma grew more urgent. Even with two of his brothers on watch in the security room, he wouldn't rest easy until he witnessed for himself that Emma was safe.

"David."

He stopped halfway up the stairs and turned to Rafe Torres, the former FBI agent. "Yes?"

"Are you sure Emma didn't break WITSEC protocol?"

David scowled.

Rafe held up a hand. "Answer the question without decking me."

"I'm positive. If she had broken protocol, Emma would have called me. Where are you going with this?"

"If you're correct, the FBI has serious holes in their security. I have to tell you, buddy, the US marshals know their job. As long as witnesses follow protocol, the chance of a breach in security is low. Something is way off if your lady's security was breached that many times."

Four times in 18 months pointed to Marshal ineptness or a leak. "Your point?"

"If the feds have that many holes in their security, then the Butcher knows exactly where Emma's hiding, and he'll be coming for her."

"This isn't on Emma."

Rafe stepped closer and lowered his voice. "That leaves two possibilities. The FBI has a hole in their cybersecurity or they have a mole."

David rubbed the tight muscles in his neck. "Tell me something I don't know." He pieced that together the first time he heard Emma's story at the FBI field office in Nashville.

"Assume anything you tell Jordan and his cronies the Butcher knows."

"Noted. Thanks." After Rafe nodded and returned to the first floor, David took the stairs two at a time.

He opened the door to the suite's living area, surprised when he noticed Emma sitting at one end of the couch. Why was she awake? He'd encouraged her to go to bed two hours earlier. "Everything okay?"

Emma tossed her blanket aside and came to him, wrapping her arms around his waist. "Even though I'm tired, I couldn't sleep. Too worried about the Butcher, I guess."

Despite the circumstances, David couldn't deny that having her in his life again, in his arms, was worth every bit of pain he'd suffered during her absence. "If he shows tonight, we'll know. The Rocking M isn't like your other safe houses, Em. We have perimeter alarms at the borders of the property as well as at half-mile increments to the ranch house. We also installed cameras with infrared capability. The Butcher won't catch us by surprise."

He tilted up her chin and captured her mouth in a tender kiss that he hoped conveyed the depth of his feelings for her. "You need to sleep, baby," he murmured, hugging her close.

"What about you?"

"I'm on night watch soon." David kissed her temple. "Sit with me a few minutes." Maybe his body heat would help her relax.

David led her to the couch, tucked her close to his side, and draped the blanket over them both. Grabbing the remote, he searched for a slow movie or television program. After he found an old mystery series he knew Emma loved, David urged Emma to lay her head against his chest.

By degrees, her muscles relaxed until she drifted to sleep. David lowered the television's volume and dozed.

Three hours later, he woke to a tap on the suite door. David's weapon was in his hand a second later and pointed at the door.

"It's Eli," Wolf Pack's leader said through the door. "I'm coming in soft."

"Come ahead." He held his aim steady, lowering his weapon when Eli walked into the suite alone. "Sit rep."

"Company." Eli inclined his head toward Emma. "She should be in the safe room while my team hunts."

"My brothers?"

"Awake and ready."

"One minute."

With a nod, Eli left.

Emma stirred. "What's wrong, David?"

"You need to go to the safe room."

She sat up. "Why?"

"Company. Put on your shoes."

Emma tossed the blanket aside, shoved her feet into her running shoes, and stood. "Ready."

David dropped a quick kiss on her mouth, anxious to assess the situation for himself. "Let's go."

At the suite door, he held up his hand for her to wait while he confirmed the corridor was clear of threats, then reached back and grasped Emma's hand.

They hurried toward the stairs. On the first floor, David led her to the library. Tugging on the designated book in the bookcase, he shifted the bookcase to reveal a door leading to the safe room. After typing in the appropriate codes, he nudged Emma inside the room where Mrs. Grady waited.

Emma hugged the housekeeper. "I'm glad you're here, too."

She patted Emma's back. "The Montgomery boys wouldn't leave me outside this room with danger looming. After what happened two months ago, they insisted I stay in here with you."

"I'm glad to have your company." Emma turned to David. "What do you want us to do?"

"Stay here, no matter what." He motioned toward the bank of screens connected to the security cameras around the property and ranch house. "You can observe what's happening from here. Stay where I know you're safe. Otherwise, my attention will be divided."

"Go. Mrs. G and I will be fine." Emma brushed a soft kiss over his mouth. "Be safe." She stepped back.

Although reluctant to go, David secured the door and returned the bookcase to its original position. He hurried to the security room where Levi and Elliot monitored the screens. "Any news?"

Elliot handed him a comm device.

Satisfaction filled him. Now, he'd be able to monitor events occurring on the ground. David slipped the communication device into his ear, hearing whispered communications between the members of the black ops team.

Levi inclined his head toward the camera feeds on the west side of the ranch. "Wolf Pack is closing in on the target."

David scanned the camera feeds in the relevant areas. "Where is he?"

"Not showing up on the monitors at the moment. Our visitor is avoiding the cameras."

His jaw tightened. This guy had explored the Rocking M in the daytime, but couldn't avoid all the cameras at night. Too dark. "He's been on our land before tonight."

"Yep."

Elliot glanced at David. "How did we miss him?"

"No system is perfect. Let's hope he missed some of our surveillance cameras. I want to see his face."

Minutes passed in silence as the three of them watched Wolf Pack close the circle on their prey.

Elliot tapped the comm device in his ear. "Movement in quadrant three, heading toward the ranch." He gave the coordinates.

"Copy," Jon murmured.

On screen, one member of the black ops team peeled off on an intercept course. Two minutes later, Jon whispered, "Target sighted."

"Hold," Eli murmured. "Almost in position." Less than a minute later, a third figure appeared on screen behind the target. "Levi?"

"No other bogeys."

"Jon, go."

The sniper closed in on the target. With a minimum of fuss, he and Eli captured the intruder.

"Returning to base," Eli murmured.

David considered the best place to interrogate the intruder. "Kitchen."

"Copy."

Although reluctant to bring the man inside the house, Emma would want to see what was happening. David headed toward the door. "Keep an eye on the monitors."

"We've got this. Get the information we need," Elliot said.

Leaving the surveillance to his brothers, David walked to the kitchen to brew a pot of coffee for Wolf Pack and his brothers. The coffeemaker signaled the end of the brew cycle as the back door opened. Wolf Pack streamed into the kitchen with a man dressed in black in their midst.

Fury burned in David's gut at the man swearing when Rafe shoved him onto a chair and secured the intruder's hands behind his back with a zip tie.

"This idiot claims he knows you," Eli said.

"Unfortunately, he's telling the truth. What are you doing here, Wells?"

"Who are these thugs?"

"Answer my question," David snapped. "You're trespassing on private property in the middle of the night. You're lucky one of them didn't shoot you. Why are you here?"

"To make sure Emma was safe."

David folded his arms. "Did you think I'd let anyone near her?"

"You don't know who you're up against," Wells muttered.

"If his stealth skills match yours, I don't have anything to worry about."

The agent scowled. "Then you're more of a fool than I originally thought."

Wells and his buddies had more information than they shared, information that could be vital in identifying the man stalking Emma.

Owen gathered coffee mugs from the cabinet and began to fill them. "And you thought we needed your help to protect Emma?"

Wells' cheeks flushed. "You're a bunch of Army grunts. What do you know about protection details?"

"More than you think. Is your memory short? We were all spec ops, Wells."

The agent strained against his bindings. "Cut me loose. I'm not a threat."

Jon glanced at David, eyebrow raised. After David's slight nod, the SEAL grabbed his Ka-Bar and sliced through the bindings. "Stay in your seat."

The agent scowled. "And if I don't?"

A slow, cold smile formed on the sniper's mouth. "Do you really want me to answer that question?"

Wells dropped his gaze. "Whatever. Look, I'm not a threat to any of you. I wanted to protect Emma."

"I have her covered," David said. "Tell me what happened, Wells."

"The Butcher sent another threat."

CHAPTER FOURTEEN

David frowned. Why did the Butcher send the threat to the feds instead of sending it to Emma at the ranch? "You should have called instead of sneaking onto the Rocking M. You're lucky one of my friends didn't shoot you on sight."

The agent glared at him. "I planned to tell you about the threat in the morning," he muttered.

He still held something back. "Spill it, Wells. No more dancing around the truth."

Wells reached inside his jacket, freezing when every man in the room pointed a weapon at him a second later. He held up an empty hand. "I'm reaching for a paper copy of the Butcher's message. No weapon, I swear. You should know I'm not carrying since you confiscated my weapons."

"Go slow," David warned in a soft voice. "We have itchy trigger fingers."

A snort, but Wells withdrew a sheet of paper from the inner pocket of his jacket. He held up the paper.

David flicked a glance at Levi who bridged the gap between himself and Wells. His brother scanned the message, a muscle twitching in his jaw. Levi brought the paper to David.

"Well?" Owen demanded. "Don't keep us in suspense, bro."

David read the message aloud. "If Emma Tucker doesn't dump her bodyguard and come out to play, I'll hunt in her backyard."

"He's expecting Emma to give herself up," Rafe said.

"Why would she agree?" Jackson asked.

David knew the answer, and one glance at his brothers told him they understood the reason. "To protect our friends and neighbors. The Butcher is a threat to people in Maple Valley. He already murdered her family. Emma won't want anyone else hurt."

"Handing herself over to die isn't an option," Levi said. "We won't let him have Emma, not even to protect the citizens of Maple Valley."

"We have to convince Emma," Owen said as he handed mugs of coffee to the Fortress operatives. He eyed David and gave a slight inclination of his head toward Wells.

He didn't want to be chummy with the agent, but he wasn't a threat to David or Emma. He gave a slight nod.

A moment later, Owen handed Wells a mug of coffee. "Cream or sugar?"

The agent shook his head. "Black's great. Thanks." Wells sipped his coffee.

David studied him. "Anything else you need to tell me?"

A head shake. "Is Emma safe?"

"Do you think I'd sit here and chat with you if she wasn't?"

The agent's shoulders relaxed. "I suppose not. Where is she?"

"All you need to know is that Emma is safe."

"I'm trying to help," Wells said.

"Don't need it, Wells."

"You don't understand who you're going up against."

"The Butcher is the one who should be wary."

"Come on," Wells sneered. "A few hired thugs can't help you deal with a serial killer."

"Their security clearance is higher than yours, and they're highly-trained black ops warriors."

The agent looked surprised. "Who are they?"

"You have a leak or a mole," David said.

Wells shook his head.

When David continued to stare at him, the agent swallowed hard. "Maybe. You must move Emma. You can't trust your ranch security. Sure, you caught me, but I didn't intend to hurt Emma. The Butcher wants her dead and doesn't care who he hurts to accomplish his goal."

"If you have a leak or a mole inside the FBI, the Butcher should know Emma can't identify him."

The agent dropped his gaze to his coffee mug.

David's eyes narrowed. "That information isn't in the file, is it?"

Again, no response.

The silence told David what he needed to know. "Where's your car, Wells?"

"In the woods a mile from the ranch."

David glanced at Owen.

His brother laid a hand on Wells' shoulder. "Let's go."

The agent scowled. "I want to help."

"Your job is to catch the killer, Wells, not protect Emma."

After a glance at David, he sighed and nodded. Wells headed for the door with Owen at his heels.

After Owen and Wells left, Eli said, "Do we move Emma now or stick to the original plan?"

He considered his options. "My gut says to stick to the original plan. We don't know how much information Wells will report to Jordan. Emma is safe for the moment. However, we should rethink the location for a safe house."

Jon held up his hand. "Wait." He glanced at Eli. "Electronics," he murmured.

Rafe set his coffee mug on the table and left the room. He returned a moment later with a black gadget in his hand. While he walked around the room, the rest of the occupants remained silent. When he'd nearly completed the circuit, Rafe paused in front of the doorway. The chaser lights on the electronic gadget turned red.

David filled a juice glass with water and handed it to Rafe. The operative turned from the doorway with a small black listening device on the palm of his hand. He dropped the bug into the water.

Rafe completed his circuit of the room. "Clear."

"Someone planted a bug in your house," Jon said. "That person knows our plans for watch shifts and the perimeter alarms you set up. Emma shouldn't remain in this house."

"Agreed. Suggestions? We can't use Emma's childhood home now."

Jon and Eli looked at each other, then Wolf Pack's leader said, "Let me make a phone call. While I do that, check on Emma." He glanced at his team. "Search the house for electronic surveillance. Be ready to go in fifteen minutes." He opened the back door and stepped outside on the deck.

David returned to the safe room. As soon as he stepped inside, Emma rushed into his arms. He hugged her tight.

"I saw Agent Wells on the monitor. What's going on?"

"He wanted to be sure you were safe."

"You don't believe him?"

"I don't think your safety is his only motive."

"What else is troubling you?"

"Someone planted an electronic bug in the kitchen."

Mrs. Grady gasped. "Oh, no. When did that happen?"

"Not sure." But he had a good idea.

"What does that mean for us?" Emma asked.

"We move sooner than I wanted. How quickly can you be ready to leave?"

"As soon as I change clothes. I packed them in the duffel bag Mrs. Grady brought me." She gave a wry smile. "I learned to stay packed and ready while in WITSEC."

"Excellent. We need to be careful what we say since Wolf Pack is still searching the house for more listening devices."

He led Emma from the safe room to the suite. "Go change," he whispered against her ear and nudged her toward the room.

While he waited, David checked with Elliot and Caleb by text. His tension subsided when they assured him no one else had triggered an alarm and the cameras at the farthest edges of the perimeter revealed nothing out of the ordinary. Didn't prevent an ambush away from the perimeter.

Emma returned with her duffel bag in hand. She'd dressed in running shoes, black jeans, and a long-sleeved black t-shirt. Perfect in case she needed to run.

David hated that Emma had to run again. This time, however, she wasn't alone. He would protect her, no matter the cost to himself.

CHAPTER FIFTEEN

Emma looked down at herself when David's gaze drifted over her. Had she chosen the wrong clothes? "Is what I'm wearing all right?"

He walked to her. "It's perfect. Your beauty blows me away, Emma." He took her bag. "I'm sorry."

Running from danger had become a way of life in recent months. At least she wasn't alone this time.

The possibility of a listening device in her suite made Emma shudder. Though this house had been her safe haven for years, she couldn't wait to see the Rocking M in the rearview mirror.

David held out his hand. "Let's go downstairs." They went to the security room where Elliot and Caleb watched the monitors.

"You okay, Emma?" Elliot asked.

She nodded. Sure, she was scared, but the only thing that mattered to her was protecting David and his brothers from the Butcher. Perhaps she should have stayed in hiding. If she had, the Montgomery brothers wouldn't now be in the crosshairs of a killer. "Thanks for asking."

"You're important to us," Caleb said. "We just got you back. Losing you to the feds or a killer isn't on the approved agenda."

That surprised a laugh out of her. "Good to know. It's not on my agenda, either."

Elliot frowned at David who responded with a hand signal.

David hadn't told her everything. When they were alone, she would ask what he left out.

She studied the setup in the room, impressed with the number of cameras placed around the Rocking M. "This is amazing," she murmured. "I'm not surprised you saw Agent Wells approaching the house with all the angles covered by your cameras."

Elliot broke away from his stare down with David and gave her a slight smile. "Wells is lucky he's not full of holes. Wolf Pack had him in their sights, and he was an unknown threat."

Eli walked into the security room. "All set," he told David. "We'll use one of our safe houses. I'll give you details on the way."

Caleb pushed away from the monitors and stood. "How are we doing this, David?" He glanced at Eli and said, "No offense, but you aren't blood kin."

Wolf Pack's leader inclined his head. "Understood."

"Has this room been scanned?" David asked Eli.

"It's clear."

"How far away is your safe house?"

"Thirty minutes. Maddox wanted to make sure your brothers could offer assistance when we need it."

Emma's heart sank. They sounded as though they were planning for a war, and, perhaps, they were. "He's one man," she said. Could the killer outwit and outgun ten highly-trained men?

"He's evaded the FBI," Eli reminded her. "If we're overreacting, you'll have bragging rights about two teams of black ops agents protecting you."

"We assume the Butcher is one man," David said. "I'd rather have more protection than we need in case we're wrong."

She flinched as something flashed into her mind and disappeared too quickly to grasp.

"Emma?" When she swayed, David gripped Emma's upper arms. "Are you okay?"

She nodded. What was wrong with her?

"Why don't I believe you?" he murmured.

Because she didn't believe it herself. Was she losing her grip on reality after holding herself together for so long? "Something popped into my head, then disappeared." Emma frowned. "I know it was important. Why can't I remember?"

"Don't push. The memory will return." His thumb brushed over her cheekbone, his confidence in her evident in his eyes.

She wished she had as much faith in her memory as David did. Emma kissed his palm. "Thanks." For his support, his care, for more things than she would name with an audience listening to each word. Did David suspect how much he meant to her? If she lost him, her life would be meaningless.

He crushed her close, then glanced at his brothers. "I'll contact you when we're at the safe house. For the moment, two of you need to be on duty at a time. You'll need more officers to share the load, so I'll swear in Rafe and Cal as deputies since they're former law enforcement. I'll help with shifts."

Elliot shook his head. "You need to stay with Emma. We'll make it work. You know the part-timers will step up. No one will question why you're working remotely, David."

Caleb squeezed David's shoulder. "Take care of Em."

David gave a short nod. "I owe you."

A quick grin from his brother. "You may regret saying that when we collect."

"Go," Elliot said, his voice barely above a growl. "If you run into trouble, call."

"Ready to go?" Eli asked, his gaze taking in Emma's bag.

"I need to grab my gear." David dropped a light kiss on Emma's mouth.

"Need a cup of tea to go, Em?" Caleb asked. "We have several to-go cups."

She smiled. The Montgomery brothers were serious coffee drinkers. "Thanks, Caleb."

"Sure thing." He left the room.

"How do you feel about log cabins?" Eli asked her.

Her eyebrows soared. "I love them. Why?"

"Then you'll like your new safe house."

A cabin sounded intriguing. She could think of far worse places to be in hiding. If the property was isolated enough, she might be able to go for walks.

Emma regretted not asking Mrs. G to buy knitting needles and yarn for her. Knitting kept her stress level down. If the safe house was located near a town with a knitting shop, perhaps she could purchase the supplies she needed.

David returned with a bag and picked up hers. "Let's go." He escorted Emma into the kitchen where Caleb handed her two cups.

"Tea for you and coffee for David."

She kissed his cheek. "Thanks. I'll take care of him," she whispered.

Caleb's lips curved.

"Where are Rafe and Cal?" David asked Eli.

Wolf Pack's leader opened the back door and stepped outside. A moment later, he returned with the other two men.

David swore in Rafe and Cal as deputies. "I appreciate the help."

"Glad to do it," Rafe said. He glanced at Eli. "We're ready to roll. The SUVs are parked near the deck stairs."

Eli handed David and Emma a small device to slip into their ears. "This will allow you to communicate with my team as we travel."

"Where are we going?"

"Archer."

David smiled. "It's at the edge of Morgan County. I know the police chief. She's a good cop and will be glad to lend a hand if we need it."

"Good to know." Eli motioned for Rafe and Cal to precede him outside. He held up his hand for David and Emma to wait.

Through the ear piece, Emma heard the low-voiced, clipped conversation between the members of Wolf Pack. Finally, Eli said, "Clear, David."

"Copy." He glanced at Levi and Owen who walked in, fully armed and wearing bullet-resistant vests, then turned to Emma. "Let's do this. I want you in the safe house as soon as possible."

Caleb took the bags from David and turned off the kitchen light. "I'm right behind you."

Levi and Owen stepped out onto the deck.

David tucked Emma close to his side. "Straight to the SUV, sweetheart." When she nodded, he signaled his brothers to move out, and hurried Emma toward his vehicle.

Covering the distance to the SUV took seconds. Levi opened the passenger door, keeping his body between her and a potential threat. Caleb tossed their bags into the back.

David lifted her to the passenger seat and closed the door. After a quick word with his brothers, he climbed behind the steering wheel. "Eli, head toward the back of the smaller barn. It's one of four access roads leading to the back of the property and away from Maple Valley. If there's an ambush, hopefully we'll avoid it."

"Copy."

The lead SUV took off with David close behind and followed by a third SUV.

"At the asphalt road, turn left," David instructed.

Eli acknowledged his direction, then the operatives lapsed into silence.

Emma found the silence more nerve-wracking than the chatter she'd been hearing through the ear piece. "It's too quiet now," she murmured. The men chuckled. She wouldn't be sharing any deep, dark secrets while connected to Wolf Pack electronically.

The vehicles traveled along the access road without interference and emerged from tree cover onto the asphalt road.

Emma breathed a sigh of relief when they traveled far enough away from Maple Valley that the likelihood of an attack seemed minimal. She glanced at David. "You were right."

He flashed her a grin. "I always like to hear that." More laughter from the operatives listening to their conversation. "What was I right about?"

"We escaped the ambush."

"The bug in the kitchen meant our plans to use your childhood home were compromised. The most likely place for an ambush was on the road to that house."

"Who planted the bug?"

David scowled. "One of the FBI agents. Probably Wells."

She blinked. "He wants to protect me from the Butcher."

"He's also the one who touched that exact place on the door frame before he left the house earlier in the day. Jordan and Jones didn't."

Emma shuddered. "He listened to us all day. What if one of the agents planted a tracker on your vehicle? They could be following us."

"We checked the SUV," Jon murmured. "No trackers."

She relaxed against the seat. "Thanks, Jon."

"We'll be at the safe house soon," Eli said. "Try to relax."

"Drink your tea," David murmured. "Eli, do you know if the safe house has a supply of herbal tea?"

"We'll check. If the kitchen doesn't have a supply, we'll buy some."

"I'll be fine without tea," Emma said.

"Hey, we need coffee to survive. Picking up a box or two of tea isn't a problem."

That made her laugh. "I don't suppose the safe house has knitting needles and yarn."

Silence, then, "Do you want knitting supplies?" Eli asked.

Excitement blossomed inside Emma. "Yes, please. If Archer has a knitting store, I can buy what I need in under ten minutes."

David wrapped his hand around hers and squeezed gently. "Stores have surveillance cameras."

"I might have a compromise," Eli said. "My wife is friends with a woman who owns a knitting shop in Otter Creek. I'll talk to the owner later this morning. We'll find a way to get the supplies you need."

"Thank you, Eli."

"Are you sure we can trust her?" David demanded.

"Positive. Her husband is a detective with the Otter Creek PD, and she's Ethan Blackhawk's sister-in-law."

David whistled. "I've worked with Ethan on a few cases. He's impressive in the field."

"No one's better," Eli agreed. "We're ten minutes from the safe house."

Emma finished the last of her tea when the three-vehicle caravan turned into an almost hidden driveway. The long, winding drive ended at a large, two-story cabin with a wraparound porch.

When they parked, David said, "Wait here." He climbed from the vehicle and walked to her door, his gaze scouring the surrounding area.

Jackson, Rafe, and Cal joined David in standing watch while Eli and Jon checked around the cabin. Within five minutes, the two men walked inside the structure. Soon, Eli stepped onto the porch and gave a hand signal.

David opened Emma's door. "Let's go." He helped her out, tucked her against his side, and rushed her to the porch and inside the cabin.

Emma removed the comm device and handed it to Eli with a smile. "I'll feel a little lonely without the voices in my head."

He winked at her. "You just let me know if you need to hear my voice."

Jon snorted as he entered the large living room. "Only if you want him to drive you crazy."

"Aww. I knew you loved me." Eli punched his friend lightly on the shoulder.

David handed Eli his comm device. "Where is Emma's room?"

"Second floor, last room on the right. Her room is the best protected. Your room is next to hers. The rest of us will occupy the other rooms on that floor. We're leaving one room open for your brothers."

"Perfect." He accepted their bags from Rafe. "I'll be back in a few minutes."

"Take your time," Jon murmured. "We'll set up watch shifts while you're upstairs." His lips curved. "Hope you don't need sleep."

David rolled his eyes and ushered Emma toward the stairs.

Emma drew in a deep breath. Maybe now she would obtain answers from David. He hadn't told her everything, and something told her the information he'd withheld was bad.

CHAPTER SIXTEEN

David escorted Emma to the second floor of the safe house and down the hall to her room. Setting his bag by the door, he carried hers to the queen-size bed.

While Emma glanced around the room, David checked the two windows to be sure no trees were close enough to be a security risk. Satisfied with what he observed, he turned back to see Emma close the door behind her and lean against it, watching him.

Uneasiness curled through his gut. "What's wrong?"

"You tell me."

David grimaced. Should have known better than to hide something from Emma. "This isn't a good conversation to have before you sleep."

She hugged him. "There's never a good time for bad news. No more secrets, David. I've had enough of those to last a lifetime."

David looped his arms around her waist with a sigh. If she wanted the truth, he wouldn't hide it from her. "The Butcher sent a message through the FBI."

She stilled. "What did he say this time?"

"If you don't dump me and come out to play, he'll hunt in our backyard."

Emma sucked in a ragged breath. "Oh, no."

When she tried to wrench herself out of his arms, David tightened his hold. "The message doesn't change our game plan."

"Everyone we care about is at risk because of me. I can't let them die." Her voice broke on the last word.

"Baby, stop. Take a breath."

"I've lived with this nightmare for more than a year. I don't want to lose my friends. I don't want to lose...."

"What?"

"You," she whispered, tears sheening her beautiful eyes. "I can't live with that. I can't lose you, David."

"You're not getting rid of me." His mouth brushed hers. "I've already lived without you once. I'm not willing to do it again." Did she feel the same about him?

"The separation would be temporary."

Even the thought of another separation sent a stab of pain through his heart. Obviously, David's explanation was lousy. Her rejection would gut him. His heart rate increased. *Man up and tell her the truth, Montgomery.* "I'm not talking about a separation."

"What do you mean?"

"I'm trying to tell you that I love you, Emma. I lost part of my soul when you were in WITSEC. You're the best part of me."

"David." She kissed him.

After a series of deep, hot kisses, David pulled back, aware that she hadn't verbally responded to his declaration. She seemed to feel the same way about him, but he needed her to say the words. If she didn't love him, he would do his dead-level best to win her heart because the alternative was a lifetime without her. No. A thousand times, no. While he'd learned to handle many things through the years, losing Emma was unthinkable.

He cupped her face. "You're killing me, baby. Do I have a chance to win your heart?"

A vibrant smile curved her luscious mouth. "You already have. I love you, David. I've loved you for so long."

David crushed her close. "Even though I don't have a ring yet, will you marry me?"

"Nothing would make me happier."

Man, he hoped she meant those words because he didn't know how long he'd be able to wait to marry Emma. "Soon? A long engagement might be the death of me."

Emma laughed. "As soon as you want." Her smile slowly faded. "What if we can't find the Butcher?"

"I'm not delaying our wedding because the Butcher is roaming free. In fact, I think he's a great excuse to marry you sooner. I'll have a legitimate reason to keep you by my side all hours of the day and night. As soon as I have the chance, I'll buy your engagement ring. I want everyone to know you're mine."

And if they were forced into WITSEC, they'd go as husband and wife. That would, indeed, tick off Agent Jordan. He wouldn't like adjusting his protection plans to include David. Tough. Emma was his to love and protect.

"I don't want our wedding tainted by the Butcher."

"Our wedding day will be about us." He kissed her until she practically melted in his arm. "Let's not worry about the date yet. Knowing you'll be my wife soon is enough for the moment."

"What about our friends in Maple Valley? Will marrying before the Butcher is behind bars heighten the risk to them?"

"We can't solve every problem tonight." He smiled. "I'm just happy you put me out my misery by accepting my proposal. Now, I'll be able to sleep."

Another laugh from his bride-to-be. "I'm not sure I'll sleep at all. I have wedding plans to make. Oh, I wish I could talk to Gigi."

David chuckled. "Soon, okay? Save some of the planning for after sunrise. Do you need anything? Water, more tea, a snack?"

She shook her head. "I have what I need most in this world. You."

Another kiss, this one soft and tender. "I'll be close." Walking away from her was the hardest thing he'd ever done. David returned to the first floor and found four of the operatives gathered in the kitchen. "Where's Jackson?"

"Manning the security cams," Eli said. "Coffee?"

"Not unless I'm on watch tonight."

"Lucky for you, your shift isn't until nightfall." Rafe tossed him a bottle of water. "How's Emma?"

"Trying to sleep."

Jon frowned. "You told her the truth, right?"

"I did."

"Huh." Cal rubbed his jaw. "She must be one strong woman to fall asleep after hearing the Butcher's threat."

"I balanced out the bad news with something else." His cheeks burned. The news would leak soon. He needed to tell his brothers.

Eli's eyebrows rose. "Must be something good."

"I asked her to marry me."

The operatives stared at him in stunned silence. "Well?" Rafe demanded. "What did she say?"

He grinned. "Yes."

A round of handshakes and slaps on the back followed his news. "Congratulations, buddy," Eli said. "You're one blessed man."

"Believe me, I know. Better than that, she agreed to a wedding soon."

A soft whistle from Cal. "Good job." His lips curved. "That's sure to tick off the feds."

"Doesn't hurt my feelings any," Rafe muttered.

David chuckled. "You used to be one of them."

"I'm a reformed fed and take every opportunity to needle them." He scowled. "Especially Jordan."

"Not a fan?"

A snort. "Not in this lifetime. Jordan is a lot of things, but a team player isn't one of them."

The operative's assessment matched David's. Glancing at Eli, he asked, "What time will Zane be at work?"

"Early. His wife and son are early risers. Need him?"

"Yeah, but I don't want to wake him."

"Send an email. If you text, he'll respond immediately." Eli squeezed David's shoulder. "Rest while you can. Things will heat up soon."

In his room, David called his brothers and shared the news about his engagement. When he finally ended the call, he debated sending Zane an email and opted to wait and text the tech wizard later in the morning.

After readying himself for bed, David stretched out on the comforter, fully dressed except for his tactical boots. Praying for a few hours of uninterrupted rest, he went to sleep between one heartbeat and the next.

He rose sometime later when Emma's bedroom door opened. "Are you okay, Emma?"

A soft gasp. "I'm sorry," she whispered. "I didn't mean to wake you."

He looked down at her beloved face. "You're up early."

"I slept."

"Uh huh." His lips twitched. "Are you hungry?"

Her stomach growled.

He chuckled. "I'll take that as a yes." David threaded his fingers through hers and started toward the stairs. "Come on. Let's see what we can find in the kitchen."

Jon turned from the stove when they walked into the room. "Morning. Hope you're hungry."

Emma gaped at the volume of food on the breakfast bar. "Good grief! You could feed an army with that amount of food."

The sniper lifted one shoulder. "We burn calories."

"I can't imagine your grocery bill," she muttered.

One by one, the other operatives drifted into the room and filled their plates.

"Better choose what you want," David murmured to Emma. "I've seen these guys eat. There won't be enough to feed a mouse in a few minutes."

"I believe it." She grabbed a plate and added small portions of everything.

When they finished the meal, David sat on the outdoor couch with Emma and called Owen. "Any problems after we left?"

"Everything remained quiet. You?"

"Nothing yet."

"It's coming."

"We'll be ready. Who's on duty today?"

"Levi and I are working until 2:00, then Caleb will take over with a couple of part-timers until 10:00 tonight. Elliot and I will work the overnight shift with Rafe and Cal."

Excellent. "We'll reevaluate tomorrow morning. In the meantime, I'll do what I can from here."

"How's Emma?"

She leaned her head against David's shoulder. "I'm fine, Owen. Your brother is taking great care of me."

"You let me know if he slacks off. I'll yank him back in line."

David snorted. "Thanks for the vote of confidence, bro."

Owen chuckled. "You bet. If anything happens, we better hear about it."

"Same." After ending the call with his brother, David called Zane Murphy.

"Yeah, Murphy."

"It's David Montgomery. You're on speaker with Emma."

"Good morning, Emma. I trust you're well."

"If you don't count a deranged serial killer scouring Tennessee looking for me, I'm great."

"Don't worry. We'll find him. What can I do for you, David?"

"Have an update for me?"

"I just sent you a packet of information two minutes ago."

He straightened. "Find anything?"

"Plenty. Our least-favorite fed has been holding back."

David growled. "Can't say that surprises me. Give me the highlights."

"Jordan and his buddies have been chasing their tails for months with the Butcher. The Tuckers aren't the first or last victims of this guy."

"How many people has he killed?" Emma asked.

"Fifteen so far, but the murder of your family is different."

David frowned. "How?"

"The rest of the victims have been individuals. That was the first time the Butcher had attacked a family."

CHAPTER SEVENTEEN

David scowled. "A serial killer doesn't generally change his MO once he has it nailed down. Any speculation as to why he changed tactics?" he asked Zane.

"Best guess is he didn't realize the family was at home."

He stilled. "The feds think the Butcher targeted Emma specifically?"

"Sorry, my friend."

Why didn't the feds tell him? David didn't know what game Jordan was playing, but he planned to get to the bottom of it.

Emma shook her head. "But if he watched the house, he would have seen me drive away in the car."

The Butcher had probably seen Emma and chosen her as his next victim. If he was smart enough to park a block or two away, he wouldn't know Emma left or that Anne was in the house. Her sister could have gone to the beach. The killer wouldn't have known Marian and James Tucker were in the house.

David frowned. Emma said she and her sister wandered all over Seagull, visiting booths during the festival. Perhaps the killer was closer than she realized. He chose Emma for a reason. If David discovered why, he might be able to stop the Butcher before he struck again.

"Not if he believed you would be in the house alone. Is that possible, Emma?" Zane asked.

"I don't know."

"Think about when you were in Seagull with Anne," David said. "While you and your sister attended the festival, did you discuss plans for when you returned to the beach house?"

Emma's hand clamped onto his forearm. "Anne mentioned a swim before dinner. Why didn't I remember that before now?"

"Your memory's been in a deep freeze," Zane said. "David's presence is thawing the ice."

"More memories will return." David stroked Emma's hair. "The killer will pay for what he did to you and your family, and his other victims. Zane, did you send a copy of the case files, too?"

"Affirmative. I'm still searching for security cam footage at Emma's safe houses. Jon's scanning for security and traffic cams on Seagull Island. Anything else you need?"

"Track down every scrap of information on Jordan and his cronies, Justin Wells and Phil Jones."

"Copy that. Later, David." Zane ended the call.

"Why are you investigating the FBI agents?" Emma asked. "They protected me for months."

"Have they?" David wasn't so sure.

"You don't trust them."

If what he suspected was true, Jordan had much to answer for. "The security breaches shouldn't have happened."

David tucked Emma close, enjoying the sun and light breeze. Though the vista before him was peaceful, gut instinct led him to believe this was the calm before the storm.

Minutes later, Emma stirred. "I can't hide here forever," she said, voice soft.

He kissed her temple. "You're right." Too many people's lives were at risk. The killer's patience would end soon. When it did, people they knew and loved could die.

"What will we do?"

"Find him, and arrest him."

"The best option," she agreed. "What's our next choice?"

One he didn't want to use, but might be the only way to draw out the killer. "Set a trap."

"You need bait." Emma faced him, her expression somber. "Me."

He gave a slight nod. "It's a last resort."

"And if you have to use that option?"

"I'll personally guarantee the Butcher won't touch you again."

She sighed. "All right. I'll be the bait if doing so will protect our friends. How do we set this up?"

"Remember, it's my last option. If we use it, we'll leave a trail of breadcrumbs for the Butcher. When he walks into our trap, we'll nab him." David cupped her cheek. "Before we set the trap, we'll put every resource we have into locating him before he finds you."

"How can I help?"

"Are you willing to tell Wolf Pack about the Butcher's attack on you and your family?"

Emma grimaced. "If it will help."

"One of them might ask a question that jars your memory." Jon might be the best option. David hoped Jon's legendary interrogation skills closed the gaps in Emma's memory.

"What else can I do?"

He studied her a moment. "We need to compare the case files of the Butcher's victims to look for commonalities, anomalies, and create profiles."

She shuddered. "I understand."

"If you can't assist with cases and profiles, no one will think less of you. I know how difficult this will be." If Emma participated in the process, she'd be forced to relive the attack on her and her family as well as discuss the breaches in her security.

"I'm tougher than I look. When do we start?"

"As soon as I talk to Agent Jordan."

"What if he's still asleep?"

He smiled. "Then I'll have the pleasure of waking him. Do you want to listen to the call or tell the others to set up for a meeting?"

"I'd rather be the message bearer. However, Agent Jordan will want proof I'm safe."

David brushed a kiss over her mouth, then called the FBI agent.

"Yeah, Jordan."

"It's David Montgomery."

"Is my witness safe?" Jordan demanded.

Emma rolled her eyes. "I'm fine, Agent Jordan."

"No thanks to your flunky," David added.

"What's that supposed to mean?"

"Keep Wells on a leash."

"Wells? What are you talking about?"

"Agent Wells tried to sneak up on my home overnight. He's lucky he didn't end up full of holes."

Jordan muttered a curse. "I'll talk to him."

"Did he act on your authority?"

"Are you accusing me of spying on you?"

"Is that what I'm doing?"

"Yeah, you are, and I don't appreciate it. We're on the same side."

"Are we?"

"Look, we want the same thing."

"Which is?"

"The Butcher behind bars before he hurts anyone else."

"How far are you willing to go to make that happen?"

"What are you getting at, Montgomery?"

"Either you or one of your agents left a bug in my kitchen."

Silence, then, "Do you know who?"

"I have a pretty good idea."

"Then you know it wasn't me," Jordan said flatly. "Wells left it, didn't he?"

"Ask him."

"I need to go."

"Hold it, Jordan."

"What? Unlike country bumpkin sheriffs, I'm busy."

"Why didn't you tell me about the Butcher's latest communication?"

Another curse from the FBI agent.

David scowled. "Knock it off. You're still on speaker."

"Sorry," he muttered. "Wells must have spilled his guts. What did you do to him?"

"Nothing."

"He better not have a mark on him or I'll file charges against you."

"Tell your agent to stay clear of the Rocking M unless he has a valid reason to be there. Everyone at the ranch is on high alert, and my people are armed."

"Are you threatening my agent?"

"I'm explaining the facts."

"Tell me where you are. I need to know in case we have to move her quickly."

David laughed. "Good try, Jordan."

"Let's at least discuss the possibility."

"If you're trying to triangulate my position, you're wasting your time. I'll be expecting your report on the package contents by noon."

"The lab is backed up," the agent protested.

"Noon," David repeated and ended the call. He stood and held out his hand to Emma. "Come on. It's time to track our quarry."

CHAPTER EIGHTEEN

Emma sat at the kitchen table with a mug of tea while the Fortress operatives assembled in the room with her and David. Rafe remained in the security room since he was on watch.

When she lifted the mug to her lips, Emma's hands shook. She sighed. Great way to look calm in front of a group of SEALs. She doubted David and the others reacted this way when faced with a question-and-answer session.

"We can find information another way if you aren't ready to talk, Emma," Jackson said. "Pushing yourself won't help."

Her brain had been hiding secrets since the night her family was murdered. David needed her to remember.

Emma wondered if her memory was returning. She kept having flashbacks of something even when she slept. Not seeing the flashback long enough to process the image was driving her crazy. "I need to do this, Jackson."

"The process will go smoother if you relax."

"Easy for you to say," she muttered. "You don't have to revisit some of the worst minutes of your life."

Wolf Pack's medic flashed her a sympathetic look. "True." He squeezed her arm gently. "Jon's the best. If anyone can help you remember more, it's him."

Jon? Emma's gaze flew to the silent, intense man as her dread built. Why Jon? She turned to David. "I thought you would ask the questions."

"Jon is an expert."

She studied the operative. Did he have a psychology degree or hypnosis skills? While Emma was willing to answer questions, she didn't know about answering them while hypnotized.

Jon grimaced. "My skills are better utilized in a different context."

His words had an ominous ring. "What context?" Emma asked.

"Interrogation."

She sucked in a breath. Oh, boy. Interrogation wasn't on her bucket list of things to experience in her lifetime. As Jackson said, there were other options to learn the information they needed to find the Butcher.

After Cal entered the room and filled his mug with coffee, David looked at Jon. "How do you want to do this?"

The other man rubbed his jaw, expression thoughtful. "Our best shot is to have Emma comfortable and relaxed. She needs you for that. Sit on the sofa and hold her close. Maybe drape a blanket over her." He looked at Emma. "What kind of white noise do you like?"

"Rain." She wrinkled her nose. "But the sky is clear today."

"I'll come up with something," Jon said. "Get comfortable. I'll be there soon."

She walked to the living room with David. He closed the curtains to darken the room, then turned the lamp to its lowest setting.

Emma sat and grabbed the lightweight blanket from the back of the sofa. David joined Emma, draped the blanket over her, then wrapped his arms around her.

Peace enveloped her. The whole world might be in chaos, but for this moment, nothing mattered but being with the man she loved.

"Comfortable?" he murmured.

Emma nodded. "What if this doesn't work?"

"We'll try something else."

"Not hypnosis, right?"

"We have many options, including hypnosis."

Her stomach knotted. Hopefully, Jon wouldn't make her cluck like a chicken if he used hypnosis.

The operative walked in with his laptop. After setting the computer on the coffee table, he tapped a few keys. Seconds later, the sound of rain filled the room.

"The acoustics are so good, it sounds as though someone opened a window to enjoy nature's symphony." Her smile slowly faded. "What do you want me to do?"

"Close your eyes, snuggle close to David, and listen to the rain."

"You won't learn much that way."

"Did I forget to mention the questions I'll be asking?" Amusement filled his voice.

"That wasn't on your stated agenda."

"Oops. My bad."

Emma smiled. Who knew that Jon Smith had a snarky sense of humor hidden behind a wall of silence?

"Close your eyes, Emma," Jon murmured. "Lean against David's chest."

She complied. "Where are your teammates?"

"Around. Do you feel David's heartbeat?"

Emma nodded.

"Allow the rhythm of his heart to ground you. Let yourself drift. The man who loves you will keep you safe.

Listen to the rain. Breathe slowly, Emma. Take full, deep breaths."

She followed his instructions and found herself relaxing in David's embrace. Perhaps this experience wouldn't be as bad as she thought.

After a while, Jon said, "Tell me a good memory from your childhood, Emma."

She stiffened.

"Easy, sweetheart," David murmured. "Think about something fun that happened with your mother and sister."

Emma's thoughts drifted back to elementary school when her home life was relatively calm. Although still demanding, her father wasn't as hard-nosed as he became when Emma grew older.

"For my eighth birthday, Mom took us to the Nashville Zoo. We had so much fun." The days following the expedition were filled with turbulence and her first trip to the hospital from a supposed fall.

"What was your favorite part of the zoo visit?" Jon asked, his voice gentle.

"The giraffes. They were elegant and majestic, graceful despite being so tall. Peaceful." Unlike her life growing up.

"Picture the giraffes in your mind. Do you see them?"

She gave a small nod.

"Keep them at the forefront of your mind as you tell me about your family vacation on Seagull Island. What was the first thing to pop into your mind when you parked at the beach house and exited the car?"

"The sea air smelled of brine and fish, and the seagulls were noisy."

Day by day, Jon led her through good memories of her beach vacation with her family. Emma snuggled closer to David.

He kissed her temple. "I love you, baby."

She smiled. "I love you, too."

"Please," Jon complained. "You're making me miss my wife."

That made her laugh.

"Tell me about the Seagull Island festival."

A kaleidoscope of memories spun through her mind. She recounted different things Anne said, the booths they visited, the items they purchased and the food they consumed. "We ate so much we didn't want to eat dinner. No choice, though."

A pause, then, "Why not?"

"Dad would have insisted we eat whether we were hungry or not. He said not eating what she'd prepared was disrespectful. Mom was a great cook. According to Dad, cooking and cleaning were her only skills."

"Go back to the festival. You and your sister arrived in Seagull. What did you do when you parked the car?"

"We walked to town. Dad wouldn't let us have the car." She recounted their day from the time she and Anne entered Seagull.

"Think about the people around you. Who did you see?"

"So many people were in town for the festival that we had a difficult time walking from one booth to the next."

"You said the first booth you visited sold blown glass. Take a mental picture of the people with you at the booth. Where did you go next?"

"A t-shirt booth."

"Did you buy anything?"

"A shirt for David. I have no idea what happened to it." That night had been so devastating that she hadn't thought about the shirt since the attack.

"What was on it?"

She smiled. "Beach Body."

David chuckled.

"The shirt made me laugh because unlike most of us, as a SEAL you always have a beach body."

"Glad you think so."

"Who did you see around you, Emma?" Jon interrupted.

"Tourists flocked around that booth."

"Compare your mental picture to the first booth. Do you recognize the same hats, sunglasses, shirts, or shorts?"

She started to say no, but a memory sparked in her mind. She frowned.

"Don't censor or analyze," Jon instructed. "Just tell me."

"At least ten of the same people were with us at both booths." She sighed. "I'm sorry."

"You're doing great. Where did you and Anne go next?"

"Pretzel booth." She laughed softly. "Anne wanted a hot pretzel with mustard. We split one. The pretzel reminded me of one David and I shared before he deployed."

"Who is around you? The same ten people?"

Emma frowned. "No," she said, the word drawn out. "We lost four, but gained others."

"Where did you and your sister go next?"

She continued to recount their journey, booth by booth until she reached the last one.

"Don't think, just respond. Did anyone follow you and Anne to most of the booths?"

A shudder wracked her body. "Yes."

"Describe him."

"Them." She gasped and sat up, her gaze locking on David's. "That's what I've been trying to remember. My family wasn't attacked by one man. Two men killed my sister and parents."

CHAPTER NINETEEN

The confirmation of what David had suspected made his heart ache. "Two men," he said. "Can you remember what they looked like, Emma?" Two men attacked his woman and killed her family. David looked forward to the day he caught up with them.

A sigh. "I remember baseball hats, sunglasses, and beach-themed t-shirts on the men trailing us around the festival. They were dressed like everyone else. But I only remember dark clothes on the killers during the attack. Maybe I'm wrong."

Jon stirred. "Don't second guess yourself. In our line of work, we don't believe in coincidences. Two men trailed you and your sister through the festival. Later at your beach house, two men attacked you and your family. Chances are good it's the same two men."

"Had any luck locating traffic or security cam footage for the day of the murders?" David asked. If Jon located an image, David stood a better chance of identifying the men responsible for killing the Tuckers and hurting Emma.

"Sorry, David. It's been too long."

That's what he'd figured. David turned to Emma. "Wasn't Anne active on social media?"

She rolled her eyes. "Very. Why?"

"If you give Jon access to Anne's accounts, he might find images from her social media pages."

"I should have thought of that sooner." Emma gave Jon the login information and a list of social media sites Anne frequented. "She uploaded pictures while we walked to the beach house. Most were of the beach and items for sale in the booths."

"It's a place to start." Jon ended the rain sounds. "You've had enough for now, Emma. We can try again later." He stood and patted Emma's shoulder. "Take a break. You'll remember more soon." With that, he left the room.

"Emma," Eli said.

She jumped and glanced behind her at other members of Wolf Pack leaning against the wall. "I didn't realize you were in the room."

Jackson winked at her. "That's what happens when you're distracted by David."

"Are you ready to talk to my friend about your knitting supplies?" Eli asked.

Emma nodded. "I only have cash on me. Will that be a problem?"

David tapped her nose gently. "I'll take care of the bill."

"Thank you, sweetheart."

That sweet name made his heart turn over in his chest. Man, he'd missed hearing Emma call him that name. He glanced at Wolf Pack's leader and nodded.

Eli grabbed his phone and made a call, tapping the speaker button.

A moment later, a woman answered. "The Bare Ewe. This is Madison."

"Hello, sugar. This is Eli Wolfe."

Madison laughed. "Don't let my husband hear you call me that. He's liable to take a swing at you the next time you're in town. How are you, Eli?"

"As handsome as ever."

"And as humble," she teased. "How's your family?"

"My girls are fantastic. Brenna sends her greetings."

"I'll have to call her. I haven't talked to her in months. Now, I know you didn't call to shoot the breeze with me or flirt. So, what can I do for you?"

"I have a principal who needs knitting supplies. Can you help her out?"

"Absolutely."

"Excellent. You're on speaker with Emma. I'll let her tell you what she wants."

"Hello, Emma. I'm Madison Santana. How can I help?"

David listened to the order Emma placed and shook his head at the foreign language they seemed to be speaking. Yarn weights and needle sizes plus several other things he couldn't decipher. When the time came to settle the bill, he started to hand his credit card to Emma, but Eli waved him off and gave her his card.

When he frowned, Eli edged closer to David. "We don't want your name out there in case the Butcher has computer skills. I'm not a stranger in Otter Creek." His expression grew smug. "My wife is a favorite author of the town's bookstore owner. You'll be familiar with Otter Creek soon if you and your brothers sign on with Fortress. Our training school is there with two teams as trainers."

David tilted his head. "Isn't that where Josh Cahill and his Delta team are located?"

Amusement lit Eli's eyes. "I see Cahill's reputation precedes him."

A soft whistle. "The rumors are true?"

A snort from Rafe. "The man's a sadist," he said as Emma handed Eli his phone and card.

"I heard that comment about my brother," Madison said.

"No offense meant, Maddie," Rafe said.

She laughed. "Based on what I hear from the trainees, that remark was mild. Eli, how do I get Emma's supplies to her?"

"Is your husband near the store?"

A pause, then, "Lucky for you, he just walked in for a cup of coffee. Hang on." After a short, muffled conversation, Madison said, "Here's Nick."

"Eli, what do you need?" a male voice asked with a light Spanish accent.

"A favor. Can you talk?"

"Hold." A minute later, Nick said, "Go."

"We're protecting an HVT who needs knitting supplies from Madison. Think you or one of your brothers-in-law will have time to make a delivery?"

"When and where?"

Eli looked at David.

"Nick, it's David Montgomery."

Silence, then, "How are you involved in this, Sheriff Montgomery?"

"It's David, and the HVT is the woman I'm marrying soon."

"This is the same woman who disappeared?"

"That's right. She was in WITSEC."

Nick whistled softly. "I'm glad to know you're reunited with her. Give me a location for the drop. Ethan is leaving the office in fifteen minutes for an out-of-town meeting. He'll be glad to deliver the supplies."

David breathed easier at the knowledge that Ethan Blackhawk, Otter Creek's police chief, would be available for a consult. The tough Army Ranger was legendary in the Special Forces community for his tracking ability and often consulted with police departments across the country on missing persons cases, especially cases that involved children.

He gave Nick the address of Bear Lake Cabins, a vacation rental business twenty minutes from the safe house, a business he'd invested in when he left the military. Although his financial support of the business wasn't widely known, there was a possibility the Butcher and his partner might dig up his involvement and stake out the grounds on the chance that David had hidden Emma in one of the cabins. "What's Ethan's ETA?"

"Ninety minutes. He'll call when he's ten minutes out."

"Tell him I appreciate his help."

"No problem, my friend. Eli?"

"Right here."

"Need anything else?"

"Not at the moment. We'll update Ethan when we see him, but we might have to hole up at PSI."

"Understood. We'll be ready if you need us. Later." Nick ended the call.

"What's PSI?" Emma asked.

"Personal Security International, the Fortress bodyguard training school located in Otter Creek," Eli said. "It's also where our black ops teams train."

"When do we leave for Bear Lake Cabins?"

"I'll leave in ten minutes," David said. "You should stay here."

"You need someone to watch your back. I want to be there for you."

"I want you somewhere safe, Em."

Eli and the other three men left, leaving David to sort things out with Emma.

She laid her hand over his heart. "I'm safest with you. Please, take me with you."

He hugged her. "I won't be gone long. I promise."

"Think with your head, not your heart. How much risk is involved with this meeting?"

"Not as much as I would face at the Rocking M or in Maple Valley," he admitted. "But it's still more than I want for you."

"Life has no guarantees of safety. I could be injured in an automobile accident, or fall and break a bone going for a walk."

He frowned. "This isn't the same. Two men are searching the county for you."

"Why did you choose Bear Lake Cabins to meet Blackhawk?"

"I'm a silent partner in the business."

She stared. "Doesn't Abe Coulter own the business?"

"Still does, but he was in a bad place financially when I left the Navy. His wife was taking cancer treatments, and he needed cash to keep the business afloat."

"Do people know you're part owner?"

"I'm not an owner," he insisted. "I invested money to help a friend. I haven't told anyone except my brothers, but someone good with computers could unearth the information."

"In other words, the risk of me going with you is low."

"Not low enough."

"I'll be safe as long as I'm with you."

"Emma."

"Please."

David sighed. "All right. But you have to do exactly what I tell you. Although the risk is minimal, it's not zero. The killers might have the area staked out. Since we haven't identified them yet, they could walk right up to us and we wouldn't know they were a threat."

"I won't leave your side." She kissed him. "Thank you."

Taking Emma to Bear Lake Cabins might be a costly mistake. Hopefully, she wouldn't pay the price for his inability to tell the woman he loved no. "Don't make me regret this," he muttered.

"Yes, sir."

He snorted. "Smart aleck." David threaded his fingers through hers and escorted her to the kitchen where Eli waited.

"Who won?"

He glared at Wolf Pack's leader. "Who do you think?"

Eli grinned. "That's what I figured. Have to love strong women."

Emma Tucker was as strong as steel.

"We're taking my SUV," Eli continued. "The vehicle is reinforced and has bullet-resistant glass."

"What about your teammates?" Emma asked.

"Cal will ride with us. Jon's remaining here to continue his search for photos of the killers. Jackson takes over the watch in a few minutes. Rafe is preparing a few surprises in case we have unwanted company." He turned to David. "Ready?"

"As soon as I make one phone call." He wanted backup at Bear Lake Cabins. He trusted Eli and Cal. He trusted his brothers more. "I'll return in a minute." He stepped outside and called Elliot.

His brother answered on the first ring. "Everything okay?"

"I need backup."

"When and where?"

"Bear Lake Cabins in twenty minutes. I'll have Emma and two members of Wolf Pack."

"Why are you bringing Em?"

He snorted. "Wait until you have a woman of your own. You'll understand."

"Won't happen on my watch."

"You say that now. I'll be the first one to laugh in your face when you fall hard."

"Why are you going to the cabins?"

"To pick up supplies for Emma. I don't want to hear it," he said over his brother's protests. "Just say you'll back me up."

"Of course we will."

"Only two of you. I don't want to pull the others off shift."

"See you soon." Elliot ended the call.

David slid his phone away, sure his brothers would tear a strip off his hide for taking chances with Emma's safety. He was already second guessing his decision.

Although he wanted to lock Emma inside a fortress for her own safety, David couldn't do that to her. Her reaction to darkness and difficulty eating all added up to untreated PTSD, another black mark against the FBI. They should have insisted on counseling for Emma.

The door to the deck opened. "Time to go," Eli said.

He nodded. The sooner they picked up Emma's knitting supplies and returned, the better for his peace of mind.

"I'll drive the SUV to the deck stairs."

David returned to the kitchen to find Emma and Cal waiting for him.

The operative looked from David to Emma and back. His lips curved. "I'll wait on the deck," he murmured.

As soon as the door closed behind Cal, Emma asked softly, "Are you mad at me?"

He blinked. "Do I look angry?"

She studied his face. "I don't know what that expression is."

"It's the I-think-I-screwed-up-and-I'm-worried expression." His lips curved. "Get used to it. The expression might be permanent until the killers are behind bars."

"Then let's find these guys so I don't have to see that expression often."

"Deal." David wrapped his arm around Emma and drew her close to his side. "Let's do this."

CHAPTER TWENTY

David scanned their surroundings, his skin prickling. Something was off, but what? He studied the cabins. According to Abe's computerized reservation program, all the buildings were occupied except for Cabin 10. The curtains were open in each cabin except that one. Vehicles were parked in front of the structures, but no one appeared to be around. Abe's vacationers must be down at the lake.

Eli said softly to Cal, "Recon."

"Yes, sir." The operative walked to the closest cabin and around the back of the building.

A sheriff's SUV drove into the clearing and parked next to the Fortress vehicle. Elliot and Levi exited the cruiser. Dressed in uniforms, their shields glittered in the bright sunlight.

"Updates?" Levi asked, glancing at Emma who sat inside Eli's vehicle.

"We're waiting for Blackhawk to deliver Emma's supplies, and don't give me grief. She needs the supplies to keep herself grounded and calm."

His brothers exchanged glances. "Didn't know Chief Blackhawk made special deliveries." Elliot glanced around, his eyes narrowing. "You feel that?"

"Oh, yeah." Levi shifted to David's other side, studying the tree line. "Emma shouldn't be here, bro."

"I won't keep her locked up."

"Better than Em being hurt or killed." Elliot's gaze locked onto the unoccupied cabin. "Cabin 10 has closed curtains. You checked it?"

"We arrived two minutes ago. One member of Wolf Pack is doing recon." He sent Elliot a pointed look as he tossed his brother the master key. "Don't shoot him on sight or arrest him."

"If I spot him, he deserves what he gets." With that, Elliot walked in the opposite direction from Cal. Within thirty seconds, he melted into the dense shadows of the woods and vanished from sight.

David's phone rang. He glanced at the screen. "Montgomery."

"It's Blackhawk. I'm ten minutes out."

"Copy that. Be careful. We could have trouble brewing."

"Sit rep."

David updated the other man, ending with, "Emma insisted on coming with me. She's inside a Fortress SUV, but I don't have a good feeling about this."

"Listen to your gut. If you suspect a trap, choose another place to meet. I'll catch up with you."

Torn, he looked at the SUV again to reassure himself that Emma was still safe. "What's your ETA now?"

"Two minutes."

"Hurry." David ended the call. He started to go to Emma when a shot rang out, followed by another, then another in rapid succession. "Emma, get down!"

He and the other two men dashed to the driver's side of the vehicle and dropped down. After a quick glance to be sure Emma was out of sight, David asked, "Anybody got a bead on him?"

After getting a negative response, David called Ethan. "We're under fire."

"Copy. Where is he?"

More gunfire gave him a general location. He relayed the information to the police chief.

"I'll come up from the south. Tell the others not to shoot me. I'm in uniform."

"One of my brothers and Cal Taylor are in the woods, probably tracking. I'll pass the word." He glanced at Eli who fired his weapon when a shooter leaned out for a better line of sight.

Loud swearing followed by more gunshots.

David glanced at Eli. "Ethan's coming up from the south. Civilians will come soon. We need to end this, fast."

"Suggestions?"

"Get in your SUV and start backing out of the clearing as though you're making a run for it with Emma."

Eli scowled. "Bad plan. I'm not leaving you and your brother out here like sitting ducks."

"We'll use the vehicle for cover. When you draw him out, we'll take him down. Head for the north end of the clearing and stop. Keep Emma as far away from the shooter as possible."

A frown from Wolf Pack's leader. "This isn't my first rodeo, buddy. I'll protect your woman. You and your brother look after yourselves. No heroics."

David gritted his teeth. He'd do whatever was necessary. Glancing at his brother who signaled that he was ready, David motioned for Eli to go.

Wolf Pack's leader maneuvered around the Montgomery brothers to open the driver's side door and climbed behind the wheel to the accompaniment of rapid gunfire. "Hang on, Emma. We're going for a slow ride." After cranking the engine, he glanced at David.

David gave a short nod. "Levi, when we're close enough, get into the trees and get a bead on this guy."

"Copy that."

Eli began to back slowly from the clearing, angling the SUV to best protect Emma, David, and Levi.

The shooter renewed his efforts to stop the vehicle. Bullets pinged off the hood and fender on the passenger side.

David kept pace with the SUV, hoping the shooter would make a mistake before an innocent civilian wandered into the line of fire.

When the SUV moved close enough to the tree line, David fired a volley of carefully aimed shots to provide cover for his brother who sprinted for the safety of the trees.

At the designated place, David signaled Eli to stop. He peered around the front of the SUV, weapon aimed. He scowled. He still didn't have a line of sight on the shooter who continued to pepper the SUV with bullets. Soon, the compromised glass would give way, endangering Emma further.

After communicating with Eli via hand signals, David shifted to the back of the SUV in a crouch and peered around the back bumper when Levi fired a shot. His brother leaned out just enough to draw the other man's attention.

When the shooter took the bait and leaned out to get a better shot, David fired. The shooter dropped to the ground, groaning and clutching his right shoulder.

"Shooter's down," David called as Levi left cover to secure the man's weapon. "Watch for his partner."

Elliot jogged from the tree line with his phone to his ear. A moment later, he said, "Ambulance is on the way."

Cal and Ethan emerged from the trees, weapons drawn and aimed at the injured man until Levi cuffed him. The shooter spewed a litany of profanity.

David hurried to the SUV. "Emma."

She dove into his arms. "Are you all right?"

He closed his arms around her and held her tight. "I'm fine. You?"

"I may be shaking for days, but I'm not hurt." She glanced up at him. "I should have listened to you. I'm sorry. I didn't mean to endanger anyone."

David kissed her. "None of us are injured. I'll take that as a win." He glanced at Eli. "You okay?"

"Yep." He inclined his head toward Emma. "I'll stay with her while you check on your prisoner."

David cupped Emma's cheek. "I'll return in a few minutes."

"Do what you need to do." She started to tremble.

He nudged her back into the SUV. After draping a blanket from the sheriff's vehicle around Emma, David joined the others keeping watch over the prisoner. Levi was on his knees, pressing his gloved hands on the bullet wound to slow the blood flow.

The injured man glared at David, eyes narrowing. "I'll sue you."

"Get in line." Something about this guy was familiar. Did he and his partner attack the Tuckers, or was this related to something else entirely?

David looked at Elliot. "ID?"

"Paul Franks. Sound familiar?"

He looked down at the man again and studied his face. "Yeah, but I can't place him."

"You didn't deal directly with this Franks. You put his brother, Gage, behind bars eight months ago. Paul decided on a little payback when he saw you standing in the clearing."

David dragged a hand down his face, frustrated. He'd hoped capturing this man would cut the danger to Emma in half. Instead, the danger to his future wife remained as high as ever. "What were you thinking, Franks? You could have hurt an innocent person in your desire for revenge."

Franks scanned the faces of the men surrounding him, his eyes filled with contempt. "Don't see no innocent people here. Just a bunch of cops."

David called on every ounce of discipline the military had drummed into him to keep himself in check. What he wanted to do was pound some sense into Franks. This idiot could have hurt or killed the woman David needed more than his next breath.

Elliot scowled. "Families with kids are in the area, enjoying the sunshine and the lake. Bullets travel a long way."

Franks frowned. "That's not true." He paused. "Is it?"

Good grief. David sighed. "Levi, read Mr. Franks his rights. I need to call the TBI." This was going to be a long, drawn-out ordeal.

Elliot grimaced. "Great."

David caught Ethan's attention and stepped away from the downed man and his brothers. "How much time do you have?"

"What do you need?"

"My brothers and I will be tied up either here or with Franks for several hours. I don't want Emma out here that long. Would you take Emma and Cal to the safe house?"

"No problem." Ethan squeezed David's shoulder. "I'll return with my SUV in a few minutes."

"Thanks." David signaled for Cal to follow him and returned to Emma. He crouched beside her as Cal took up a defensive position to best cover him and Emma. "How are you?"

"Better." Her shaking hands told a different tale. "Are we leaving now?"

"You and Cal are leaving with Otter Creek's police chief in a few minutes. Ethan Blackhawk will drive you to the safe house."

"What about you?"

"Unfortunately, I have to stay for a while. I'll come to you as soon as I can."

Emma glanced across the clearing. "Is he one of the men who killed my family?"

He shook his head, regret twisting his stomach into a knot. "I'm sorry, baby. The shooter was after me, not you."

"Why?"

"Revenge for putting a family member in prison." He cupped her cheek. "While this isn't the norm, Emma, I can't guarantee someone else won't try something similar. Family and friends of people we arrest aren't afraid to let us know how they feel."

"That won't scare me off, Sheriff. I love you too much to give you up."

"I'm glad because I'm not above begging to keep you in my life."

She smiled. "No need to beg, love. You're stuck with me."

Ethan drove into the clearing.

"There's Ethan. Do you need anything before you go with him?"

"Something carbonated, please."

"I'll get it," Cal murmured. "Where do I go?"

"Abe has a vending machine in the lobby of the main office. You'll be able to get in although he's down at the lake this time of day." Good thing he was out, or his friend would have been caught in the crossfire. Abe would consider it his duty to protect his guests.

With a nod, the operative jogged to the main office.

"Come on." David lifted Emma from the SUV and carried her to Ethan's vehicle.

"I can walk," she protested.

"Maybe I need to hold you close." Not a lie.

Emma melted against him. "I won't complain, then."

He set her inside the vehicle. "Emma, this is Ethan Blackhawk, police chief of Otter Creek. Ethan, my future bride, Emma Tucker."

Ethan smiled. "It's good to meet you, Ms. Tucker."

"Call me Emma. Thank you for driving me to the safe house."

"I'm happy to help." He inclined his head toward the large bag on the dashboard. "Madison said she included a few extra supplies for you. If you don't like them, return them when you have the chance."

Cal handed one soft drink to Emma and one to Ethan while keeping the third for himself. "You're on your own, Montgomery."

"Thanks a lot, buddy. Better get going, Ethan. I don't want to delay you." He also didn't want Emma here when the Tennessee Bureau of Investigation showed up to start their work. If they realized she witnessed the shooting, the investigators would separate him and Emma for questioning.

David kissed Emma, then stepped back and closed Emma's door as Cal climbed into the backseat.

He waited until the SUV carrying Emma to safety was out of sight before calling the TBI. Once that was done, he and Elliot set up a perimeter around the area since David couldn't take an active part in the investigation. The afternoon promised to be a long one.

CHAPTER TWENTY-ONE

Emma stared through the front windshield of Chief Blackhawk's SUV. She shouldn't have left David. Yes, his brothers were with him, but she wanted to be with David to offer moral support.

If she'd stayed, though, he would have worried about her safety. News of the shootout would spread like wildfire in the community, and people from every corner of the county would come to see for themselves what was going on. Standing in the open with people staring at her, possibly the men who killed her family, sent a shudder cascading over her body. With her at the safe house, David could concentrate on protecting himself instead of her.

"Cold?" Chief Blackhawk asked.

"No, sir." She tugged the blanket tighter around herself for comfort and, yes, maybe to fight the trembling that still wracked her body.

"Call me Ethan." He placed the bag of knitting supplies on her lap. "Check the contents. Madison will ask what you thought about her choices when I return home." He glanced in the rearview mirror. "Cal, you're navigating. I'll watch for a tail, but no detours unless we run into a problem. I'm consulting on a case in another county."

"Yes, sir."

After sipping her drink, Emma peered inside the bag of supplies. Her eyes widened. "Oh, wow." She hadn't expected Madison to include so much in the bag.

"Good or bad?" Ethan asked.

"It's wonderful." Emma fingered the yarn, many more skeins than she'd requested. So soft and delicate, and the colors were gorgeous. Socks were the perfect small, portable project. The rosewood needles Madison included were smooth enough for yarn to glide along the surface. She couldn't wait to start on her first pair of socks.

Emma dug deeper into the bag and found a book of sock patterns she'd seen advertised and planned to order, but the Butcher and his partner broke into her last safe house before she followed through.

"What should I tell Madison?" Ethan asked.

"That I'm not giving anything back. I love it all. In fact, The Bare Ewe might become my go-to knitting store."

"Excellent. My sister-in-law will be happy to hear that. The store has a website so you can order whatever you need. If Madison doesn't have what you want, she'll find it for you."

"Madison seems very nice."

"She is. Once your problem is resolved, you and David should visit Otter Creek. Madison would love to talk shop with you. Have you been a knitter long?"

"Since I was six. My grandmother taught me." She smiled. "You should have seen my first project. My scarf had more holes than a piece of Swiss cheese. I made the scarf for her. Nana wore that scarf with pride until I begged her to stop."

Ethan's phone signaled an incoming call. He glanced at the name on his dashboard screen. "That's my wife. Mind if I take the call?"

"Of course not." She was curious about Ethan's family.

He tapped the screen. "Hello, beautiful. You're on speaker with Emma and Cal."

"Hello, handsome." A slight pause, then, "Cal Taylor?"

"I knew you loved me," Cal said.

"If you know what's good for your health, you won't flirt with my wife, Taylor." Ethan glared at the man in his rearview mirror.

The other woman laughed and said, "Hi, Emma. I'm Serena."

"Hello."

"What do you need, baby?" Ethan asked.

"Lucas wants to talk to you."

"Yeah?" The policeman's mouth curved into a smile. "Hold the phone for him."

A moment later, a toddler babbled into the phone.

Ethan chuckled. "Hey, buddy. Is Mommy treating you right?"

More babble. The only word Emma recognized was something that sounded like Dada. Her eyes stung. Would she and David have a child one day who wanted to call and talk to his dad?

"Is that right?" Ethan turned left at Cal's direction. "Be good. I'll be home before bedtime."

More garbled words.

"I love you, too, buddy. Let me talk to your mom."

A moment later, Serena's voice filled the SUV's cabin again. "Thanks for letting us interrupt, love. He kept pointing at the phone and saying Dada. Nothing I did would satisfy him until he heard your voice."

"I love hearing from you both. I'll be home in a few hours." After telling Serena he loved her, Ethan ended the call.

"You are a blessed man," Emma said.

"Believe me, I know. Serena owns my heart. And Lucas?" Ethan grinned. "That boy has me wrapped around his little finger."

"How old is he?"

"Eighteen months." The police chief made the final turn into the long, winding driveway leading to the safe house. "Wait in here until we're sure it's safe."

He exited the SUV along with Cal. The two men scanned the area for signs of danger. Seeming satisfied that the area was clear, Ethan opened Emma's door. "Let's go."

The police chief escorted her to the front door with Cal at their backs. Jackson opened the door as they climbed the porch steps.

The medic frowned as he stepped back to allow Emma and Ethan to enter the cabin. "Where are Eli and David?"

"Still at Bear Lake Cabins," Ethan said. "They ran into trouble. Emma and Cal will explain." He looked at Emma. "Need anything before I go?"

She shook her head. "Thank you for everything, Ethan."

"I hope we see you and David in Otter Creek soon." He nodded at Jackson, clapped Cal on the shoulder, and left.

"What happened?" Jackson demanded.

"Chill." Cal nudged Emma toward the kitchen table, draped the blanket around her shoulders again, and set her soft drink and bag on the table within easy reach as Jon walked into the room. "Eli and David are fine. A family member of a man David arrested decided to get a little payback. David shot him in the shoulder. He and Eli will be tied up with the TBI for a while."

The medic turned his attention to Emma. "You're okay?"

"Thanks to David, I'm fine. He didn't want me outside of the vehicle, a wise move on his part." She tried to smile, but figured she failed when Jackson's eyes narrowed.

The medic filled a coffee mug with water and dropped an herbal tea bag into the liquid. When the microwave heating cycle ended, Jackson set the mug in front of her along with a packet of sugar and a spoon. "I know you drink unsweetened tea. Make an exception today."

She nodded, unable to speak. Emma did not want to cry in front of these big, tough SEALs.

Jon joined her at the table with a mug of coffee. "What's in the bag?"

"Knitting supplies." Grateful for the distraction, she unloaded the contents of the bag and spread them out.

"Is knitting difficult?"

Her gaze shifted from the yarn to the operative. "Not really. There are only two stitches, knit and purl. The patterns are made with combinations of the two stitches. Do you want to learn?"

His lips curved slightly. "My wife, Dana, loves to learn new skills, especially skills that help her cope with stress."

"I'd love to teach her to knit, but you probably don't want me near her right now." With a pair of serial killers dogging Emma, being around her wasn't safe.

"What about books, websites, or teaching videos?" Jon asked.

"I can write a list of resources I've found helpful along with a list of basic supplies."

"That's perfect." He left the kitchen and returned with a notepad and pen. "Do you need anything else?"

Amusement filled her when she realized the quiet operative was probably trying to keep Emma's mind occupied, but Dana might use the information. Emma recognized that she was dealing with adrenaline dump again, but she was also worried about David's safety. "This is perfect. Thanks."

After removing the tea bag and adding sugar to her drink, earning a nod of approval from Jackson, Emma picked up the pen and made a list of supplies and two instruction books appropriate for novice knitters.

She glanced at Jon. "I don't have a computer or cell phone. I need to search for the best websites and instructional videos."

He tapped a few keys on his keyboard and slid his laptop across the table to Emma. "You're free to surf without risk of detection online. Don't access your accounts, including the ones set up while you were in WITSEC. We have to assume those accounts have been compromised."

Emma focused on making a complete list for Dana while Jon, Eli, and Jackson talked among themselves. She surfed the web, blocking out the conversation of the operatives. While locating information for Dana, Emma found a few websites she wanted to explore for herself.

A long while later, Jon set a glass of ice water by her hand. "Having fun?"

Emma blinked and looked up at the operative. A slight smile curved his mouth. Glancing at the time, she gasped. "I'm sorry. I didn't realize I'd been using your computer so long."

He shrugged. "I used a computer in the security room to continue my research." Jon inclined his head toward the water. "Drink or David will be angry with us for not taking care of you."

"Can't have that." She wrote the final website address for Dana, then exited from the search engine. "Thanks for the use of your computer." After tearing out the page with the websites she wanted to follow up on later, Emma handed the notepad, pen, and laptop to Jon. "This will help Dana get started."

He skimmed the list. "If she has questions, are you willing to talk to her?"

"Of course. I love to teach others to knit. It's a passion of mine."

The front door opened.

Between one breath and the next, Jon was out of his chair, his weapon in hand and pointed at the doorway to the kitchen.

"It's Eli and David," Wolf Pack's leader called. "We're coming in soft."

Jon didn't holster his gun until his friend and David walked in.

Emma hurried into David's open arms. "Hi."

"How are you?" he murmured.

"Better now that you're here."

He squeezed her tighter. "Any problems while we were gone, Jon?"

"Nope."

"Sit rep." This from Eli.

"Rafe set the traps we discussed. He's in the security room."

A frown. "He's off duty."

"He wanted Jackson to keep an eye on Emma."

David drew back to look down at her. "Em?" Concern filled his eyes.

"I'm fine. I was shaky when we first arrived, but thanks to the tea Jackson made for me and Jon's distraction, I'm back to normal."

Jon chuckled. "Caught me."

"Will your wife be interested in the list I put together?"

"Of course. I didn't lie to you. Dana loves to learn new things, and she's always looking for ways to cope with anxiety and stress." His expression darkened. "Some days are better than others for her."

Hmm. Sounded like Dana had a traumatic past. The knowledge sent a surge of sympathy rolling through Emma. "If she needs a sympathetic friend, give her my number."

The operative studied her a moment, then gave a slow nod. "I'll do that, but Dana is slow to warm up to strangers."

"She does have someone to talk to?"

"She and Eli's wife, Brenna, are best friends as well as sisters."

"What else happened, Jon?" David asked.

The sniper scowled.

Eli and Jackson chuckled. "Losing your ice-man persona?" Eli teased.

"Shut up. You are expendable, you know."

"Aww, now. Don't be like that. Besides, Dana loves me, and you hate to make your sweet wife angry."

Jon rolled his eyes as the others in the room laughed.

David dropped a light kiss on Emma's mouth, then nudged her back to the table. "What's all this?"

"My haul from The Bare Ewe." Emma rubbed the strands of a skein between her fingers. "I'm going to enjoy working with this yarn. Madison sent me a book of patterns, too. I can't wait to try the sock patterns."

"It's easier to buy them at the store," Jackson muttered.

"Easier, yes," Emma admitted. "Making my own is more fun."

"If you say so." He didn't sound convinced.

"What did you find out, Jon?" David asked.

The sniper glanced at Emma before focusing on David. "I hacked into the security cams at Emma's safe houses."

"And?"

"I have photos you need to see."

CHAPTER TWENTY-TWO

Adrenaline poured into David's bloodstream at Jon's news. "Enough to get an ID on the perps?" he asked. They needed a break. He desperately wanted Emma to be safe. For that to happen, the Butcher and his partner must be behind bars.

"The men were careful to keep most of their faces averted."

Most, but not all. He smiled. "But you caught enough."

A slight nod. "We won't have to look far."

What did that mean? "Let's have a look."

Emma gathered her supplies and returned them to the bag. Her hands shook.

David wrapped his arm around her shoulders. "Have you looked through the book yet?"

She shook her head.

"Choose a pair of socks for me." He wouldn't wear them on the job, but he'd definitely wear the socks at home and treasure them. The task gave Emma something pleasant to focus on despite the topic of conversation.

The conversation in the room came to a halt as the operatives stared at him. He glared at the lot of them. They would have done the same thing if their girlfriends or wives needed the distraction.

Emma glanced at David. "You'll wear them?"

"Absolutely."

Her face lit with pleasure. She removed the book from the bag and pulled out two rolls of yarn. Thankfully, one roll was dark gray and the other was black. He could live with either of those colors.

Jon snorted, then returned his attention to his laptop.

"I wouldn't laugh too loud, dude," Jackson said with a grin. "If Dana knits socks, you'll be wearing a pair of those handmade beauties, too."

"No way. That's not going to happen."

"You say that now. Aren't you the ice-cold sniper who drops everything the minute his wife calls?"

Jon narrowed his eyes. "I can kill you from one thousand yards away."

The medic shrugged. "True. If you do, you'll have to sew your own bullet and knife wounds in the field."

"Not a deterrent, Conner. I've stitched my own wounds before."

A snort from the medic. "Dana won't like you adding more scars to your already impressive collection. You don't want to worry her, do you?"

Another glare from Jon before he returned his attention to his computer. After a few rapid-fire taps on his keyboard, the operative looked up. "Emma."

Her shoulders tensed under David's arm. "Yes?"

"Look at the screen when you're ready."

"Show me."

Jon looked at David, eyebrow raised.

"Go ahead." The more information he had to work with, the faster Emma would be safe.

The sniper turned his laptop around as Jackson shifted to stand near Emma. The screen was filled with a still shot of a man dressed in dark clothes, most of his face averted from the camera.

Emma leaned closer to the laptop. "Can you enlarge the picture?"

"What do you see, Em?" David asked.

"There's something on his wrist."

The tattoo she'd noticed when the killer attacked Emma and her family in Seagull?

Jon came around the table, angled the computer away from Emma, and typed in a few commands. A second later, the view on the screen shifted and focused on the intruder's wrist. He typed in a few more commands, and the picture sharpened slightly. "That's the best I can do." He turned the computer to face Emma and David again. The intruder had two letters tattooed on the underside of his wrist. HC.

Emma gasped, blood draining from her face.

David covered her hand with his. "Emma?"

"That's the tattoo I saw." She turned to him. "I remember seeing HC on the wrist of the man who attacked me. What does it mean?"

Good question. David studied the photo. "Jon, focus in on the man's face." When the picture on the screen shifted again, a surge of anger swept over David. He needed to talk to Zane. Would Emma recognize the jawline and ear? "Look at his face now, baby."

Emma didn't say anything for a minute as she stared at the photo on the screen with a puzzled expression on her face and a hint of fear in her eyes.

He squeezed her hand. "What is it?"

"What I'm thinking can't be right. I have to be mistaken."

"Tell me."

"That man resembles Agent Wells from this angle." She shook her head. "Agent Wells wouldn't hurt me or murder my family." Emma turned her hand over and threaded her fingers through David's. "Would he?"

"We'll find out." David looked at Jon. "Can you focus on the man in the background?"

A head shake. "This is the best I can do."

"What other photos do you have?"

Jon leaned over and tapped a few more keys.

The photo on the screen changed, the background indicating a different safe house. In the foreground, the camera had captured the image of two men, side views again. Both intruders wore identical skull caps.

David didn't recognize either of the men. "Does anything about this guy look familiar, Emma?"

She shook her head.

"Jon, can you give us a better look at the man in the background?"

More keys tapping, then the photo on screen shifted.

Although grainy, the jawline was clear enough to determine this man wasn't captured on the security cams at the other safe house. David's stomach knotted. "Do you remember this guy?" he asked Emma.

Eyes wide, she again shook her head. "What does this mean?"

Nothing good. Instead of answering, he lifted her hand to his lips and kissed her knuckles.

"Have you looked at the FBI's crime scene reports, David?" Cal asked.

"Jordan hasn't given me anything."

"Don't insult my intelligence. You asked Z to do some digging for you. He knows his stuff and lives to defeat fed cybersecurity without leaving electronic tracks behind. Nothing makes that SEAL happier than to frustrate the federal government. Unless Zane was slammed by other priorities, he would have sent you something by now."

David chuckled. "He did send files, but I haven't looked at them yet." His smile faded. "Unfortunately, there are many. The Butcher and his partners have been busy."

"Partners?" Emma echoed, her voice faint. "More than one?"

He cupped her cheek. "You know the answer to that question, baby. You saw the evidence for yourself." Worse, David was almost positive more than these four men were involved in hunting Emma.

"How can we help?" Eli asked.

"I need to print photos of each of their victims and create a murder board." David lifted one shoulder. "It's easier for me to see patterns that way."

A nod from Wolf Pack's leader before he glanced at his partner. "Any more photos to show Emma and David?"

The sniper brought up another photo of two more men. Nothing about them was familiar.

Cal whistled softly. "Any tattoos on this pair?" he asked Jon.

The operative enlarged the portion of the screen where the wrist of one man was visible. HC, the same tattoo seen in the other photos.

David rubbed the back of his neck, frustration building. How were these men able to avoid the cameras so effectively? "Do you have a better camera angle of these two?"

"Sorry. The rest of the angles were worse."

"Show the photos from the third safe house," Eli ordered, his expression grim.

A moment later, the screen filled with the profiles of two more men. The one in the foreground wore an earring. Emma leaned closer to the computer, her gaze intent.

"Do they look familiar, Emma?" Jackson asked.

"Maybe. Jon, can you enlarge the earring?" When he complied, she gripped David's hand tighter. "I remember seeing that earring. But where?" She was silent a moment, then groaned. "Why can't I remember?"

"You will. Look at the men. Do you recognize them?" David murmured.

"Emma." Jon waited until she focused on him. "Study their faces, then close your eyes and think about the location of your third safe house."

"Where were you?" David prompted.

"Cherry Hill."

He frowned. "That's an hour away from Otter Creek." And two hours from Maple Valley.

She shrugged. "Agent Jordan told me to keep a low profile, so I didn't travel around the area much."

David blew out a breath as frustration continued to build inside of him. "You could have gone to Chief Blackhawk or the Fortress training school for help. Fortress has a Delta team stationed there to train bodyguard recruits."

"I never heard of Fortress until you told me about the company, and I didn't know Ethan until today." She smiled. "I wish I'd known about The Bare Ewe. I would have been a repeat customer."

"Focus," Jon murmured. "Study the faces of the men, then close your eyes and picture your favorite places to visit in Cherry Hill." The perspective on the photo shifted again to crop out the background.

Emma studied the screen for a long minute, then closed her eyes.

David prayed this worked. They needed information as fast as possible because his future wife was in grave danger. He and the other men in the room remained silent as Emma focused on her time in Cherry Hill.

Emma had been so close, yet the FBI had refused to allow her to contact him. David had lost too much time with her. Worse, he could have been at Emma's side when these men breached her safe houses and possibly brought this nightmare to an end before good agents paid the ultimate price.

Emma's eyes opened. "I saw them when I attended an arts and crafts festival in Humphrey, a town on the opposite side of Dunlap County from Otter Creek."

Cal grunted. "That wasn't a good idea, Emma. The key to keeping yourself safe in WITSEC is staying away from anything associated with your past."

"I didn't introduce myself to the vendors and didn't stay long. I bought a pair of knitting needles and three skeins of yarn, and returned home. Cherry Hill didn't have the supplies I needed."

"But those men knew where to find you," he pointed out gently.

David looked at him. Cal sighed and held up his hand to forestall David from telling him to back off.

"These men had access to the US Marshals' database or a mole in the FBI," Eli said. "Otherwise, they wouldn't have known where to start looking for Emma. There must be thousands of arts and crafts festivals held all over the country every year." He turned to Emma. "Assuming you followed the rest of the WITSEC protocols."

She frowned. "Like I told the FBI, I didn't break the rules except to go to one festival for ten minutes."

"How soon was your safe house breached following the arts and crafts festival?" David asked.

She shifted her guilt-filled gaze to him. "The same night. I barely escaped. They still hurt me."

He gritted his teeth. "How? Their MO thus far has been using a baseball bat and knife to attack their victims."

"This pair cheated. One of them brought a gun and grazed my arm with a bullet."

David stared. "How did you escape?"

"I climbed out a second-story window and shimmied down a tree. They fired on me when I ran."

"Did you notice these men at the festival or feel as though someone watched you?"

"I didn't notice anyone following me. I felt as though spiders crawled on my back. Does that count?"

Despite the seriousness of the discussion, the men chuckled. "Oh, yeah," Cal said. "We're all familiar with the fake spiders. You might not have noticed these men, but your subconscious gave you a warning. You didn't visit other booths at the festival?"

She shook her head. "After I bought the knitting supplies, I went home." She sighed. "I must have led them right to my safe house."

Jon shook his head. "They already knew where you were hiding. My guess is these two followed you from the safe house to the festival and back home again. They waited until they thought you were asleep to break in. Were you sleeping when they arrived?"

"No, thank goodness."

"It's good that you were awake," he murmured.

Emma shuddered. "I may never sleep well again," she muttered.

David glanced at Jon. "Show us the pictures from the safe house in Rock Harbor."

A moment later, another photo of two men filled the screen. "Do you remember seeing these men, Emma?" Eli asked.

She studied the screen, but finally shook her head, a troubled expression on her face. "I don't recognize them, either. I don't understand, David. What does this mean?"

"Trouble with a capital T."

"David, send me Zane's email. I'll print the files, and we'll get started." Jon sent him a pointed glance. "Sounds like you have a call to make."

Yeah, he did. "Have you searched Anne's social media pages?"

"My priority was the safe house photos. The social media pages are my next project."

"I need it yesterday."

"Understood."

David kissed Emma lightly and stood. "I'll be back in a few minutes." He looked at Eli who gave him a slight nod. Knowing his bride-to-be would be well protected, David walked outside to the deck. As he shut the door behind him, he heard Eli ask Emma to show him her book of sock patterns.

David grabbed his phone and strode to the railing. He checked his emails and saw what he'd expected to see from Jordan. Nothing. The special agent wanted to play hardball? Fine. David relished a good game.

Seconds later, his call was answered. "Yeah, Jordan." The special agent's voice sounded surly and clipped.

"This is Montgomery. We need to talk."

"So, talk. I'm busy."

"Where's my file on the threat delivered to the Rocking M?"

"This is my case. I have more important things to do than cater to your curiosity, Montgomery. How's my witness?"

"Safe, no thanks to you. You have until 8:00 a.m. to send me the information I asked for, or I'll contact Whitehead."

Jordan hissed out a breath. "Look, I told you I might not have all the results back as soon as you wanted them. I don't. The lab's backed up."

"Then pressure the lab to send the results."

"If the only reason for this call is to threaten me, you've accomplished your goal. I have to go. Unlike you, I have real work to do."

"Hold it, Jordan."

A muttered curse. "What else?"

"You have a serious problem."

"I have several, and you're at the top of my list."

"When were you going to tell me that Emma has a crew of men hunting her?"

CHAPTER TWENTY-THREE

Satisfaction filled David at the silence from Special Agent Craig Jordan. Guess the agent hadn't expected a country bumpkin sheriff to uncover information pointing to a group of men hunting Emma.

David didn't understand why the men wanted to kill her. Was Jordan's assumption that the group wanted to finish what they started correct?

"I don't know what you're talking about," the FBI agent said finally.

"Don't lie to me, Jordan. I'm not in the mood."

After a muttered curse, "How did you find out?"

David's hand clenched around his phone. If Jordan stood in front of him, David would punch him. "You should have told me the truth. By holding back, you endangered Emma."

"The more people who know, the greater the risk for a leak."

He snorted. "If your agency was a ship, it'd be on the bottom of the ocean." When Jordan protested, David cut him off. "How many people in your agency know about Emma and the crew of men hunting her?"

"It's a tight group."

"How many? Remember, I will confirm your claim."

More cursing. "The circle is smaller than it was two days ago."

"How many, Jordan?"

"It was twelve people."

David blinked, stunned at the revelation. "Are you kidding me?" His voice rose. "You call 12 people a tight circle?"

"I'm down five marshals because of your girlfriend."

"You're down five agents because of your own incompetence," he snapped.

David dragged a hand down his face. Good grief. Any number of people could have accessed the information in the database, including a mole. "What do the letters HC stand for?"

A hiss of annoyance from the agent. "I'll learn who told you this information and arrest him."

"Good luck with that." If Zane was as good as Wolf Pack said, Jordan would never trace the leak to him. "Answer my question."

"Hunt Club," he muttered.

David's eyes narrowed. He'd never heard of this group. "Who are the members?"

"Do you think I'd be sitting here talking to you if I knew that?"

"What do you know about them?"

"They're dangerous."

"Tell me something I don't know."

"No one knows who's involved in this group. Their identities are a closely held secret, but rumors say the only way out of the group is in a body bag. Makes people unwilling to talk about their little fraternity of blood brothers."

"Where do they operate?"

"All over the country." Bitterness filled Jordan's voice. "Look, I can't tell you anything else. If I do, my badge is on the line. If your sources are so good, dig up the rest for yourself."

"So much for sharing information."

"I can't give you what I don't know. I have one witness who can't recall the faces of her attackers, and there's no forensic evidence to work with. So, you tell me how I'm supposed to build a case on nothing but supposition."

"Is Wells a member of this group?"

"No." Jordan ended the call.

David shoved his phone into his pocket and leaned against the railing. Unbelievable. This group of hunters had been operating all over the country for at least 18 months, and the FBI had nothing to show for their investigation?

No way. Jordan had just lied to him, and David wanted to know why. Was he protecting Agent Wells? Maybe Jordan didn't have enough evidence to arrest him.

As he turned to go inside, Rafe walked around the corner of the house with a pack on his shoulder. The former fed gave a chin lift in silent greeting.

"Finished your security shift?"

"Yep. I wanted to check the perimeter." Rafe's eyebrows knitted. "What's up?"

"It's that obvious?"

The other man lifted one shoulder. "Want to talk or should I mind my own business?"

David motioned toward the chairs at the far end of the deck. He'd share the information with the others soon.

"Talk to me," Rafe said as he sat and set his bag beside the chair.

"Just got off the phone with Jordan."

"Bet that was unpleasant. The dude's a jerk."

"I confronted him about information he didn't share."

A snort. "What else is new? Jordan has a rep at the Bureau for holding information close to the vest."

"This information is a game changer in how we protect Emma." David rubbed his jaw. "Jordan neglected to tell us Emma has a crew of men stalking her."

Rafe stared. "Who are they?"

"He says he doesn't know, but they're part of a group called the Hunt Club."

The former agent surged to his feet and stalked to the deck railing. Rafe gripped the wood hard enough that his knuckles turned white, the muscles in his arms bunching. After several minutes of silence while the operative pulled himself together, he turned back to David. Eyes glittering with fury, he said, "Details?"

"You know this group."

"You could say that. They murdered the woman I planned to marry three years ago."

Oh, man. "I'm sorry for your loss, Rafe."

The operative gave a short nod. "Now you understand why I will do anything necessary to protect Emma." His eyes darkened. "No one should have to experience that loss."

"Did you investigate her death?"

"Not officially. My supervisor said I couldn't be objective."

"But you did nose around."

A slight curve of Rafe's lips. "Of course."

"Come inside. We'll brief everyone at one time."

The other man grimaced.

"They don't know about your girlfriend?" David asked.

"No." He sighed. "Let's go. Protecting Emma will be worth the pain of talking about Callie." Rafe snagged his bag and led the way into the cabin.

Cal's eyebrow rose at the sight of his teammate. "That was fast. You finished checking the perimeter already?"

David held up his hand to hold off more questions. He turned to Eli. "Can Jackson join the discussion without compromising our security?"

Jon said, "I'll monitor the security cams from here." He indicated his laptop.

Cal left the room and returned with Jackson.

"What's going on?" the medic asked as he sat across from Emma.

"I spoke with Special Agent Jordan," David said. "At first, he denied knowing about the men searching for Emma. After a hard push, Jordan finally admitted the letters HC stand for Hunt Club."

Rafe's hands fisted.

Eli narrowed his eyes as he took in his teammate's reaction.

"Jordan said the only way to leave the Hunt Club is in a body bag," David continued.

Cal whistled. "Harsh."

"How long has this club been in existence?" Eli asked.

"At least three years," Rafe answered. He jammed a hand through his hair, his expression bleak. "Two members of this club murdered the woman I was planning to marry."

"Oh, Rafe," Emma murmured. "I'm so sorry."

He cleared his throat. "Thanks."

"You joined the FBI to hunt for her killers." Jon glanced at his teammate. "Knew something prompted your decision. You aren't fond of the federal government."

"What do you know about the Hunt Club, Rafe?" Eli asked.

"Not enough. They're like ghosts. A friend in the Bureau gave me a copy of the crime scene reports from Callie's murder. The team found evidence of two killers, but not much else. No fingerprints, no murder weapons. Like Emma's family, she was stabbed multiple times. The killers bypassed Callie's security system. The outside camera caught less than the photos Jon pulled from

Emma's safe houses. The men knew the location of the external cameras and sprayed the lenses with black paint."

He scowled. "These men are treating the US as their hunting ground." Rafe looked at Emma. "Where were your safe houses located?"

"Arkansas, Louisiana, Tennessee, and Kentucky. My family was attacked in Alabama. The marshals were discussing moving me from Rock Harbor right before the last team found me."

David stiffened. "The FBI suspected your security had been breached?"

"I don't know. They only told me if I was relocated again, they hoped it was the last time."

Rafe growled. "They were setting a trap."

She blinked. "A trap for the Hunt Club?"

"For one of the teams, and they were using you as bait."

"Some trap," Cal said. "They not only didn't catch the hunters, they lost the bait."

"I thought Agent Jordan wanted to keep me safe." Emma looked stricken.

"He does," Rafe said. "But his priority is catching a group of killers."

"You said the teams have been operating for at least three years." Eli frowned. "If there are teams all over the US, why haven't they caught the attention of the media?"

"The teams use different methods to kill their victims."

David groaned as realization sank in. Had one of these teams killed Emma's grandfather, too? "And law enforcement may not realize a team is hunting in their area." He turned to the woman he adored. "I'm sorry, Emma. If I had known this, I would have safeguarded your grandfather."

Emma laid her hand over his. "You had no way to know. Even if the FBI had shared the information with you, you couldn't have anticipated they would target him."

"What purpose would killing Mr. Watts serve, David?" Jackson asked.

"I think the men killed Mr. Watts while trying to force him to tell them where Emma was hiding."

"But he didn't know." Her voice broke. "What must Grandpa have thought if he learned I was alive but didn't contact him?"

"He'd be thrilled that you were alive and safe. If he'd known where you were, Mr. Watts wouldn't divulge the information. He was a tough cowboy."

"Because of me, they tortured him. I should have defied the FBI and contacted Grandpa. He might still be alive if I had called him."

"Wouldn't have mattered if he gave away your location or not," Rafe said. "The men would have killed him anyway. They don't leave witnesses behind. It's one of their trademarks."

"That's why they're desperate to kill Emma." Cal pushed away from the table and refreshed his coffee. "She's the one witness who escaped." With an apologetic glance at her, he added, "Since they fancy themselves as professional hunters, the men will hate that their prey outwitted them. Worse, you escaped from at least four teams, possibly five. That makes you a prized target."

Emma sighed. "What kind of men hunt people instead of wildlife?"

"Evil ones."

"Men who think they're untouchable," Jon added. He looked at Rafe. "If the FBI used Emma for bait, why wasn't a team of agents on her at all times to catch the crew who stepped into the trap?"

"From what Emma said, the agents were stationed close to the safe house. Jordan probably hoped to capture the images of the hunters on camera to identify them all and scoop them up at one time."

"But I can't identify any of them," Emma said. "At least, not yet."

"The hunters don't know that. I'm betting the information isn't anywhere in the FBI files. Craig Jordan is a glory hound. He wants to make a name for himself by busting this crew of hunters and parading them in front of the cameras. I've always believed there are more victims than the FBI realizes, but the feds are keeping the information quiet instead of contacting law enforcement agencies across the country."

David slammed his fist on the table, making Emma jerk. His face burned. "The hunters could have killed Emma. She was lucky to escape and almost didn't the last time they found her. The Marshals didn't survive Jordan's plan."

"That wasn't the only possible flaw in his plan," Eli pointed out. "If the mastermind behind this system is smart, one member of a team only knows his partner, but not the identities of other teams. Jordan would have captured the hunters and missed the mastermind."

Rafe's expression grew dark. "If word leaks that the FBI is looking for members of the Hunt Club, there's a good chance the members will go underground until the interest dies down. Then, they'll start the game again."

Shoving aside his fury, David focused on what was important. "How do the teams choose their victims?"

"The teams are autonomous. Once they pick their target, they stalk and kill their prey. I'm assuming they report their success to the mastermind and are credited with the kill. I don't know what the reward is for success."

"A team in Alabama killed my family," Emma said. "Have other teams murdered multiple victims at one time?"

"Not that I know, but I haven't been part of the FBI for several months."

Jon frowned. "The mastermind has to be keeping track of the hunts and teams."

"I agree, but the FBI hasn't captured a team and traced an electronic trail from them to the mastermind."

"Then that's part of our new mission. We nab a team and trace them to the mastermind." He turned to Eli. "Agreed?"

"Yep. Emma's safety is first. After that, I say we go after the Hunt Club and take them down." He looked at David. "We have to bring Maddox into the loop."

A nod. "If this crew is as large as Rafe says, we'll need more than Wolf Pack and my brothers."

"Unless we take them down one pair at a time." Cal pushed aside his empty coffee mug.

"Too risky. All it would take is one nervous team to alert the mastermind."

"We need to know how many teams are operating," Jackson said. "Tracking them down will take a coordinated effort, especially if they're stalking their next victims."

"They can't hunt all the time," Emma said. "Unless they're independently wealthy, they have to have jobs to support their disgusting hobby."

"We'll find out." David squeezed her hand. "I need to update my brothers since there's a good chance at least one of the teams is in this area now."

Eli glanced at his watch. "Your brothers should be here soon."

"Owen and Caleb are on duty in two hours."

"I called Elliot while you on the phone with Jordan. We can't have information gaps between the teams. Elliot asked the part-timers to cover the shift for four hours while we discuss Emma's protection plan. He sent a text five minutes before you came inside to confirm their arrival time."

He would have to rework the shift schedule. Although David was on administrative leave while the TBI investigated the shooting, the massive amount of paperwork required to keep his department running didn't stop. At least he could help his deputies take care as much paperwork as possible. His top priority, though, was to ensure Emma's safety and that of his family and Morgan County citizens.

"What's the scoop on Agent Wells?" Jackson asked.

"No scoop." David scowled. "When I asked about his role, Jordan said he wasn't involved and ended the call."

Cal snorted. "And, of course, you're supposed to take his word on that."

"But we saw him on the security photo." Emma turned to David. "How did Agent Jordan explain that?"

"He doesn't know I have photos from the safe houses." He looked at Jon. "Are the security cam photos good enough to run through facial recognition systems?"

He nodded. "Can't guarantee we'll get a hit based on what we have, though."

"Does Fortress have a facial recognition system?"

"Zane designed one for us." A pointed look. "The system isn't connected to law enforcement in any way."

"Excellent. Run the photos. The FBI has a leak, and I don't want to alert the wrong people. If the Hunt Club goes underground, Emma will continue to be at risk until we smoke them out and take them down."

Those hunting teams would be like snakes in the grass, lying in wait to strike when he least expected. Unless David captured them all, Emma would never be safe.

CHAPTER TWENTY-FOUR

While they waited for David's brothers to arrive, Emma discovered her concentration was too fractured to knit. She walked to the refrigerator and peered inside, needing to do something to distance herself from the nightmare of her past. How could she have stumbled into a sick game to hunt people? What attracted the men to her family?

With a cabin soon to be full of hungry cops and operatives, the most useful thing she could do for them and herself was to prepare dinner.

Pushing her worries to the back of her mind, Emma perused the supplies available in the refrigerator, then walked to the pantry. After taking stock she decided on spaghetti and a salad. The kitchen had enough food to withstand a siege.

She gathered the ingredients for spaghetti sauce and set them on the counter. After locating a large pan, she added chopped onion and green pepper to the hamburger meat, and turned on the burner.

"What are you making?" David asked. He wrapped his arms loosely around her waist and planted a kiss on the side of her neck, sending a shiver of delight through her.

"Spaghetti. I hope that's all right with everyone."

His arms tightened. "Please tell me this is your recipe."

She laughed and turned her head to press a kiss to his jaw. "Of course. You requested my spaghetti every time you came home on leave. I thought you might like that choice."

"I don't know about the rest of this bunch, but I'm looking forward to dinner. Your cooking is one of the many things I missed while you were gone."

Emma smiled as she stirred the mixture in the pan. "Would you like brownies? I think I have the ingredients to make them."

"I'd love a brownie if you don't mind the work." David turned her to face him. "You don't have to cook meals for this motley crowd, Emma. We can take turns or pick up something."

"Not Jackson," Eli chimed in. "He burns water."

"Hey!" the medic protested. "I resent that. I make a mean chili."

The members of Wolf Pack groaned. "Mean is the perfect description," Cal muttered. "I haven't forgotten the upset stomach your concoction caused the last time I had the misfortune to eat it."

Emma laughed along with the others. If this was the norm for Special Forces teams, no wonder David missed his teammates so much.

"How can I help?" David asked her.

She handed him the wooden spoon. "Stir this while I add the rest of the ingredients for the sauce."

By the time the Montgomery brothers arrived, the spaghetti sauce was simmering, filling the air with a mouth-watering scent.

Caleb strode to the stove and kissed Emma on the cheek. "What's cooking, Em?"

"Spaghetti sauce." She smiled. "And, yes, there's enough for you and your brothers."

"Excellent. You sure you want to marry David? If you switch your loyalty, I promise to treat you like the queen of the universe."

"Hey." David punched Caleb on the shoulder. "No flirting with my woman."

"Just reminding her that she had better options than you."

Levi shook his head. "You just like her cooking."

"Maybe."

Elliot snorted.

"Give it up," Owen said. "You don't have a chance, bro."

Caleb winked at Emma and walked to stand in front of the large white board the operatives had found somewhere in the cabin and set up in the dining area of the large kitchen. "What's this?"

Emma half listened to the conversation as she continued meal preparations. By the time David's brothers were up to speed on the Hunt Club, the salad and spaghetti were finished.

After setting up the breakfast bar with plates, bowls, and the food, she said, "Dinner's ready. Drink options include coffee, water, soft drinks, or iced tea."

Eli gave Emma a one-armed hug. "Thanks for preparing dinner, sugar. Have a seat. I'm volunteering David to prepare your plate. The rest of us will serve ourselves and handle the cleanup. You've done enough."

David seated her at the table with her back to the white board of victims. She breathed a sigh of relief. Seeing names and faces of the victims upset her, especially the pictures of her parents and sister. Thankfully, the photos were from either social media pages or provided by families.

Throughout the meal, talk around the table focused on funny stories from military and Fortress deployments. Emma laughed more in that hour than she had in months. As the meal concluded, David made another mug of tea for her, this time a wonderful aromatic mint.

"Thank you," she murmured. "You're spoiling me."

He dropped a light kiss on her mouth. "That's my new mission in life."

She smiled, grateful to be with the man she adored. David Montgomery was a definite keeper.

Eli stood. "Kitchen detail before we make plans."

Without protest, the men stood and began to clear the table.

"Plastic containers for leftovers are in the left cabinet," Emma said.

Rafe chuckled. "What leftovers?"

She stared. "I prepared enough food to feed an army."

"Face it, Em." Levi patted her shoulder as he carried several empty glasses to the dishwasher. "You fed an army of hungry guys. Look at it this way. We showed our appreciation for your fine culinary expertise by eating every bite."

Good grief. "Do you have room for brownies?"

Elliot's eyes narrowed. "I don't see brownies anywhere. Did you leave David alone with them? You know he can't resist your brownies. If he ate them all, we'll have to hurt him. You know that, right?"

Emma laughed. "Relax. I haven't made them yet. As soon as you finish in the kitchen, I'll start on them."

Two minutes later, the table was clear and the dishwasher loaded. After washing the pans she'd used, the men vacated the kitchen.

"How long will the brownies take?" Owen asked. "Caleb and I need to be in Maple Valley in two hours."

"About forty minutes."

"Are you sure you're up to it?" David asked. "Don't let Owen or the rest of us guilt you into doing more if you're too tired."

"I'd rather be busy than think too hard about the board behind me." She laid a hand on his arm. "I'm fine. Let me do this."

Understanding filled his eyes. He hugged her. "All right. I'll wash the bowls and spoons you use, though. After the brownies are in the oven, why don't you start on your first pair of socks?"

Emma sighed, lingering in David's arms a few seconds longer. He understood her so well.

She returned to the kitchen to gather ingredients for brownies as the men began discussing options. Again, she half listened while she mixed the batter, then poured the mixture into two prepared pans. If dinner was any indication of their appetites, the operatives and the Montgomery brothers would polish off the brownies fast.

After sliding the pans into the oven, Emma retrieved her knitting supplies, chose a pattern for David's socks, and cast on the required number of stitches. As the men debated the best way to protect her and locate the hunting teams, she knitted round after round, occasionally stopping to measure the growing length.

She made a mental note to contact Madison Santana and thank her for the wonderful yarn and needles. The sock yarn she had chosen for Emma was so easy to work with and created a soft, beautiful knitted fabric that David should enjoy wearing.

"Caleb and Elliot, we need more information about the Hunt Club," David said. "Tap your sources for information on them. Whoever you contact must be someone you trust implicitly. If word gets back to any of the members, we'll lose our chance to capture them."

"Don't expect them to testify against these guys in court," Caleb said. "These folks work in the dark and intend to stay there. They're not fans of law and order."

"I want Emma safe."

"Even if we have to go around the law to do it?" Levi asked.

"You know the answer to that."

He rolled his eyes. "We're law enforcement. Everything we do must hold up in court." The Army Ranger slanted a hard look at his brother and boss. "Even if we could take care of business and bury the evidence where no one would find it."

David's eyes lit with amusement. "That's right. Our job is to protect and serve. Get the information, Caleb and Elliot. Once we have that, we'll have a place to start, including methods that can be used in court to convict these criminals."

"The teams might not be interested in surrendering," Rafe said. "If the only way out of the club is in a body bag, they probably won't cooperate with law enforcement, either."

"All we need is one man or one team to turn on the others."

Rafe looked skeptical. "I don't know, David. If we're right, the only person who knows all the players is the mastermind. Besides, the traitors would be fair game in prison."

"Then I need an airtight case on each team so I don't have to depend on a confidential informant."

"Or we have to find a way to draw them all into a trap at one time."

Emma froze. Even though she would gladly offer herself up as bait again to protect her friends, she couldn't be a big enough prize to tempt all the teams at once.

"Let's not go there yet," David said. "We'll hold that option in reserve as a last resort. First, let's identify as many teams as possible. Even though the feds haven't been interested in sharing intel with local law enforcement, I believe that's a viable choice. If we have enough proof, the local agencies will be glad to capture the teams and hold them for the feds."

Rafe shook his head. "You have to include the FBI for that plan to work. The teams may be stalking a victim, but not actually have committed a crime in the local jurisdiction yet."

"And if we include the feds, we risk tipping off the teams," Eli chimed in.

"The plan will work if we're able to identify a hunting team and connect them to murders," David insisted.

"Only if we have agents involved who know how to keep their mouths shut. I still have contacts inside the FBI," Rafe said. "Agents that I worked with and trust. They might be able to help."

"Maybe. Depends on how many teams are operating. If we involve too many agents, the bad ones will notice."

"What do you want me and Levi to do?" Owen asked.

"Search for unsolved murders in our surrounding counties that fit the brutality of these crimes." David indicated the murder board.

"What will you be doing?"

"Checking our surrounding states for the same types of crimes."

"Big pool," Jon murmured. "We need a better plan, David. If Rafe is correct and these teams are trolling the US for victims, the best model would include all 50 states. They're probably in territories assigned by the mastermind."

"We have to start somewhere."

"If someone else will search Anne's social media pages, I'll focus on compiling the most likely unsolved murders that fit our parameters."

"I'll take the social media pages," Jackson said.

"Funnel the likely cases to the rest of us, Jon," Eli said. "Cal and Rafe, you still need to help the Montgomery brothers with patrol duties. Between the ten of us, though, we should be able to make good progress in a short amount of time."

Emma glanced up from her knitting. "I'll help Jon."

The men stared at her.

She frowned. "No, it won't be pleasant, but I can help Jon create a spreadsheet to group the teams and their potential victims to particular sections of the country." She looked at the operative. "If you don't mind me helping, that is."

"I'd appreciate it. I'll pull the cases and dump them into files by state. We'll start organizing them into groups from there." He turned to the others. "I might locate photos of the teams from the police files, but locating photos from other sources will take a long time and might be impossible."

David rubbed his nape. "Time isn't our friend. Do what you can. Would Zane be able to give us a hand with this search?"

Jon looked at Eli, eyebrow up.

"I'll talk to Maddox," Wolf Pack's leader said as he stood. "Rafe, Cal, if you have trusted friends in law enforcement with connections, contact them while you're on patrol tonight. Find out what they've heard. Jon, you and Emma get to work on finding and organizing the potential cases. Start in the southeastern US first since we know of five incidents involving Emma. That will give us an idea of the magnitude of the task ahead of us. Focus on murders similar to that of the Tuckers."

"Why?" Emma asked.

"Easier to find a pattern. Once we identify the other teams who attempted to kill you, we'll track their movements and figure out if they're operating in the same territory as the original team or if they were allowed to cross into another territory to finish the first team's hunt."

Her stomach churned as the reality of her situation struck her anew. Eight, maybe ten people tried to kill her. What happened when a team failed? Was the team punished somehow?

"We need to involve the Fortress research department," Jon said.

Emma dragged in a sharp breath. "You think the teams have murdered that many people?"

"Not necessarily. I think a large number of murders would garner too much attention. However, if we enlist help from the tech team, we'll have data to organize that much faster."

"Are they good at their jobs?" David asked.

"If they weren't, Maddox wouldn't hire them."

To Eli, David said, "Call Maddox."

"What about you and your brothers?"

"Owen and Caleb, you're on patrol tonight with Rafe and Cal. Split up and keep your eyes open for anything out of the ordinary. Elliot and Levi, keep six ranch hands on watch tonight around the house while you two get some rest. I'll rework the patrol schedule and start plowing through the paperwork." He glared at his brothers. "You owe me big for taking that responsibility off your plates."

Emma rose. The brownies should be finished baking now. She opened the oven and withdrew the two pans. Perfect. "If you wait fifteen minutes for the brownies to cool, I'll wrap several pieces for you to take with you."

"Individual packages," Levi insisted, eyeing his brothers. "We don't share well."

Amused, she agreed with his stipulation. "Is there an extra computer I can use?" she asked Jon.

He chuckled. "This is a Fortress safe house. We always provide laptops in case our operatives need a backup computer. I'll set you up."

Eli motioned for his partner to stay seated. "I'll bring a computer to you. David, come with me. Maddox will want to talk to you."

David rose, squeezed Emma's shoulder, and followed Eli from the room.

After Wolf Pack's leader brought the laptop and left again, Jon waited for Emma to cut and distribute or package brownies, then waved her to the seat beside him. "Time to get to work."

CHAPTER TWENTY-FIVE

David dropped into a chair in the safe house office. "Will Maddox still be in the office?" He glanced at his watch and grimaced. Probably not. It was almost 8:00. Fortress Security's CEO must have a family.

"We'll soon find out."

"Does he have a family?"

"Yep. An amazing wife and beautiful daughter. We try not to interrupt his family time unless it's necessary, but your request is time sensitive. He'll understand."

If Emma's life wasn't on the line, David would delay contacting Maddox until tomorrow morning. He wondered how many other times Maddox's family time was interrupted? His lips curved. Probably as often as David's own off time.

Eli called his boss.

"Yeah, Maddox."

"It's Eli. You're on speaker with David Montgomery."

"Hold." After a short, murmured conversation and the sound of a door closing, he said, "Go."

"Sorry to interrupt your night, Brent."

"You can make it up to Rowan by bringing her a signed copy of your wife's latest book."

Eli chuckled. "Deal."

"Sit rep."

Between them, Eli and David updated Maddox on the situation.

"What do you need, David?"

Relief swept over him. "Tech support and possible operative involvement in the near future."

"Explain." After David finished, Maddox said, "No problem on the tech support. Eli, contact Z and tell him what you need. As far as the operative support, I'll check potential availability as soon as Rowan and I put Alexa to bed. Keep me updated on everything. If we go after each team simultaneously, the op might be larger than one or two teams can handle." He was silent a moment, then said, "We have to involve Darren Whitehead in this setup."

David straightened. "I know Director Whitehead. His son and I served in the Teams together."

"Have you talked to the director yet?"

"No, sir."

"Why not?"

"I threatened to contact him if Craig Jordan didn't pony up the crime lab results from the threat to Emma that was delivered to the ranch."

He groaned. "Jordan, huh? Wish I could say I'm surprised to hear his name connected with this mess. Deadline?"

"Twelve hours from now."

"Contact Whitehead at home. Tell him not to contact Jordan until the deadline has passed without the report. Between Whitehead and Rafe, you should have a list of agents you can trust to be part of a task force. One other person to consult is Stella Armstrong. She was a US Marshal before she married one of our operatives and joined the Otter Creek police department as a detective. Her former partner is on staff at PSI as a trainer for our search and rescue teams."

David's eyebrows rose. Fortress offered several avenues of training and services.

"I'll contact Stella in a few minutes," Eli said. "I should have thought of her and Deke before now."

"Need anything else from me? Alexa is ready for her bedtime story."

Eli glanced at David.

He shook his head. Maybe, just maybe, they were lining up the exact help they needed to pull off this half-formed plan.

"Nope," Eli said to Maddox. "Give Alexa a hug from me." He grinned, amusement dancing in his eyes. "And be sure to give Rowan a kiss from me. Better yet, I'll give her one myself the next time I see her."

Maddox growled. "You are expendable, Wolfe. Don't forget that. I have dozens of men willing and able to take your place at a moment's notice. So, keep your hands and kisses to yourself if you want to live."

Eli laughed at the threats from his boss.

"David?"

"Yes, sir?"

"Thought any more about my offer?"

He smiled. Should have figured that Maddox would revisit the topic at the first opportunity. "I have. I don't have an answer yet." Although he could guess what his brothers would say. They, like him, were restless. "I haven't had time to consult with my brothers."

"Get on it. I need you."

"Yes, sir."

"If anything flares up, call me. Day or night."

"Thank you, sir."

Maddox ended the call.

A smile curved Eli's mouth. "The boss is recruiting you and your brothers."

"He says he'll call us the M team."

The operative rolled his eyes. "And people say Wolf Pack is a lame name."

"At least our name isn't associated with a college sports team."

Eli narrowed his eyes as he grabbed his phone again to make another call. "Don't knock it, buddy. After all, we might be called to back you up one day soon."

David sobered. True enough.

A moment later, Eli's call was answered by a woman. "Armstrong."

"It's Eli, sugar. Can you talk?"

"I have five minutes before I arrive at a crime scene. Talk fast."

"First, you're on speaker with David Montgomery, Sheriff of Morgan County." Eli laid out what was going on in short, concise sentences.

A soft whistle from the lady. "Your girlfriend was lucky to escape that many times, David. What do you need?"

"Names of FBI agents who can't be bought." Her list along with the one from Whitehead and Rafe should give them a solid group of trustworthy agents.

"I'll talk to Deke, and we'll send Eli a list. With Zane's encryption, no one will intercept the information or trace it from Fortress to you."

"I appreciate the help."

"No problem. Let me know if I can do anything else."

Eli chuckled. "We might need to borrow your husband."

"You planning to blow something up?" Stella teased.

"Maybe."

"He loves keeping his hand in that part of the business. Later, guys." She ended the call.

David wondered about her comment concerning her husband. "What does her husband do?"

"Nate's a member of Durango, the Delta team Brent recruited. He's their EOD expert and, oddly enough, a professional chef."

"That's handy."

"Tell me about it. His team never has to worry about edible food. Nate has the skills to make almost anything taste good."

He grunted. "My team could have used that skill more than once on deployment."

"Yep. My team ate more MREs than I care to remember. Do you want to wait while I call Zane or start on your own work?"

He felt a strong urge to keep an eye on Emma and probably would for a long time to come. Didn't matter that this cabin contained other SEALs capable of protecting Emma. She was his to care for and protect.

And, yeah, he'd missed her so much when she was in WITSEC that he almost went through withdrawals when he was separated from her now. No use kidding himself. He was head-over-heels in love with Emma Tucker and craved spending time with her.

David also needed to start on the paperwork involved in the shooting incident with Paul Franks. He might as well satisfy his desire to have Emma within sight and take care of the necessary paperwork at the same time. "You explain what we need. Before he sets up the search parameters for the unsolved murders, ask him to locate Justin Wells. I want to talk to him, preferably face to face."

A nod.

Retrieving his laptop from his duffel bag, David returned to the kitchen. After pouring himself a cup of coffee, he settled in a seat beside Emma.

He logged in and began the long process of filling out reports on the shooting incident. David worked steadily for several minutes as Jon and Emma consulted on their project. When he finished his first report, Wolf Pack's leader walked into the room.

David paused, hands hovering above the keyboard. "Well?"

"Got it. Zane sent the information to your email along with a link to track his movements as long as he stays with his phone."

He studied Eli's expression. "That's good news. So, what's wrong?"

"Wells never left Morgan County."

David sat back. "Where is he?"

"At the Archer B & B."

Emma gasped. "That's Gigi's place."

David's blood ran cold. The B & B was only fifteen minutes from this cabin. Had Wells tracked them to this location?

Jon paused in his work. "Field trip?"

"Depends," Eli said. "Can you set the computer search to run automatically?"

His partner just stared at him.

A slow smile curved Eli's mouth. "Hey, I had to ask. We need that information as fast as possible. Will Emma be able to access what she needs to group cases?"

"You're ticking me off," Jon muttered, glaring at his friend.

That earned him a good-natured chuckle from Wolf Pack's leader.

"Wells is a federal agent," David reminded them. "I don't know what techniques you use for interrogation, Jon, but he still has the power to arrest you."

"Let me worry about that. Give me a minute to show Emma what she needs to do, then we'll have a chat with Wells."

Within minutes, David climbed into the passenger seat of the Fortress SUV. He checked his email for information from Zane on Agent Wells as he gave Jon directions to the

B & B. "I should call the police chief of Archer and let her know I'm paying a visit to Wells."

"Why?"

"In case this visit goes south. Wells may not be inclined to cooperate."

"He'll talk."

David slanted a look at the operative. "You know something I don't?"

"Maybe."

He snorted. "Don't overwhelm me with your chatterbox tendencies. Do I want to know how you learned this information?"

"What do you think?"

"That I'm better off not asking."

"Wise man."

David shook his head as he called Blair Hoffman, the call on speaker. His fellow law enforcement officer answered a moment later. "It's David Montgomery."

"I heard what happened at Bear Lake Cabins. Anybody hurt?"

He sighed at her question. Man, cop shops were hotbeds of gossip. "Perp has a bullet wound to the shoulder. No injuries to officers on scene."

"Good. What can I do for you, David?"

"I'm in Archer, getting ready to visit an FBI agent staying at the B & B."

A pause, then, "I wasn't aware of a fed operation in the area."

Her clipped words made David smile. "I can't say if there is an official op in Morgan County or not."

"Can't or won't?"

"Can't tell you what I don't know." What he suspected didn't count.

"You're in my town, Montgomery. You know something. Spill."

Having worked with the lady on several cases, he knew she disliked working with alphabet soup agencies. Blair was also an Army veteran and knew how to keep her own counsel. David gave her a concise version of events, ending with, "I need answers from Wells, answers he may not be willing to divulge without a little persuasion."

"You're risking your badge, my friend."

"Understood. It's necessary."

"And if you lose your job?"

"I won't regret anything as long as Emma is safe."

"Need backup?"

He relaxed, not surprised by the offer of help. "I have backup, but thanks."

"One of your brothers?"

A logical question since he and his brothers usually worked cases together, but he wondered if Blair was looking for information on Elliot. He'd seen the way the pretty sheriff looked at his brother when Elliot wasn't watching. He'd also noticed Elliot returning the favor.

David had considered teasing his brother about it more than once and chose to leave that hot potato alone. If Elliot could find happiness again, he wanted his brother to have the chance.

Besides, Elliot was stubborn and hardheaded. Blair would have to use some sneaky tactics to slip past his guard. David silently wished her luck. No matter what Elliot believed, he deserved happiness. "I have a friend from Fortress Security with me." The term friend might be stretching things although Jon didn't object to the claim of friendship.

Blair was silent for a moment. "I've heard of that outfit. Are they as good as the rumors claim?"

"Better."

"Huh. Well, I'm a phone call away if you need me. I'll also have dispatch notify me personally if a complaint comes in from the B & B. Make sure I don't receive a call, David."

He smiled. "Thanks, Blair."

"Yep. Keep me in the loop, all right?"

"Will do." He ended the call.

"Interesting lady," Jon murmured.

"Turn right at Dunmore."

Within minutes, Jon parked at the back of the bed and breakfast. The two men exited the SUV and headed for the front door. When they walked into the receptionist area, the owner met them in the lobby.

"Sheriff Montgomery." Virginia Warren's eyebrows rose. "Is there a problem?"

"Nothing like that, Gigi. I want to speak to one of your guests. He has information on one of my cases." Gigi would be so angry with him for not telling her that Emma was back. Soon, though. Hopefully, he could get back into her good graces.

"I see." She walked behind the receptionist desk. "What's his name?"

"Justin Wells."

She brought up her reservation system. "He's in Room 8. I'll ask him to come down. Would you like coffee or iced tea in the library?"

That approach might work better. The library was on the ground floor with a sitting room on the floor above it. David had noticed the sitting room lights were out when they drove up. "That would be great, Gigi. Thanks."

"Go into the library. I'll call Mr. Wells and bring a tray."

Jon followed David to the Victorian house's library, a room David loved as much as the Rocking M's library. Gigi's parents had been professors at a private college and instilled their love of learning into their only child before they retired from teaching and relocated to a beach house on the Florida coast, leaving their daughter the Victorian to do with as she pleased.

Two minutes after Gigi brought a large tray loaded with a carafe of coffee, three mugs, and a plate of cookies, Justin Wells walked into the room. His eyes narrowed when his gaze landed on Jon. Wells shifted his attention to David. "How did you know I'm staying here?"

"Have you forgotten I'm a cop?"

The agent waved that aside. "Is Emma safe?"

"She's fine, no thanks to you."

"What's that supposed to mean?"

"Since when is a federal agent allowed to plant a bug in a private residence without a warrant?"

Pink tinged the agent's cheeks. "Jordan already tore a strip off my hide for that. I need to help protect her."

He understood Wells wanting to protect Emma, but *needing* to help? What was the agent keeping from him? "Bugging my kitchen isn't the way to go about it. You also neglected to mention a few things when you were at the ranch, Wells."

"Like what?"

David motioned to the sofa. "Do you want coffee? Gigi makes the best in the county."

"Tell me what this is about. Otherwise, I'll return to my room. I have work to do."

David poured coffee in the mugs and handed one to Wells after he sat. "Let's start with why you neglected to mention your connection to the Hunt Club. We'll go from there."

Wells froze with his coffee mug halfway to his mouth. "Hunt Club?"

He waited the agent out.

"I'm investigating them." When David remained silent, Wells scowled. "I'm trained in interrogation techniques, too. If you think I'll spill my guts, you're wasting your time and mine. Besides, this is an FBI case, not yours. We have jurisdiction."

"You said you wanted to help Emma. I'm giving you that chance."

The agent straightened. "What happened? You should have let me protect her."

"Last chance, Wells," David warned softly.

"Or what?" he scoffed. "You'll beat the information out of me? I'll have your badge and press charges against you. Then, I'll protect Emma myself. By the time you leave prison, she will have moved on to a better man than you." Left unsaid was the implication that Wells might be that man.

Fury burned through David with the power of a raging inferno. Was this a ploy to sweep David out of the way and leave the path clear for Justin Wells to make a play for Emma, a woman the agent claimed he wanted to protect? Who would protect Emma from Wells?

Jon caught David's eye and shook his head slightly.

Shoving his anger behind a mental wall, David leaned forward, gratified to see Wells flinch. "You want to play hardball?" David gave a slow nod. "Fine. I can do that. Fair warning, though. I'll tear your life apart and expose every secret. I will ruin you," he vowed. Nothing and no one meant more to him than Emma Tucker. If destroying the career of this FBI agent was the cost of protecting the woman David loved, he'd do it without one second of regret.

Wells paled. "You're threatening me?"

"Am I threatening Agent Wells, Jon?" David kept his gaze locked on his quarry.

"I didn't hear one."

Wells shifted his attention to Jon. "Who are you?" he demanded.

"No one you want to know." The sniper's thousand-yard stare focused on Wells.

The agent swallowed hard. He ripped his gaze from Jon and turned back to David. "You brought a thug with you?"

As much as David would love to plow his fist into Wells' face, he wanted to return to the safe house and Emma.

He reached into his pocket and withdrew a copy of the photo of one of the teams hunting Emma. David unfolded the paper and laid it on the coffee table without saying a word.

Wells stared at the photo, sweat beading on his forehead. "Where did you get this?" he said, voice hoarse.

"Explain it."

The agent shook his head. "It's not what you think."

"This is your last chance to explain before I contact Director Whitehead." He planned to contact Whitehead anyway, but the added pressure might encourage Wells to talk. David inclined his head toward the photo. "Jordan says you're not involved with the Hunt Club."

"I'm not," Wells snapped.

"You aren't," Jon murmured. "But your cousin is, a fact Whitehead would be very interested to know."

CHAPTER TWENTY-SIX

Wells set his coffee mug on the coffee table with a thud and dragged a shaking hand down his face. "Estranged cousin," he muttered. "How did you find out?"

"Doesn't matter how we know," David said, drawing the agent's attention back to him. "Director Whitehead doesn't know the truth or you wouldn't be involved in this investigation at all. Jordan shouldn't have let you be part of the team investing this. You aren't objective."

A scowl. "You're not the poster child for objectivity, Montgomery. Besides, my cousin and I aren't close, and I haven't seen him in years."

"Try again." Jon pulled a sheaf of papers from the pocket of his cargo pants, unfolded one page at a time, and laid each on the coffee table.

Although difficult, David managed to keep his expression neutral. How had Jon located those so fast?

"Where did you get these?" Wells demanded.

"You should be more concerned about what I'll do with them."

"You can't show them to the director. Please."

"Your career is on the line, Wells." David almost felt sorry for the special agent. Almost. "Why are you so sure you're the only one who can protect Emma?"

Wells sighed. "I should have known this would come back to bite me."

"Explain," David snapped, his sharp tone making the agent's spine straighten. He'd used the same tone to obtain a response from the men under his command in the Navy.

"It was a stupid childhood game we invented."

David stilled. "You stalked people as a kid?" Wells couldn't be serious.

"With a camera, not a weapon. Marty and I made a game out of catching people off guard with a camera. It was supposed to be innocent fun."

"Until it wasn't. Let me guess. Your cousin took it too far and started using the photos to blackmail people." Moving from voyeurism to blackmail was a logical step. When had good old Marty gone a step further into murder?

Wells winced. "When I found out what he was doing with the pictures, I refused to play the game anymore. Marty continued the challenge without me. He not only blackmailed people, he turned into a Peeping Tom, taking pictures of sleeping women through their windows."

"How long before you discovered the new game?"

Wells looked ill. "When Marty became obsessed with one of the women he was stalking and broke into her house."

Jon's eyes narrowed. "Was she there at the time?"

A short nod. "He beat her when she tried to call the police."

"Was he arrested?"

Wells shook his head. "His family is wealthy. The vic refused to file charges. Couldn't prove it, but I know Marty's family bought the woman's silence."

"Did the pattern of assaults continue?" David asked.

"Of course. Unfortunately, Marty developed a taste for violence and blood. None of the women or their families would call his hand on it." Bitterness filled his voice. "Marty Grisham and his family move in high-powered, wealthy circles. People were either too afraid to stand up to him or they were willing to be bought off with money or favors.

"Marty is charming. Women fall all over him until he shows the real man behind the charm and smooth moves. At first, everyone loves him. Once they see the real Martin Grisham, they don't want anything to do with him personally. He's also a shrewd and ruthless businessman. The family continues to cover for him because he's feeding the family coffers."

Jon grimaced. "He must have practiced his craft often enough to perfect the attacks."

"No forensic evidence to tie him to the crimes." Wells jammed his hands through his hair. "When Jordan showed me the security cam photo, I hoped this time evidence would put him behind bars. Didn't work out that way. What we have is circumstantial. All we can prove is that Marty and his buddy followed Emma and Anne around the festival in Seagull. There's no law against following pretty women."

And there was the confirmation he'd needed. All he needed was a picture of Marty Grisham to show Emma. Maybe the full-on view of Grisham would jog her memory. "Fast forward to the night of the Tucker murders." David tapped the photo of Grisham and his partner that Jon or Jackson had unearthed. Now that he knew about relationship between Grisham and Wells, he saw the difference in the jawline and the nose. "Where were you the night the Tuckers were attacked?"

The agent swallowed hard. "On Seagull Island. Another agent and I were investigating a different case. I heard about the murders the next morning, along with the whole island. I didn't know Marty was on the island until Jordan brought me into the case later."

"Jordan believed you when you told him you didn't know about Marty's presence?" Jon asked.

Wells sent Jon a dark look. "Why wouldn't he? My partner and I were in a hotel across town. We never left the room."

"Neither of you went out to purchase drinks or food?"

"We ordered room service. We worked the whole night on the case. We were searching for a missing child. The first 48 hours are the most crucial."

"Did you find the kid?" David asked.

A faint smile curved his mouth. "Yeah, we did."

"Good. Let's try this again. What do you know about the Hunt Club?"

The smile faded. "Not enough. If I did, don't you think I would have found a way to shut it down by now?"

"Is Grisham the mastermind of the game?"

"I don't know."

David's eyebrow rose.

"I don't," Wells insisted. "He could be the mastermind or just one of the players. The only reason I knew Marty was involved in the Hunt Club was because of the security cam photo." He frowned. "Some of those photos are out of our case files. Did Jordan give you a copy of them?"

"Show me your forearms."

"You can't be serious."

Jon clamped a hand on his shoulder.

A second later, blood drained from Wells' face. He moaned.

"Do as the man asked," the sniper murmured. "His woman's life is at stake."

When the agent gave a slight nod, Jon released him. Wells shuddered with relief. "You're lethal, man," he muttered.

"So they tell me."

The agent unbuttoned his shirt sleeves and rolled them up. He turned his arms over so the men could see that his skin was unmarked by a tattoo. "Satisfied?"

"Not even close. Who's your cousin's partner?"

Wells remained mute.

David waited 30 seconds, then headed for the door. "You'll be hearing from Whitehead soon."

"Wait."

He paused at the doorjamb.

"You can't tell Jordan I talked to you. He'll force me to return to D.C. and block me from having access to any part of this investigation."

"Name."

A sigh. "Jerome Burke. He attended the same college as Marty."

"Are they behind bars?"

"I wish."

David spun on his heel. "Why not? If Marty and his partner remain loose, they're a threat to Emma."

"It wasn't my call, all right?"

"Jordan is allowing two known killers to roam free?"

"I told you the Grishams are a powerhouse. They know people with clout in the Justice Department."

A river of ice water flooded his veins. "Your cousin worked out a deal."

A nod. "If he and Jerome testify in court, they walk."

For a split second, David saw red. "They murdered Emma's family."

"I know. I'm sorry. The Justice Department wants the Hunt Club shut down. Marty and Jerome are the only two members we've been able to identify. Jordan saw the resemblance between me and Marty, and showed me the photo. I identified them and asked Jordan to allow me to work with him on the case. I feel responsible since Marty and I were the ones who created that stupid game. I want the chance to help shut down the Hunt Club."

"Can you identify the other teams?"

A head shake.

"How many other teams are playing?"

"I don't know that, either."

"What do you know?" Jon murmured.

"That Emma Tucker is in grave danger."

"That's not news," David said, hands fisting.

"Marty doesn't give up on a quarry."

David stared. "What are you saying, Wells?"

"Marty failed to kill Emma twice." The agent inclined his head toward the two photographs that showed the deadly duo. "Deal or not, he won't quit until he succeeds."

"He might be your cousin, but if he comes after Emma again, he's dead. I will kill him."

Wells gave a short nod, his expression grim.

"Are the feds tracking Marty and Jerome's movements?"

A slight hesitation, then, "We are."

David walked further into the room, suspicion growing. "But?"

"Marty runs one of the Grisham multinational corporations. He travels frequently."

He remained silent, waiting for the bomb to drop.

A sigh. "The Grishams own several jets, and so do their wealthy friends."

In other words, Marty could give the feds the slip and continue to play his sick game without anyone knowing.

"Look, I know you want to protect Emma, but you don't want to get on the wrong side of the Justice Department."

Did Wells really think David cared what the Justice Department thought? "Jordan took you off the case, didn't he?" If he was still assigned to the investigation, Jordan and his other henchman would be staying in Gigi's B & B, too. They weren't. David had seen the reservation list when Gigi brought up the computer program.

"Maybe."

"Since you're still in Morgan County, you're either on suspension or waiting to be reassigned to another case. Which is it?"

Another flinch. "Suspension," he muttered.

"Go home, Wells."

The agent scowled. "I'm allowed to stay wherever I want."

"Not when you staying in this area puts Emma in more danger."

"You want to help Emma?" Jon asked, his voice soft. "Go home. Your cousin has made a point of finding you in several cities where you're working a case." He waved toward the photos. "Don't bother denying it. There's the proof. What are we going to find when we track your movements and Marty's? More murders?"

The guilt in Wells' eyes confirmed the truth of Jon's question.

"Jordan might have believed you, but I don't think Director Whitehead will," David said. "Go home before you sacrifice your career."

"What about yours?" Wells challenged. "Your law enforcement career is in jeopardy, too."

"I have other options. Do you?" With that, he and Jon left the B & B.

When they reached the parking lot at the back of the business and neared the Fortress SUV, David pulled up short. "Blair, did Gigi call you?"

The Archer police chief pushed away from the side of her cruiser. She eyed Jon curiously before she focused on David. "Thought I'd make myself available faster by hanging out in the parking lot." Blair inclined her head toward Jon's vehicle. "Nice wheels." She held her hand out to Jon. "Blair Hoffman."

"Jon Smith." At Blair's skeptical look, the operative held up a hand. "Truth."

With a snort, she turned to David. "How did it go?"

"No screams or visible injuries."

"Good to know. Find out anything?"

"Enough to know that Emma's life may never return to normal."

"And neither will yours?"

He shrugged. Emma was his life. "Gigi doesn't know Emma is back. It's for her own safety."

"I hope you know what you're doing, my friend." She circled the hood of her vehicle. "I'm here if you need me. Good to meet you, Jon. Keep an eye on this guy. I'd hate to lose a friend." Blair climbed behind the wheel, gave a wave, and left the lot.

"Let's get out of here." David rubbed a knotted muscle in his neck. He wanted to see for himself that Emma was safe before calling Darren Whitehead.

Back at the cabin, he strode into the kitchen with Jon close behind. There she was. He drew in a deep breath as some of his tension dissipated at the sight of Emma, safe.

Eli gave a chin lift in greeting as he poured himself a mug of coffee.

Emma smiled at David. His heart turned over in his chest. Would he ever get used to seeing that look in her eyes, the one that said he was her whole world? "Hey."

She came around the table and wrapped her arms around him. "I don't see blood anywhere. I assume Agent Wells is still alive?"

David dropped a light kiss on her lips. "For the moment."

"Did you learn anything useful?"

He debated how much to tell her. The last thing David wanted was to terrify Emma. She was already afraid. However, they couldn't build the life they both wanted unless their relationship was founded on truth and trust. Sure, there would be times he couldn't tell her everything. More of those instances were ahead if he agreed to work for Fortress and managed to keep his job as sheriff. Now, however, the most important case of his career involved Emma. She needed to know as much as possible to be prepared in case the worst happened. God willing, it wouldn't. "The photo wasn't of Wells. It was, however, a photo of his cousin, Marty Grisham."

She frowned. "Do you have a photo of Marty?"

He glanced at Jon. The operative handed him the photo. David unfolded the picture and showed it to Emma.

Blood drained from her face.

"Baby?" David cupped her cheek. "Emma, talk to me."

"It's him."

"Tell me."

"He killed my family." Her stricken gaze shifted from the paper to David. "I remember now. He's the one, David."

David gathered Emma close. At least now they had a positive identification. While holding her, he told her the rest of the information he and Jon learned from the agent.

"If Wells was suspended, why is he still in the area?" Eli asked.

"He feels responsible for what's been happening because he helped create the hunting game in the first place."

"He really is trying to protect me." Emma eased away and grabbed two mugs from a cabinet. She poured coffee into both and handed one each to David and Jon. No one mentioned her trembling hands.

"That's what he says. At the moment, he's more of a hindrance than a help."

"Why?"

He looked at Jon. "Tell her."

"Grisham shows up frequently when Wells is working a case. The fact that Wells is here could lure Grisham to the area if he hasn't arrived already."

Emma sat in her chair abruptly. "You think he's still hunting me despite the fact he plans to testify against the members of the Hunt Club?"

David crouched at her side and took her hand in his. "Look at me, Em." When she did, he her gaze. "I will not let him near you."

"But you believe he won't give up."

"Do you?" After all she'd been through, Emma knew how determined the Hunt Club members were to eliminate her. She had the power to bring down their whole organization, especially now that she remembered the night she was attacked in Seagull and could testify in court.

She sighed. "No. Grisham is obsessed with completing his horrible mission. Why isn't he in jail where he can't harm me or anyone else?"

"If Jordan arrests him and his partner now, the other Hunt Club members and the mastermind will know they've been compromised. They'll go to ground and resurface later when we aren't expecting them." Although he understood, David still didn't like it.

Emma linked their fingers. "Let's identify and find the rest of these people. The sooner we identify them, the better. Somewhere, these teams are hunting their next victims, whether it's me or other innocents." She squared her shoulders. "It's time the hunters became the hunted."

David pressed a kiss to the back of her hand, proud of her strength and resolve.

Jon's lips curved. "Good girl." He looked at David. "You heard the lady. Let's get to work."

Right. Nothing like being called to task by the woman he loved. When Jon sat next to Emma, David stood. "I need to call Whitehead." He kissed Emma's forehead. "I won't be long." He looked at Jon, who acknowledged his silent order to watch over Emma with a slight nod.

In the office, David sat behind the desk and made the call.

After two rings, a deep masculine voice said, "Whitehead."

"This is David Montgomery. I'm sorry to call so late, sir."

A slight pause, then, "I'm always glad to hear from you, son. It's been a while. Your brothers are doing well?"

"Yes, sir."

"I don't imagine you called just to shoot the breeze with a friend's old man. What can I do for you?"

"I need two favors."

"Shoot."

"I need a list of agents you trust without a doubt."

"You're in trouble?"

"Not me, sir. The woman I love is."

"What's going on?"

He explained, ending with, "I know I'm asking a lot, but if this plan is going to work, the FBI has to be involved. I need agents who can't be bought."

"And you don't trust Craig Jordan."

"Do you blame me?"

A sigh. "Can't say that I do. He's not known for being a team player. I'll look into the case myself. If Jordan doesn't send the forensic report by your deadline, text me. I'll make sure you receive a copy. I'll compile a list of agents and send them to you before midnight. I'll contact each of them personally and make them aware that they may be needed for a special assignment. Anything else?"

"No, sir. Thank you."

"I expect to be updated regularly, David."

"Yes, sir."

"Best of luck to you, son. If what you're saying about this group is accurate, you'll need every bit of skill and luck to protect Ms. Tucker." After giving David a brief update on his own family, the FBI director ended the call.

He returned to the kitchen where Emma and Jon were hard at work. Eli was nowhere to be seen, but Jackson was now sitting at the breakfast bar working on his laptop, a mug of coffee close at hand.

David joined Emma and Jon at the table, and returned to filling out the reports on the shooting incident. Paperwork was one of the things he hated most about his job. He loved helping the citizens in his community and providing protection for them. Politics and paperwork? Not so much.

Near midnight, his phone rang. David glanced at his screen and frowned. "What's wrong, Blair?"

"A boatload of trouble. I need you and your friend to return to the B & B."

He straightened. "Why?"

"Justin Wells is dead."

CHAPTER TWENTY-SEVEN

Blair met David and Jon at the back entrance of Gigi's B & B, her eyes narrowed. "You're not staying at the Rocking M, are you?"

"Emma is in a safe house not far from here," David confirmed. "Was anyone else hurt?"

"Gigi suffered a blow to the head. EMTs are checking her now."

Oh, man. "Does Owen know?"

Blair's eyebrow rose. "Why would I notify Owen?"

"He cares about her." More than his brother would admit.

She frowned. "Why didn't I know about this? I hear everything in Archer."

"My brother is careful not to let anyone know, including Gigi. Nobody does stealth like Force Recon." He smiled. "Unless it's a Navy SEAL."

The police chief rolled her eyes. "Call him. Gigi is shaken, and she won't call anyone for support. I'll meet you in the kitchen." Blair motioned for Jon to follow her into the house.

David called Owen.

"Miss me already, bro?" Owen asked in greeting.

"Come to the Archer B & B."

"Is Gigi all right?"

"Someone attacked her and killed Wells."

A cruiser's siren blared and its engine roared as Owen said, "I'll be there in fifteen minutes or less. Stay with her." His brother ended the call.

David's lips curved. He suspected his brother would arrive sooner than the fifteen-minute ETA. He hoped Owen wised up and staked his claim before some other man beat him to the punch. The B & B owner was beautiful. If Owen didn't make his move soon, he might lose his chance with her.

Shoving his phone into his pocket, David entered the kitchen where Blair and Jon sat at a table. "Where's Gigi?"

"Living room. Your brother?"

"Ten minutes out. I'm under orders to keep an eye on her."

"We'll talk after Owen arrives."

"Yes, ma'am." He paused at the threshold. "You'll need to inform Special Agent Craig Jordan about the death of Wells. I have his contact info." He texted her Jordan's contact information.

Blair groaned. "Great. Just great. Will the feds take over my case?"

"What do you think?"

A sigh. "That I don't have a chance of keeping them out of my town."

"You know this murder isn't a coincidence. Wells was a threat to the Hunt Club. Mind if I look at the crime scene and body before Jordan arrives?"

"Be my guest. It will be a circus anyway. You know the drill. Don't disturb anything. Wells' body is in the library. I told the guests to remain in their rooms for the moment."

Wells must have been killed soon after he and Jon left. David entered the living room a moment later. Gigi sat on the sofa holding a chemical cold pack pressed to the back of her head.

Her eyes widened. "David, what are you doing here?"

"Blair called me." He glanced at the EMT packing his gear. "How is she, Duke?"

"Hard headed and stubborn." The medic frowned. "Gigi refuses to go to the hospital. She says she has a house full of guests who might need something."

"Does she need to go?"

"Hey." Gigi glared at him. "I'm sitting right here. I can answer for myself. No, I don't need to go to the hospital. I'm fine."

"Your opinion is duly noted. Duke?"

"Since she was unconscious for a time, she should be checked out by the doc."

"Traitor," she muttered, glaring at Duke.

"I'm looking out for your best interests," the EMT protested. "If my girlfriend had been knocked out by a thug, you can bet your boots I'd insist she see a doctor." He stood. "Gigi's refusing transport to the hospital, and we can't force her go. She should have someone keep an eye on her."

"I'll be here a while." He figured Owen's priorities had shifted from patrol to Gigi. His brother would stay close to her tonight.

Duke rattled off a list of things to watch for, then left.

"Thanks a lot for the support," Gigi said crossly.

"He's right, and you know it. Head injuries can be serious."

"You're making my headache worse."

David sat next to her. "What happened tonight?"

"Since you and your friend were talking with Mr. Wells, I decided to bake the muffins for breakfast tomorrow. My chef is out for the next three days, so breakfast is my responsibility until she returns. Anyway, after you left, I finished baking, cleaned the kitchen, and walked to the library to see if Mr. Wells needed more coffee. He told me he would be working in there for several hours."

"Did he say why?"

"Something about an electronic trail on a case. He seemed excited about it."

David wished Jon had access to Wells' computer. "How long after I left did you go to the library?"

"I don't know. Maybe two hours. I baked several batches of muffins." She frowned. "You wouldn't believe how many muffins guests eat each morning."

"What happened after you went to the library?"

"I heard a thump inside the room. I knocked on the door. Before I could turn the knob, the door flew open." She fell silent.

"And?" he prompted softly.

"Everything happened so fast."

"Gigi, look at me." When her gaze locked on him, he squeezed her free hand briefly and released her. "Anything you remember will help."

"This sounds stupid, but a wall of black rushed toward me, and hard hands shoved me against the wall. When I regained consciousness with this killer headache, Mr. Wells was sprawled on the floor of the library." She swallowed hard. "So much blood everywhere." Gigi swiped at the tears trickling down her face. "Sorry."

"Don't apologize. I'm sorry that you have to deal with a murder in your home."

"Will you and your brothers investigate?"

"Not directly. This might be related to another case we're investigating. For the moment, Chief Hoffman is lead investigator." But he bet that didn't last long. Jordan was territorial, and the vic was his colleague.

Headlights lit the room and a siren cut off. David glanced at his watch. Owen. Until he was sure, David moved in front of Gigi, weapon held by his side.

Seconds later, Owen opened front door and rushed into the room with Cal following in his wake. David moved aside as his brother made a beeline for Gigi.

"Owen," she said, her voice husky.

He crouched in front of her. "You okay, G?"

"Why are you here?" she asked.

Owen captured Gigi's free hand. "Answer the question."

"I have a goose egg and a massive headache. Otherwise, I'm fine."

He glanced at David, an unspoken question in his eyes.

"The EMT said she needs to go to the hospital."

Gigi sent David a dark look that spoke of payback. Guess he wouldn't score muffins and coffee on his early morning rounds for a while.

Without a word, Owen stood and scooped the B & B owner into his arms. He headed for the door which Cal opened for him.

"Put me down, Owen," Gigi protested. "I have guests. I can't leave them, especially now."

"This place is full of cops and will be for several hours. Your guests will be fine. If they need something, one of the cops can get it for them. I'm more concerned about you."

"Owen...."

"Hush, G. I'm taking you to the hospital. Cal, you're with me." He angled Gigi through the doorway and carried her away from the house without a backward glance.

Cal whistled softly. "I hope your brother knows what he's doing. The lady looks seriously ticked off."

"She'll get over it. Go. Watch his back. He'll be focused on Gigi."

"Is this murder related to Emma's situation?"

"Probably. I haven't looked at the crime scene or body yet. For now, assume one of the teams took out Wells and may come back for Gigi. Make sure they don't have a second chance."

With a nod, Cal left, closing the door behind him.

After updating his brother Caleb and contacting a part-time deputy to cover the rest of Owen's shift, David returned to the kitchen. Jon looked relaxed while Blair's frustration was almost palpable.

"If you're holding out on me, Smith, you'll regret it." Blair threw down her pen.

"Why would I hold out?"

She stared at Jon a moment before turning her attention to David. "You're next. Sit." Blair stabbed her finger in the direction of the chair beside Jon. When he complied, she said, "After I notify Agent Jordan of Wells' death, how long do I have before the feds descend on me like a plague of locusts?"

"If he's still in Nashville, about 90 minutes."

Jon snorted. "Less."

Blair flinched. "Great. Give me your side of the story before I contact him, David. Afterward, you're free to go. Don't leave town until this mess is either cleared up or off my plate."

"No guarantees. I might need to move Emma."

"When the feds take over, your location won't be my problem." Mischief gleamed in her eyes. "On second thought, go where you want. I don't mind being a thorn in the side of the FBI."

David and Jon chuckled, then David said, "If Wells' death is related to the Hunt Club, Gigi could be in danger. These teams don't leave witnesses behind."

"She didn't see anything."

"Doesn't matter. She's a loose end."

"Is she still on the premises?"

"Owen took her to the hospital. He'll stay with her tonight and let you know when he needs to leave."

"The feds might shut down her B & B while they process the scene," Jon murmured.

"He'll take her to the Rocking M." In fact, the more David thought about that idea, the better he liked it. The ranch had good security, and some of the hands were former military.

"Excellent idea." Blair picked up her pen again and flipped to a new page in her notebook. "Tell me everything from the beginning, David."

He recounted his arrival at the B & B with Jon, their conversation with Wells, and the time they left the house. "You witnessed our departure, Blair."

"Yeah, yeah. Neither one of you looked as though you were sporting injuries. Too dark for me to see blood on your clothes."

David's eyebrow rose. "We haven't changed clothes. You want what we're wearing?"

"You have a spare set of clothes with you?"

"Hazards of the job. I'm sure you have a Go bag in your cruiser."

"Yeah, all right. Point taken. If you don't mind the inconvenience, I'd appreciate it." She smiled. "I'll have the clothes transported to the state crime lab immediately."

He and Jon retrieved their bags from the SUV. After changing, David gave Blair the clothes sealed and labeled in bags. "I want to see the crime scene and body now."

She waved him on. "Go. Agent Jordan will be breathing down our necks soon."

"We'll leave before he arrives." Talking to Jordan could wait.

At the library, Jon remained in the hall while David accepted protective coverings for his feet and hands, and walked inside the room he'd left hours before.

Careful to stay in the cleared path, he greeted the coroner. "What do we have, Gordon?"

The older man stood. "Blunt force trauma to the back of the head and multiple stab wounds. The ME will give an official cause of death, but I'd say the vic bled out."

Since neither Gigi nor the guests heard anything, the killers must have knocked out Wells with the blow to the head, then finished the job with the knife. David's jaw tightened. The scene reminded him of the Tucker crime scene photos. Was this Marty's handiwork?

"Are you investigating?" Gordon asked.

David shook his head. "It's Blair's case." At least for now. "I'll get out of your way." In the hall, he peeled off the gloves and shoe coverings. "Let's go," he murmured to Jon.

Blair ended a conversation with one of her officers when David caught her eye. "Observations?"

"Wells' injuries are similar to the Tuckers' injuries."

Her gaze darkened. "Same team?"

"Another team might have used the same method."

"But you don't think so."

He shook his head as he pulled up the photo of Marty and his partner. David turned his screen toward Blair. "Be on the lookout for these men."

She studied the photo a moment, then said, "Send that to me. Who are they?"

"Martin Grisham and Jerome Burke. Grisham is Wells' cousin."

A soft whistle. "Cold." Once the photo appeared on her phone, Blair inclined her head toward the door. "I want you long gone before Jordan arrives."

She'd get no argument from him. David doubted he would sleep much tonight, but Wells' death would complicate an already difficult case. He and Jon returned to the SUV.

Jon cranked the engine. "Where to? Safe house or hospital?"

"Hospital. I want to check on Gigi, and update Cal and Owen." He gave Jon directions and sent Emma a text.

Minutes later, Jon parked in the lot in front of Archer Hospital. Since David was a frequent visitor because of his job, the nurse at the desk buzzed him into the ER without questions. Cal stood watch outside one of the exam rooms.

"Any news?" Jon asked his friend.

"Not yet. Owen's inside with Gigi and the doctor." He lowered his voice. "Sit rep."

David updated him, making a mental note to do the same with Blackhawk, Whitehead, and Maddox by email. No need to wake them. His brothers, however, would expect a call.

Cal frowned. "What about Gigi? We can't leave her without protection. She's a target now."

"If the feds close the B & B while they investigate, Owen will want her with him at the ranch."

Minutes later, the exam room door opened, and Dr. Stringer walked out. He greeted David with a nod.

"How is Gigi, Doc?"

"Mild concussion, a headache, and a few bruises. She'll recover quickly."

"Are you keeping her for observation?"

"Since Owen assured me that he or another member of your family would watch over her for the next 24 hours, I'm releasing her."

"We'll take good care of her."

After a quick rundown of symptoms to be on the lookout for, Dr. Stringer walked into the next exam room.

"Gigi was lucky," Jon said.

Cal folded his arms. "We need to identify and locate the Hunt Club teams, fast. Based on what she told Owen, Gigi can't keep her business closed long, and she won't understand the necessity. She saw less than Emma did when she was attacked."

"The teams don't like loose ends. They'll come for her." David's gut churned. Instead of one witness to protect, he had two.

When Jordan interviewed Gigi, he'd want to place her in protective custody. Owen wouldn't allow her out of his sight, not after the agent's track record with Emma.

David sighed. Looked as though he'd be calling Whitehead. Otherwise, his brother would be arrested and detained, leaving Gigi at the mercy of Craig Jordan.

The exam room door opened, and Owen escorted Gigi into the hall, his arm wrapped around her shoulders. "We're ready to leave." Owen said, expression grim.

"Take her to the B & B."

Owen scowled. "No. I want her in a secure environment. The B & B might be overrun with cops, but it's not secure."

"Jordan needs to question her. You and Cal will stay with her."

Gigi glared. "I'm standing right here, and I can make my own decisions. Take me home, Owen."

"Agent Jordan will probably shut down your B & B for a day or two."

Her mouth gaped. "He can't do that, can he?"

"It's a crime scene. Jordan only accommodates himself." He turned to David. "I'll take her to the B & B, but Jordan's not taking her into protective custody."

The B & B owner stared. "Custody? But I didn't hurt Mr. Wells."

"Come on," Owen steered her toward the lobby. "Being in the hallway makes me twitchy."

David, Jon and Cal formed a triangle around the couple and escorted them to the cruiser. Once Gigi was inside the vehicle, Owen turned to David. "Do I need to go off the grid with her?"

"Not yet. I'll call in a favor with Whitehead and request Gigi be placed in our protective custody. If Jordan shuts down the B & B, take Gigi to the Rocking M and have the military-trained ranch hands form a perimeter around the house."

"I'll do it your way for now."

David understood the unspoken threat. If the security at the ranch was breached, Owen would hide Gigi where no one would find her whether it cost his badge and freedom or not.

CHAPTER TWENTY-EIGHT

David and Jon followed the police cruiser to the B & B to ensure Owen, Gigi, and Cal arrived safely, then returned to the safe house. Although they arrived without incident, David couldn't shake his sense of uneasiness. Trouble was coming, but when and where?

As soon as they entered the kitchen, Emma hugged David. He held her close, breathing in the familiar vanilla scent of her shampoo. "Hey," he murmured.

"You're okay?"

An invisible band tightened around David's heart. "I am now that I'm holding you."

"What about Gigi?"

"A mild concussion, headache, and bruises. The doc said she'll be fine in a few days."

"Thank God. I wish I could talk to her. I've missed her."

"You'll see her soon."

She eased back. "What happened to Agent Wells?"

"Come with me." He guided Emma to the living room sofa and tucked her close to his side. "He died in the same manner as your family, Em."

"Oh, no." She leaned her head against his shoulder. "Although I didn't like the man, he didn't deserve that. No one does."

"We may have to relocate."

A sigh. "I understand. I'm bringing my knitting this time."

David smiled. "Good idea."

"Where will we go?"

"Not sure yet." He couldn't leave with Emma until he'd spoken to Jordan. If the agent insisted on taking Emma into protective custody, David would go off the grid with her.

"I don't want to run anymore."

"I understand."

"No, sweetheart, you don't. You haven't spent more than a year on the run. You were right. It's time to take a stand and fight back. No more running."

Yeah, that was before he realized more than one man wanted to kill the woman he loved. "Don't ask me to do this, Emma." David didn't know if he could risk her life. He shuddered at the possibility of losing Emma. Facing an endless, empty existence without her wasn't an option. He couldn't do it again. During the past year, he'd been living a half-life. "I love you too much to risk your life."

Emma cupped his face with her soft hands. "Do you love me enough to help me bring my family's killers to justice?"

"I don't have to risk your life, our life together, to find these men and take them down. Trust me. I'll get the job done."

"How many innocent people will die while you, your brothers, and Wolf Pack identify and locate the teams?"

He flinched.

She brushed her mouth over his in a gentle caress. "I know you and the others will find them, but time isn't on our side. We have to end this nightmare soon. The Hunt Club can't continue operating."

Emma was right, but that didn't make the decision easier. "One more day, Em. If we don't make enough progress by then, we'll revisit your option."

Emma's expression softened. "All right."

The reprieve wasn't long. David prayed Zane, Jon, or a contact would come through before the woman he loved risked her life to stop the Hunt Club.

He stood and held out his hand. "I'll walk you to your room. You need rest."

Emma sent him a sideways glance. "So do you."

True, but he wouldn't get it. Hopefully, he'd have time for a nap when he was off guard duty. "I have work to do before I sleep."

At her bedroom doorway, David captured her lips in a blistering, lengthy kiss that set his blood on fire and left her trembling. Long minutes later, he broke the kiss to Emma's soft moan of disappointment. Leaving her at the doorway took every ounce of discipline he had when he wanted to follow her inside the room, lock the door, and forget the world for a few hours.

David blew out a breath as he descended the stairs. Around Emma, his legendary control was almost nonexistent. His SEAL teammates would howl with laughter if they saw him now. He headed for the coffee pot and poured the hot black liquid into a mug.

"How's Emma?" Jon asked as he typed.

He leaned back against the kitchen counter. "She wants to use herself as bait."

The operative froze. "Will you let her?"

"As a last resort." He sighed. "I convinced her to give me one more day."

A slight nod. "We need to work fast."

David grabbed his laptop. "I'll be in the security room." He walked down the hall, making enough noise to alert the operative on watch.

Eli turned at his entrance. He motioned to an empty chair and returned his attention to the screens. "Sit rep."

He updated Wolf Pack's leader, ending with, "If we don't make significant progress by tomorrow night, Emma will insist we use her as bait."

"Keep Maddox in the loop. He needs to know how fast to mobilize our units."

David tapped the lid of his laptop. "Updating him is the next thing on my agenda."

"I'll wait until you finish the email before I hit the rack for three hours."

"Thanks." Ten minutes later, David sat back. "Go sleep, Eli. I have the watch."

Eli stood and stretched. "Alert me if there's trouble."

David saluted. Turning to the security screens, he studied each of the views, memorizing them so he would recognize a change.

That done, he glanced at his watch and grimaced. He hated to disturb Whitehead, but the situation had changed.

Whitehead answered after two rings.

"It's David Montgomery, sir. I apologize for calling this late."

"What happened?"

He explained about Wells' death and the likelihood that Jordan would insist on protective custody for Gigi and possibly Emma.

"Might be best for both women, David. Having them in separate safe houses divides your resources."

"No offense, sir, but I don't trust Jordan with Emma or Gigi's safety."

"You want to protect the women yourself."

"Yes, sir, with help from my brothers. We're all law enforcement and trained Special Forces operators."

"Your attention will be split between protection and the search for the Hunt Club teams."

"We can handle it, sir." Between the Montgomerys and Wolf Pack, the women were well covered. If Maddox reassigned the Fortress unit, David would reevaluate.

"Are you sure? Failure will be costly for you and the women."

A truth the director didn't have to stress. "I'm sure." He was staking his life and that of the woman he loved on his skills and experience.

"All right. If Agent Jordan tries to take the women into custody, contact me."

"Thank you, sir. I owe you."

"No, David. I'm the one who owes you for saving my son's life more than once when you served on the Teams together. In light of the injuries you suffered to protect him, this is a small enough favor. If you change your mind about utilizing an FBI safe house, call me. Don't let pride stand in the way of the best protection option for Emma and Gigi."

Ending the call a moment later, David called his brother Levi.

"Seriously, bro?" his brother groused. "Do you have any idea what time it is?"

"I'm awake. Figured you should be, too."

Levi groaned. "You're evil, man. Hang on a second." A thump sounded over the speaker as his brother dropped the phone without ending the call. Water ran. Seconds later, his brother said, "Go."

David told him the latest developments.

Levi whistled softly. "Gigi's a lucky woman. I'm glad she's okay, but why didn't they finish the job?"

"I believe having guests in the house held them back. Maybe one of the guests came out of a room or made noise, and the team feared being caught."

"Makes her a target."

"We'll stop them."

"No other option," Levi agreed. "What's the plan?"

"We have one day before Emma insists we use her as bait."

A groan. "Lousy plan."

"Agreed. She's worried someone else will die because of her."

"None of this is her fault. It's on the Hunt Club members. If Emma offers herself as bait, too many things could go wrong. We could lose her in a split second."

"Preaching to the choir, Levi."

"What do you need from us?"

"Push hard for information from your sources. We need to know who these men are and locate them."

"You know the old saying. Follow the money."

"Find me a trail."

"I hear you. Give me another hour to sleep, and I'll start working my sources again."

"Check the ranch security. Owen will probably take Gigi to the Rocking M tomorrow. I've already contacted Caleb. Update Elliot when he wakes."

"Copy that. Elliot's probably awake, though. He doesn't sleep much these days." Worry filled Levi's voice. "Watch your back, David." Levi ended the call.

David sipped his coffee. For the next two hours, he watched the security monitors.

When David went to the kitchen for water, Jon said, "Fortress tech support came through. I'm compiling data and dividing the likely cases into areas of the country. Once that's complete, we'll assign two or three people to evaluate the cases in a particular region."

Progress, but not enough to dissuade Emma from her plan. "How long until you finish?"

"An hour, maybe less." Jon looked up. "I know, David," he murmured. "We're working as fast as we can."

"I've been thinking about Marty and his friend. They're wealthy, graduates of Harvard, and part of a powerful, influential circle of people."

"Your point?"

"Someone is coordinating this group of hunters."

"Wells said he didn't know who was running the group."

"Marty and Justin created the game. I can't see Marty, a man Justin said never gives up on a quarry, handing over the reins of this game to someone else."

Silence, then, "You have a point. The feds must have torn apart Marty's life, looking for anything to bring down this group. FBI hackers are excellent. I can't see them missing a money trail."

"I'm told you and Zane are better."

The operative grunted. "What am I looking for?"

"A hefty fee for joining the Hunt Club and perhaps a fee per hunt. I doubt Marty pays it, but perhaps his partner, Jerome, contributes something per hunt."

"Maybe." Jon looked thoughtful. "Once we identify another team, I'll have more information with which to work."

"Look for a shell corporation buried in other shell corporations, possibly set up with a Cayman Islands account or a Swiss bank account."

"You don't ask for much, do you?"

"Hey, that's why they pay you the big bucks, buddy."

Jon's lips twitched as he returned his attention to his laptop.

Thirty minutes before his shift ended, David's gaze locked on one screen displaying the south perimeter. As he watched, a figure dressed in black moved from the shadows of the trees. "Jon!"

David studied the screen intently. Where was his partner? He scanned the other screens. Shadows everywhere. At the corner of one screen, a shadow moved, but when he looked more closely, everything was still.

The back of David's neck prickled. Was there a blind spot in the coverage or had someone hacked into the security system to prevent him from seeing danger from another direction?

Seconds later, Jon entered the security room. "Where?"

"South perimeter, quadrant three. I only see one man."

"We'll deal with it. Wake Eli and get your woman to safety. I'll scan for another intruder and keep an eye on this one. He's half a mile out. We have time."

Not enough to suit him, especially with a second intruder lurking nearby. David pushed back from the desk, jogged from the room, and took the stairs two at a time. How had the team located the safe house? He tapped on Eli's door.

The door swung open almost immediately. "Sit rep."

"One man in the south quadrant, half a mile out. Jon's tracking him on the security monitor."

A frown. "Where's his partner?"

A question that had been plaguing him. "I don't know, and I don't like it."

"Wake Emma. There's a full security setup in the safe room in the office. She'll be able to see everything going on without risk to her safety. Do you remember the code?"

When David nodded, Eli reached into his Go bag for two extra magazines for his Sig and an ear piece for his comm system. "Gear up, and don't let your guard down. I'll wake Jackson when Jon and I leave the cabin. Your job is to protect Emma."

David hurried to his room to grab extra magazines for his own weapon and shoved them into his pocket. That done, he hurried to Emma's room and knocked on the door.

Emma threw open the door seconds later, eyes wide, fully dressed except for her shoes. "What's wrong?"

"Company. We need to move you into the safe room."

She rushed back into the room and returned with running shoes on her feet and knitting bag in hand. "I'm ready."

David led her to the first floor. As they hurried toward the safe room, a wave of dizziness hit David. He pressed his hand to the wall to steady himself, frowning. Was he more tired than he realized? The hallway tilted.

"David?" Emma stumbled into his side. "I feel strange."

A heavy thud came from the security room.

David shook his head, hoping to throw off the dizziness. Although he tried to continue toward the safe room with Emma, his body wouldn't cooperate, limbs grew heavy and brain sluggish.

Eli stumbled into the hall. "Gas." His knees gave out. "Save Em." The operative collapsed on the floor, unmoving.

David clumsily wrapped his arm around Emma to help her to the nearest window. At that moment, Emma went limp and slid from his grasp to the floor.

Fighting the lethargy sweeping over him in a tidal wave, David bent to drag Emma to safety, but listed sideways, falling against the wall.

As he slid to the floor, David mustered enough strength to drag himself over Emma in a last-ditch effort to protect her. He'd failed the most important person in his life. The darkness closed in. *I'm sorry, baby.*

CHAPTER TWENTY-NINE

Emma woke in total darkness on a vibrating floor. She frowned. That didn't make sense. Remaining still, she evaluated the sounds and scents around her.

As the fog in her mind cleared, Emma realized she wasn't in the safe house. The sound of an engine grew louder, and her head thumped against the floor.

She was in a vehicle? Emma moved her head and felt material tug against her skin. Her heart skipped a beat. She had a blindfold over her eyes. Did a Hunt Club team kidnap her?

She had to escape from this vehicle. The greater distance she traveled from David and the others, the less likely help would reach Emma in time to spare her life.

Emma refused to consider that a rescue might not come at all. The last thing she remembered was feeling weak and dizzy while rushing to the safe room at the cabin. If one of the Hunt Club teams had poisoned them, what were the chances they left David and the others alive, but kidnapped her? Slim to none.

Tears burned her eyes. Agent Jordan was right. She should have remained in WITSEC instead of dragging

David into this mess. If the Hunt Club team had murdered him and his friends, she would never forgive herself.

Ironic that she'd been willing to use herself as bait, and now she truly was bait. But would anyone mount a rescue?

Hearing faint male laughter, Emma listen to their voices. Were these the men who murdered her family? A few minutes later, she gave up the futile effort. The engine and road noise were too loud.

Emma started to reach for the blindfold, but realized couldn't move her hands. She scowled. Fantastic. The jerks had restrained her.

After another hard jolt, her head slammed against the floor of the vehicle. She hissed as pain ricocheted through her head.

A soft groan sounded nearby.

Emma's breath caught. Who was with her? From the sound of the groan, her companion was a man. A member of the Hunt Club wouldn't groan as though he was in pain, would he? That left another victim. The question was, who?

Another hard thump as the vehicle hit a pothole caused the man to groan again. Emma's heartbeat increased. She knew that groan. "David?" she whispered.

Emma struggled to sit up on the uneven metal floor. A van. Did the van have windows in the back?

A sharp turn had her slamming against the outer wall. That would leave a bruise, adding to the others she suspected were already forming. Her whole body ached.

Another turn, and the van left the asphalt road. Rocks pinged against the underside of the vehicle. She had a feeling this journey would end soon. She didn't want to contemplate what happened when the van stopped. "David?"

Nothing.

Rats. Emma needed to wake David. Every second counted if they were to formulate a plan.

The van swung to the right, throwing Emma to the other side of the vehicle. This time, however, instead of slamming up against a metal wall, she fell against a hard, muscular body. Thank God. Now all she had to do was stay next to David instead of rolling around the back of the van like a pinball.

Emma twisted around to face David. "Sweetheart, wake up." She brushed his mouth with her own. "Come back to me."

Over and over, she pressed light kisses to his mouth and cheek until finally he responded by nuzzling against her. "David? Are you with me now?"

"You okay?" he murmured.

"I think so. I'm blindfolded, and my hands are restrained behind my back."

His muscles flexed, then, "Same. Scoot down, and use my shoulder to slide off the blindfold if you can."

She wiggled down a few inches and located David's shoulder. Slowly the blindfold shifted upward, but not enough. Emma huffed out a breath. "It's not working. I can only raise one side a little before the material slides back into place."

"Stay where you are. I'll sit up and work the blindfold off with my hands."

She felt a moment of disorientation as David rolled away from her, then his fingers brushed against the top of her head.

"Hold still." He worked his fingers under the black band covering her eyes and tugged the material up and off. "Better?"

Emma blinked, praying her eyes adjusted quickly. Epic fail. The van was pitch black inside. "I'm happy the material is out of the way, but we're in the back of a van without windows."

"Can't say I'm surprised."

David was taller than Emma by several inches. If she stood up in the van to tug off his blindfold, she'd go flying. "Lay on your side with your back to me. I'll slide off your blindfold, too."

A moment later, she felt his back against her hands. "Hold still." After trailing her hands up David's back to near the top of his head, Emma tugged the material off.

"Thanks."

"Now what?"

Before he could respond, the van slowed and came to a stop. "Put your back against the wall and get behind me, baby."

She scrambled to do as he ordered, dread building with every beat of her heart. Would the men shoot them in the van and leave their bodies somewhere deserted?

They waited in silence, tension building as the seconds passed in agonizing slowness.

Two doors slammed shut, then footsteps came closer and closer. The doors at the back of the van opened, revealing two figures dressed in unrelieved black.

"Well, look who's awake," the taller thug said to the shorter one.

"You were right, Marty. The gas worked like a charm, and the timing was perfect. They're awake to play."

Marty Grisham? Both men's faces were still in shadow, preventing her from positively identifying either one from the security cam photos. The Hunt Club team had arranged this night's events.

"Aren't I always?" Arrogance filled Marty's voice. "Out of the van, Montgomery. You, too, Ms. Tucker."

David glanced over his shoulder. "Stay behind me," he whispered.

Easier said than done, but she nodded.

"Move, Sheriff, or I'll shoot you now and save all the fun for your woman."

What did Marty mean by that? At his words, Emma felt those invisible spiders crawling along her skin.

David slowly moved toward the men, doing his best to keep his body between their captors and Emma. The men backed up, their guns trained on David. Smart. Emma wasn't a threat.

"Stand where I can see you, Ms. Tucker," Marty ordered.

"No, Em," David said.

"Don't listen to him, sweet Emma," the second thug said. "Unless you want to watch your boyfriend die now instead of later. Don't be a spoilsport."

Emma pressed closer to David's back. "David, please," she whispered.

His jaw hardened, but he gave her a slight nod, his gaze locked on their captors.

She eased out far enough for the men to see her while still remaining partially hidden behind David. "Why are you doing this?"

A slow smile curved Marty's face. He chuckled, his glee sending a cold finger of fear trailing down her spine. "Unfinished business. And for the money, of course. I don't like to lose."

"Money? Someone is paying you to do this?"

Jerome laughed. "We pay to play, sweet Emma. The hunting fees are dumped into an account. The team with the most kills at the end of the year wins the pot of money." A sly grin. "Minus a hefty fee, of course."

Marty chuckled. "The teams made a side bet that we'd fail to bag you and your boyfriend. They were wrong."

Emma's breath caught in her throat. These men planned to hunt them like wild animals.

"You don't want to do this," David said, voice soft.

"Oh, we definitely do. This hunt will be more fun than stalking people in a house. If it's as entertaining as we hope, we'll create a higher-stakes game for members to play."

"You want a challenge? Let Emma go free, and take me on alone."

An outright laugh. "Good try, Montgomery. Not going to happen. Besides, if we let your lady go free, we'll lose the bet, and one of the other teams will have a chance to bag her. Since she escaped the first time, she's been the ultimate prize."

"They'll keep coming for her?"

"Of course. Emma has proved to be quite elusive. That makes her more valuable." Marty's smile faded. "I won't lose this bet. Doesn't matter to me what kind of secret background you have. You can't outrun a bullet." He smirked. "I know your greatest weakness, Montgomery. Emma. You won't leave her behind. She'll be the death of you."

"How much did you pay to get into this club?"

A snort. "Nothing. It's my club."

"You're the one who runs the game, aren't you?"

"We both do." He inclined his head to his partner. "But I'm the game master. Jerome is the computer genius and money man. Together, we make an unbeatable, extremely wealthy team."

"How did you find us at the safe house? No one followed us."

"Didn't have to. While you were inside the B & B admiring our handiwork, I slipped a GPS tracker on your vehicle. Jerome hacked into the security cams and played a loop while I hooked up the gas into the air and heat system. Easy as pie."

"You killed your cousin."

"Did you think I'd let him live after what he did?" Marty scowled. "He betrayed me and tried to come between me and my prize. I couldn't allow that to happen. He also threatened to have our deal with the Justice

Department revoked." A shrug. "He connected too many dots."

"Why did you kill my family?" Emma asked.

"We didn't know the old people were in the house until we were inside. They were collateral damage. We wanted you and the blond, a prize for each of us and the beginning of a new game if it had worked out right." Marty glared at Emma. "You screwed that up for us, something you'll pay for."

Her stomach churned at the realization that her parents were dead because they were in the wrong place at the wrong time. "You killed my grandfather, too."

"That was on him. The old goat refused to tell us where you were hiding. All he had to do was give us the information, and we would have left him alive."

Liar. "No one knew I was alive, not even David."

"We found that out too late."

"A good man paid with his life for your mistake." Emma's voice broke.

Jerome nudged Marty with his elbow. "Time's wasting, Marty. I'm ready to hunt." His eyes gleamed with anticipation.

"Be patient, buddy." He looked at David. "I'll give you and Emma a ten-minute head start. If I were you, I'd leave her behind to give myself a chance to escape."

"Never."

"Yeah, didn't think you'd take that choice. Makes the hunt more fun for us. Run far and fast, Montgomery, because we're coming for you."

"Rules?"

"There aren't any. Run or die. When we catch you, you die."

"And if we elude you?"

A snort. "Won't happen."

"But if we succeed?"

"You won't escape the second team who will also be hunting you."

David stiffened. "Second team?"

"Oh, did I forget to mention them?" A low laugh. "Sorry about that. They're friends of ours who want to play."

Horror filled Emma. Oh, man. Another Hunt Club team was in the area.

"What about you and Jerome? You failed to kill Emma in Seagull. Isn't this about redemption for yourself?"

Jerome bristled. "We knocked you out and brought you here, didn't we? You're helpless to stop the game. I'd call that a win already."

"Hardly seems fair. Four against two." David's smile held no humor. "You don't win until we're dead, right? We're still breathing."

"Our game. Our rules." Marty snapped. He and Jerome backed away several paces, guns aimed at Emma and David. "Better run," Marty said. "The game starts now."

CHAPTER THIRTY

David nodded at Emma. "Go, baby." When Emma broke into a stumbling run, he fell into step behind her to block a cheap shot by one of the so-called hunters jeering and laughing at them. Once he and Emma were out of the deadly duo's direct line of sight, David caught up with Emma. "Wait."

She skidded to a stop. "We have to keep going. Those men are too close, and I don't trust them to give us a ten-minute head start. They're too eager to play their horrible game."

"Running with our hands tied behind our back throws us off balance." He turned his hands until his wrists faced each other, fisted his hands, bent over slightly, and whacked his wrists hard against his backside twice. The zip tie snapped, and David's hands were free.

Marty and Jerome had removed David's Sig and cell phone. With any luck, the phone was in the front of the van. Had the men discovered his knife?

"Hurry, David."

He checked his boot and breathed a sigh of relief. The Hunt Club team missed his boot knife. Excellent. At least he had a weapon. Even if he'd been without weapons,

David wouldn't let the two teams win this sick game. He'd kill them with his bare hands if he had to in order to protect Emma.

He loosened Emma's zip tie. After shoving the plastic strip into his pocket, David clasped Emma's hand and led her toward hard-packed earth and rocky surfaces. No time to teach her how to avoid leaving telltale signs of their passage.

As they ran, David scanned the terrain ahead. Where had Marty and Jerome taken them? Couldn't have been far from the safe house. Based on the position of the moon in the night sky, he and Emma had been unconscious for perhaps an hour or less.

As long as the Hunt Club team hadn't killed Jon, Eli, and Jackson, the operatives should be awake and aware that David and Emma were missing. Since he and Emma would have been dead weight, Marty and Jerome must have driven the van to the cabin and dumped them into the back of the vehicle. With the security cams around the cabin, one of them must have captured a shot of the van and hopefully the two men. Photos plus a lock on his cell phone would lead Wolf Pack and David's brothers to this general area. If his phone was in the van, and if the operatives were still alive.

Were they still in Morgan County? The area seemed familiar, but David couldn't quite place it. Up ahead, the land rose at a steep incline. In his tactical boots, he could navigate the terrain without a problem. Emma, on the other hand, would be at a disadvantage in her running shoes. Not enough traction.

David changed direction, heading toward the right where the tree cover was thicker and the land rose at a gentler incline. He needed a higher elevation to orient himself. What he wouldn't give for a good pair of night-vision goggles about now.

A twig snapped nearby.

David froze, stilling Emma, his attention shifting ahead of them and to the left.

A brush of fabric against a tree followed by a muffled curse.

One of the members of the second team closing in on their location? If one of his brothers or a member of Wolf Pack were here, the approach would be silent.

David searched for a safe place for Emma to wait while he slipped behind the approaching hunter. Spotting a large bush with dense foliage that stood in front of a thick stand of trees, he tugged Emma that direction. He motioned for Emma to hide behind the bush.

Once Emma was out of sight, David hugged the shadows, placing his feet carefully to silence his approach as he circled closer to his quarry.

What if this was a legitimate hunter? Although unlikely, he had to be sure before he did something irreversible.

A rustle fifty feet ahead. A faint light glimmered, then, "What?" a man said, voice pitched low. "Nothing yet. They can't be far. The woman will slow him down. You see anything?" A pause. "They have to be close. I can't wait until I get my hands on her. Might have a little fun before we kill her. Text if you spot them. The man's dangerous." The light disappeared.

David had his confirmation. This man wasn't an innocent hunter. He was part of the second team hunting for him and Emma. Waiting until the hunter moved past him, David came up behind the man and caught him in a sleeper hold. Seconds later, the hunter lay on the ground, unconscious. One glance at the man's face confirmed he was a member of the Hunt Club team who breached Emma's second safe house.

Working fast, David confiscated the man's handgun and shoved the Glock into his own empty holster. He removed the hunter's boots and socks, then the laces, and tied the hunter's wrists and ankles together. David shoved the socks in the boots. After stripping the hunter's belt from his pants, he used the strip of leather as a gag, cinching the belt tight at the back of the man's head.

That done, he hoisted the man over his shoulder and carried him to an outcropping of rocks. He'd hoped to find a deep crevice to dump the man in. Instead, he found a ravine steep enough that the hunter wouldn't be able to get out on his own, and the fall wouldn't be fatal. Not ideal, but it would have to do.

David heaved the hunter off his shoulder, laid him on the ground, and pushed him off the side. The man rolled down until he hit the bottom and remained motionless. One down, three to go, and he'd scored another weapon.

The Glock wasn't his first choice of weapons. A gunshot would bring the other hunters running.

Alert for the hunter's partner who must be in this area, David retrieved the hunter's boots and worked his way back to the place he'd hidden Emma. "It's safe for the moment, Em." When she came out of hiding, David tossed the boots into the darkened interior of her temporary shelter and held out his hand.

She slid her hand into his and squeezed. "You're okay?"

"Yep. Let's go." Hoping the hunter's partner was looking for him and Emma in a different quadrant, David tugged Emma in the direction where he'd encountered his quarry. How far behind them were Marty and Jerome?

As they hurried up the incline, he scanned ahead for the easiest path for Emma. The moonlight was a blessing and a curse. The light that allowed David to navigate with ease also made them easy to spot if they weren't under cover.

"Where are we going?" Emma whispered.

"Higher ground. We need to know where we are." The skin at the back of his neck tingled. Not a good sign. He urged Emma to move faster. The sooner he oriented himself, the better.

Near the top of the rise, he dropped to his stomach and tugged Emma to hers. They moved cautiously the last few feet to the top. David's eyebrows rose as he stared down the hill, recognizing landmarks he'd seen most of his life.

Marty and Jerome were arrogant fools. Did they think he wouldn't recognize his own land? Granted, he and Emma were at the outer edges of the Rocking M, but a quarter of a mile ahead, David and his brothers had installed security cameras.

"Do you know where we are?" Emma whispered.

"The Rocking M. We're five miles from the ranch house."

"Let's go."

When she started to rise, David clamped his hand on Emma's arm to hold her in place. "We can't travel in a straight line to the house," he murmured.

"Why not?"

"Too much moonlight and not enough cover. We'll have to stay in the tree line as long as we can." Hopefully, help would arrive before they had to make a run for it across open terrain. "Come on."

David led her down the hill a few feet, then they hurried toward dense tree cover and the nearest perimeter security camera.

Nearly at their destination, he pulled up short and tugged Emma behind a large rock outcropping. David pressed a finger to his lips to signal for silence as he tucked her behind him and waited for an approaching intruder to walk closer.

A figure dressed in black stumbled in the darkness and uttered a soft curse. He righted himself and continued forward, walking within a few feet of David and Emma's hiding place.

David remained motionless, alert for another hunter. Nothing. Something about him was familiar, but what?

Although reluctant to leave Emma when his gut told him that Marty and Jerome were closing in on them, capturing this hunter would improve David and Emma's odds of surviving.

David waited until the hunter passed their location, then slipped up behind the man. Although intending to knock him unconscious with a sleeper hold as he had the man's partner, some sixth sense must have alerted the hunter that danger was closing in because he swung around at the last instant, weapon up and aimed at David.

Phil Jones. Guess David had found the mole in the FBI. Had Jordan suspected his agent was on the take?

Without giving Jones time to pull the trigger, David kicked the weapon from his hand and tackled him. They rolled on the ground, fighting for the upper hand and exchanging multiple blows.

David slammed a fist into the other man's face, breaking his nose. When Jones released his grip to clutch at his face, David knocked him out with an elbow strike to the temple.

Working fast, David slid Jones' gun into his own pocket, secured his hands with the zip tie, and gagged him with his belt. Conscious of time slipping away, he jerked off the agent's boots and socks, and carried him back to the place he'd left Emma.

Her eyes widened as David shoved Jones between two boulders where he wouldn't be able to escape without help. He doubted Marty and Jerome would be sympathetic to their competitor's plight and help him. That done, David hustled back to grab the socks and boots, and tossed them into the thick undergrowth.

He held out his hand to Emma who ran to join him. Together, they hurried through the woods toward the tree with the closest security camera.

When he reached his goal, David stopped and looked up at the camera he'd placed in the notch of the tree seven weeks earlier. With a series of hand signals, he warned his brothers of the two remaining hunters and conveyed the route he planned to travel. That done, he grabbed Emma's hand and tugged her into motion again.

"What was all that about?" Emma whispered.

"You didn't see the security camera in the tree?"

A soft gasp. "No."

He squeezed her hand. "I warned my brothers about our pursuers. We should have help soon."

"But it's the middle of the night. They must be asleep."

By tripping the early-warning system in place at the perimeter's edge and triggering an alert with the motion-sensitive camera, his brothers were already on the move. Levi and Elliot were the closest to David and Emma. Caleb could be anywhere in the county. If Wolf Pack was still at the safe house, they were thirty minutes away. His brothers and the ranch hands were his and Emma's closest source of help.

For several minutes, David and Emma rushed through the woods, picking their way around fallen trees and skirting terrain too dense to traverse without alerting Marty and Jerome to their position.

When Emma stumbled, David wrapped his arm around her waist and propelled her forward. Fury at the two men chasing them burned in his gut. Emma had been through so much, and now she was running for her life again. The unfairness of it all raked his insides and stoked his desire to see the members of the Hunt Club behind bars or dead.

"Sorry," Emma whispered. "I'm trying not to slow you down."

"You're doing great. Just a little farther, and we'll take a short break." Although he could press on for a long while, Emma couldn't. He was amazed she'd lasted as long as she had.

She shook her head. "We have to keep going."

Mocking male laughter came from the woods behind them. "Told you she'd be the death of you. Run, little rabbits."

CHAPTER THIRTY-ONE

David pushed Emma in front of him. "Run!" As she sprinted through the woods, he stayed a few paces behind Emma to better protect her, mentally urging her to run faster.

More mocking laughter followed them through the darkness as the hunter continued taunting them.

"Veer to the right, baby." A few hundred feet ahead was a stand of rocks he and his brothers played on as kids and was the last place of safety before the open fields leading to the ranch house. The only problem? They had to cross open terrain to reach the rocks.

When Emma broke out of the trees, she faltered, glancing back at him.

"Rocks!" David ordered.

Emma resumed her dash, legs and arms pumping as she ran toward the rocks.

Gunshots peppered the night air, kicking up dirt around their feet as more laughter came from behind them.

David frowned. The hunter laughing like a loon wasn't trying hard to hit them. Was he was herding them toward the rocks? Adrenaline poured into his veins. "Emma, stop!"

She pulled up short, spun, and reversed course, but not fast enough to prevent the second hunter who emerged from the shadows of the rocks from wrapping an arm around Emma's neck and jerking her against his chest. He jammed a gun against the side of her head.

Between one beat and the next, David's weapon was in his hand and aimed at Jerome's head. "Let her go." Ice water flowed through his veins as he struggled to push his fear for Emma's safety aside and focus.

A slow, smug smile formed on Jerome's mouth. "I don't think so, Montgomery. I have the advantage." When he tightened his hold around Emma's neck, she clawed at Jerome's arm to no avail.

Behind David, Marty said, "Drop the gun, Sheriff, or Emma dies in front of your eyes. Jerome has an itchy trigger finger. You don't want the game to end too soon, do you?"

David could make the shot, but if Jerome's finger twitched against the trigger, he could shoot Emma in the head. If he killed Jerome without the other man injuring Emma, Marty would shoot David in the back, possibly leaving the love of his life without protection.

"Drop it, Montgomery," Marty snapped. "Last chance."

David slowly lowered his hands and spread them wide, weapon easily visible. "Ease up, Jerome. Emma can't breathe."

When Emma gulped in several deep breaths, David bent and placed his weapon on the ground. "What now, Marty?"

"Get on your knees."

"No!" Emma renewed her fight to escape from Jerome. "Don't hurt him. I'm the one you want, not David."

"Aww, listen to that," Marty said. "She's begging for your life instead of her own. A waste of breath, but I guess she really does love you."

"I like this new game," Jerome said, his smile broadening. "I think we should allow the teams to hunt couples from now on."

"It's a rush," his partner agreed. "We'll double the game fee and buy a large, remote wooded property to hold the hunts. Should be more fun."

"David!" Emma wrenched out of Jerome's hold.

He caught her in his arms, holding her close. "I have you, baby," David whispered as he turned them at an angle away from the two men.

"I'm sorry I involved you in this." Tears streamed down her face, breaking his heart. "I love you."

Jerome hooted with laughter. "The good-bye scene of the century, Marty. Too bad we don't have a camera to record this."

"We'll set up the camera for next time."

David captured Emma's hand and brought it to his mouth. He kissed her palm, placed her hand over his heart, and slowly eased his hand to his pocket where the second gun was hidden beneath his shirt. "I love you, Emma. Do you trust me?"

"Yes." No hesitation in her response.

He bent his head until his mouth brushed hers in a gentle kiss, then trailed his lips across her cheek until they were against her ear. David wrapped his hand around the weapon's grip. "Be ready to drop."

A slight nod.

"You had your chance to say good-bye," Marty snapped. "On your knees, Montgomery. The game's over, and you lost."

Jerome chuckled. "Should have left your woman behind, man. You could be home by now."

David ignored the two men. Anchoring Emma against him with one arm, he murmured, "Kneel with me, then kiss me."

A faint smile. "Kissing you is one of my favorite things to do."

"Tell me that again when we're alone."

"Deal."

He freed his weapon as they sank to their knees. David turned his head slightly to pinpoint Marty's location. A second later, Emma pressed her mouth to David's.

"Oh, come on, Marty," Jerome complained. "Let's kill them and leave. I'm getting cold."

A sharp, familiar whistle broke the silence of the woods.

David took Emma to the ground, firing at Jerome as they fell. Other gunshots rang out in the clearing. With his body covering Emma's, he twisted to fire at Marty. The game master was already down, writhing on the ground and shouting curses.

Seconds later, Elliot and Levi emerged from the woods, weapons aimed at the two hunters. David didn't relax until Marty and Jerome had been stripped of their weapons and restrained.

"Clear," Elliot said. "Wolf Pack's ETA is five minutes." He inclined his head toward Marty. "Jackson can patch him up before we haul him to the hospital."

"Jerome?" A slight head shake was his answer. David didn't regret taking the shot to protect Emma. He helped Emma sit up, scanning her for injuries. "You okay, Em?"

"I think so." She started to look toward Jerome.

David caught her chin and gently turned her face back to him. "Right here, baby." He'd hit his target in the heart. Emma had seen enough violence to fuel her nightmares for years to come without adding more visual images.

"Is Jerome dead?"

If she saw his handiwork, would she view him as a killer rather than the man who loved her enough to die for her? "I was a SEAL sniper. What do you think?"

"You don't miss. I need to see for myself that Jerome isn't a threat, or he'll continue to haunt my dreams. I want to be free of him, David."

Although he understood her reasoning, David dreaded her reaction. If he lost her now, his life would be empty. As much as he longed to prevent her from looking at Jerome's body, David refused to cage Emma or he could lose even a small chance of convincing her to remain with him despite his deadly skills.

He stood and tugged Emma to her feet. Praying this wasn't a mistake, David escorted her across the twenty-foot gap between them and the dead hunter. She stared down at Jerome's face for a moment before turning back into David's arms.

Holding her close, he led her away from the body. When her knees buckled, David scooped her into his arms and carried her to a fallen tree at the edge of the clearing. After setting her on the trunk, he crouched in front of her. "You still with me?"

"Always." She brushed his mouth with hers. "You're amazing, David Montgomery, and I'm blessed that you're mine. Thank you for saving me."

Just like that, the tension wracking his muscles disappeared. He captured her mouth in a hot, deep kiss that chased the chill from his bones and sent his heart rate into the stratosphere. He was so in love with this woman.

"You didn't need us for anything but mop up," Eli said as he emerged from the trees with Jon and Jackson close on his heels.

David breathed easier at the sight of the operatives. Thank God Marty and Jerome had been in too much of a hurry to shoot Eli and Jon.

"Took you boys long enough," Levi drawled. "Have a nice nap?"

A scowl from Jon. "I'm not in the mood, grunt."

A chuckle was his reply.

Jackson slid a mike bag from his shoulder as he knelt at Emma's side. "At least the effects of the gas didn't last long."

"And who woke from the gas all comfy in his bed?" Eli said, voice mild. "Jon and I weren't so lucky."

"Hey, you're the one who decided to nap on the floor." Jackson patted Emma's hand. "Any injuries, Emma?"

"Thanks to David, no."

The medic looked at David. "You good, frog boy?"

"Yeah." He inclined his head toward the still-groaning Marty. "Keep him alive. I want him to have a nice, long stay behind bars."

"Copy that." He grabbed his bag and headed for the injured hunter.

"David!" Caleb jogged into the clearing with Rafe a step behind.

"We're fine. Two more hunters are restrained in the woods." He told his brother the approximate locations. "One of them is Phil Jones, the FBI agent."

Caleb nodded. "Excellent. You found the mole. Rafe and I will round them up. Cal and Owen are at the ranch house with Gigi. She and Mrs. Grady are in the safe room. The hands set up a tight perimeter around the house."

"Good. How did you get here so fast?"

His brother inclined his head toward Jon. "You can thank him. As soon as he regained consciousness, he accessed the security feeds at the safe house, identified Marty and Jerome, and pinged your phone which Marty and his partner left in their van. He called Rafe and we alerted the others. Once we knew where your phone was located, we began to converge on this general location."

David rose. "Excellent work, all of you."

"Who's responsible for the Hunt Club?" Rafe said, his voice a fraction above a growl.

"Marty and Jerome. Jerome's dead."

"Good." The operative fixed his gaze on Marty and stalked toward the injured hunter. "One more piece of garbage to take out."

David stepped in front of him. "Rafe."

"Out of my way, Montgomery."

He understood the other man's drive for vengeance. As much as David wanted to let the other SEAL have a few minutes with Marty, he couldn't. They needed information from the game master. "Can't let you do it, buddy. I'm sorry."

"Look the other way." His gaze locked onto David. "If he'd murdered Emma, would you uphold the letter of the law?"

"I'd like to think I would." But he wasn't sure. Hopefully, one of his brothers would have kept him from killing the man and ending up behind bars himself. "Don't give him an excuse to send you to prison, Rafe. He's not worth throwing your life away."

"Avenging Callie would be worth every minute I spent behind bars," Rafe whispered, hands fisting.

David laid his hand on the other man's shoulder and squeezed. "She wouldn't agree. Callie would want you to live your life in freedom. Go with Caleb and round up the other two hunters. You need to stay away from Marty."

"David...."

"We don't know if Marty and Jerome were the hunters who killed your girlfriend. We need your help to locate and capture more teams. Go. They'll pay, Rafe. All of them."

Rafe stared at him for a long moment before he gave a slight nod and left with Caleb.

After Rafe was out of earshot, Eli murmured, "Nice job, Sheriff. When do you want to call Jordan?"

"After Jon talks with Marty." He glanced at his fellow sniper. "Do you mind?"

"It will be my pleasure." Jon inclined his head toward Emma. "She should leave before I begin."

"No marks."

"No promises."

David's lips twitched as he approached Levi. "I want to take Emma to the house before I call Jordan."

His brother tossed him a set of keys to the ATV and told him where he and Elliot had left the vehicle. "We have this, bro. Take care of your girl."

"Thanks. I owe you."

A quick grin. "You owe me about a hundred, but don't worry. I'll collect."

He punched his brother lightly on the shoulder and returned to Emma. He helped her stand. "Come on. Let's go home."

As he passed Jon, he murmured, "You have twenty minutes before I make the call."

"Won't take that long."

Listening to Marty groan and whine to Jackson about his shoulder wound, David agreed with Jon's assessment. "Wait five minutes."

A nod.

When they were out of sight of the others, Emma asked, "What's Jon going to do?"

"Find out everything Marty knows."

She blinked. "Why are we leaving the scene?"

"First, it's cold out here. Second, you don't want to be here when Jon questions Marty."

"Interrogate, you mean?"

"That's right. We need information, fast. Time isn't on our side now that the game master has been captured. If word leaks, members of the Hunt Club will go to ground." They couldn't let that happen.

Emma shivered. "I am cold," she admitted. "Please tell me we have a ride to the house. I don't think I can walk the rest of the way."

He held up the ATV key. "Your chariot awaits, my lady."

"Thank goodness."

David wrapped his arm around her shoulders, as much to remind himself that his Emma was alive as to share his body heat. "We're in for a cool ride, I'm afraid, but we'll get you warm once we reach the house." He kissed the top of her head. "Owen probably took Gigi to the ranch house."

Her breath caught. "Oh, I can't wait to see her." Emma's steps quickened.

As David climbed onto the ATV and helped Emma settle behind him, a scream sounded in the distance.

Emma froze. "Was that…?"

"Let's go." After he took care of Emma, David had phone calls to make.

CHAPTER THIRTY-TWO

Emma snuggled close to David's back and held tight as he drove the ATV toward the Rocking M's ranch house. The brisk breeze and cold temperature chilled Emma to the bone. Shudders rolled through her body, one right after another in a continuous stream.

"Almost there," David said over his shoulder. "You'll be warm soon."

Couldn't be soon enough for her. She rested her head against David's back, thankful he was safe for the moment. She knew David wouldn't rest until every member of the Hunt Club was either behind bars or dead. Though he might enlist the help of other law enforcement agencies, her SEAL would insist on having a hand in bringing those hunters to justice himself. As though sensing her disquieting thoughts, her husband-to-be patted her hand.

Soon, the lights of the ranch house shone like a beacon in the night, guiding them home. When David parked the ATV at the back of the house minutes later, the back door opened and Owen stepped out, upper body covered by a bullet-resistant vest, a gun in his hand. He holstered the weapon when he recognized them. "Everybody okay?"

"Three perps captured, one dead." David climbed off the ATV and helped Emma down. "Any problems here?"

A head shake. "Jordan is spitting mad."

"Not that I care, but why?"

"I brought Gigi here as soon as I learned the safe house had been breached. He hadn't finished questioning her. Do we know how the perps found you?"

"Marty and Jerome planted a tracker on the Fortress SUV when we were at the B & B." David sounded disgusted. "The breach is on me for not checking the vehicle before we returned to the safe house." He ushered Emma into the house with his brother following in their wake.

Cal greeted them with a nod as he filled his coffee mug.

"Where is she?" a familiar woman's voice demanded from the kitchen entrance.

Emma's attention focused on Virginia Warren, the friend she'd missed almost as much as she missed David while in hiding. "Gigi!" She hurried toward the other woman.

"You're really here." Gigi hugged Emma, her grip tight. "I thought you were dead, Em."

"I know. I'm sorry."

"Why didn't you call me?"

"I couldn't. It's a long story, one that will have to wait until I'm not shivering so hard."

Her friend nudged Emma toward the closest seat at the kitchen table. "I'll find a blanket for you." She turned as Mrs. Grady hustled into the kitchen. "Em's freezing. Do you mind making her a cup of hot tea while I bring her a blanket?"

"I'll be happy to. I'm so glad you're safe, my dear." The housekeeper filled a mug with water and dropped a tea bag into the liquid. By the time the microwave heating cycle finished, Gigi had returned with a blanket for Emma.

The B & B owner scowled at David. "You should have told me Emma was alive."

He winced. "Does this mean I won't have your coffee and muffins for a while?"

"I'm still deciding. I'm so happy to have Emma back I might give you a pass."

Emma thanked Mrs. Grady for the tea and wrapped her hands around the mug, reveling in the warmth seeping into her cold fingers. "Cut him a break, Gigi. David didn't know I was alive until a few days ago."

"We'll see." Her friend sat across from her. "Now, where have you been?"

"Before I go into everything, are you okay? David said those horrible men hurt you."

Gigi brushed her concern aside. "Just a headache. No detours. Talk, Em. The suspense is killing me."

David leaned down and dropped a quick kiss on Emma's lips. "I have calls to make. I won't be far." After glancing at Owen, who nodded, David left the room.

Emma sipped her tea and told her best friend everything that had happened since the last time she and Gigi were together. By the time she finished the story, Emma's mug was empty, and her shivers were gone.

"Oh, Emma." Gigi gripped her hand. "I'm sorry you had to go through that alone."

"Now you understand why I stayed hidden. Everyone in my life is in danger because of the Hunt Club. That's why Agent Jordan convinced me to stay in WITSEC so long. I missed you like crazy, Gigi."

"Same, my friend." Gigi frowned at Owen when he handed her an ice pack. "I don't need that."

"Yeah, you do, G. You're squinting again."

Muttering under her breath about high-handed men, she pressed the ice pack to the back of her head with a hiss.

Owen's mouth curved as he went to the coffee pot to refill his mug and talk to Cal.

Emma stared at her soon-to-be brother-in-law. Had a relationship been brewing between Gigi and Owen while Emma hid from murderers?

Owen's cell rang. He snatched it up and spoke briefly, grimacing as he ended the call. He looked at Emma and Gigi. "Agent Jordan's at the gate. He'll be here in a minute with his flunkies."

Gigi groaned. "Is it too late for me to cut and run?"

"If you're too tired to deal with him, go upstairs. He won't get past me. It's your call, G."

"Does that go for me, too?" Emma asked.

Sympathy filled his gaze. "Sorry, Em. You and David are the stars of the hour."

She blew out a breath. "Lucky us."

The next two hours passed in agonizing slowness as she and David repeated their story multiple times to Agent Jordan. Brent Maddox and Darren Whitehead listened to the debrief via phone. More than once, David and the FBI agents got into heated arguments about the best way to proceed. Ultimately, Director Whitehead settled the dispute by siding with David.

"But, sir, this is my case," Jordan protested.

"Enough, Jordan," Whitehead snapped. "You had more than a year to solve this case. The Montgomery brothers and the Fortress team have come up with a viable plan. Work with them, or you'll be manning a desk for the foreseeable future. Am I clear?"

The agent's face flushed red. "Yes, sir," he muttered.

"David, did you receive the list I sent you?"

"Yes, sir."

"The agents are ready to go at a moment's notice. Do you need computer support?"

"No, sir. We have Fortress tech support."

"Good. If you need anything from me, pick up the phone. I'll get it done."

"Thank you, Director."

After Whitehead hung up, Maddox said, "I have Fortress teams ready to assist. When it's time to scoop up the hunters, call me."

"Yes, sir. Thanks." David ended the call and looked at Jordan. "Ready to get to work?"

"Do I have a choice?"

"Sure. You can sit this one out."

Jordan dropped into a chair across from David. "How do you want to do this?"

"Not me. All of us, you included."

The agent stilled. "You're not shutting me out?"

"Wells was your agent and your friend."

Jordan grimaced. "So was Phil Jones. I have no idea how many cases he's compromised."

"You'll find out and do what's necessary to bring justice to the victims. It's what we do."

The agent gave a slight nod.

"Elliot transported Grisham to the hospital in Maple Valley," David continued. "Find out the names of the Hunt Club members. We'll rip apart Jerome's computer records and trace the money."

A scowl. "You need a warrant to access the computer."

A slow smile. "I have one. Do you want control of the crime scene on Montgomery land? It covers about three miles."

Jordan was silent a moment, then shook his head. "Since, as you and the director say, our security is compromised, can your department handle the scene?"

"With help from the TBI, yes."

"Call them. I'll concentrate on Grisham." He inclined his head toward one of his agents. "I would like Agent Garrison at the crime scene. He'll keep me informed and lend a hand."

"Of course. I'll ask one of the men to drive him out there." David left the room and returned a minute later with a ranch hand. "This is Rusty. He'll take Garrison to the main site. Our coroner just arrived on the scene."

Jordan rose and glanced at his second agent. "Mayfield, you're with me. Montgomery, I'll be in touch. I promise you, I'll get the information we need."

"Jordan."

The agent paused at the threshold. "Yes?"

"Marty and Jerome killed Emma's grandfather. One of the Hunt Club teams murdered former agent Rafe Torres' girlfriend. Find out who killed Callie."

Jordan's face hardened. "Two more charges to add to the growing list. We'll talk to him about those accusations as well." He and his co-worker walked out.

David held up a hand to forestall any conversation until the front door closed behind the three federal agents and Rusty, then he turned toward Cal. "Tell Eli to bring his team here. My brothers brought in the part-timers to help with the scene and prisoner transport to the Sheriff's office. We need to move fast."

Emma frowned. "I thought you were going to work with local law enforcement and the FBI to capture these teams."

He smiled.

Gigi groaned. "Don't ask questions, Em. It's obvious the Montgomerys and their friends have a secret plan."

Oh, boy. She should have realized something was up when David ceded even a smidgen of control to Agent Jordan.

Emma wanted to help David and the others, but fatigue hit her with the force of a sledge hammer as her energy level hit rock bottom. Every muscle in her body hurt as well as her head. Nap first, then she could offer her assistance. "Is it safe to take a nap?"

David was on his feet a second later. "Absolutely." He held out his hand. "I'll walk you up to my room. No one will disturb you there."

"Come on, G." Owen tugged the B & B owner to her feet. "You've been through the wringer yourself."

She cast him a suspicious glance. "Is this an excuse to get rid of me?"

He frowned. "I'm trying to take care of you," he said as he led her upstairs.

"Is something going on between the two of them?" Emma murmured to David.

He chuckled. "Oh, yeah. Don't say anything, though. They haven't figured out what it is yet."

She smiled. This would be fun to watch. She loved Owen and Gigi. Although she'd never thought of them as a couple, sparks flew between them when they were together.

David wrapped his arm around Emma's shoulders as he walked upstairs with her. At the door to his bedroom, he gathered her in his arms. "Do you need anything?"

"I could use over-the-counter pain medicine," she admitted.

He stiffened. "You said you weren't hurt."

"Muscle aches. I don't think Marty and Jerome were gentle when they hauled us out of the cabin. I also got tossed around in the back of the van. Some of us aren't used to three-mile runs in the woods in the middle of the night."

"You'll find an OTC in my nightstand." He brushed his mouth over hers. "You were amazing tonight, Emma."

"All I did was follow your instructions. You did the hard work."

David cupped her nape. "Are you sure you're okay with what happened?"

"You protected me, David. How can I fault you for that? The hunters would have killed us if you hadn't acted in our defense."

He kissed her again, then stepped back. "I better go downstairs while I still can. If you need me, I'll be close." With that, he left.

Emma closed the door to David's room and stretched out on his bed. The scent of his soap wrapped her in comfort as she drifted to sleep.

When she woke five hours later, Emma saw that her bags had been brought from the safe house and left just inside David's bedroom door.

After a quick shower and change of clothes, she went to the kitchen which had been turned into a war room while she slept. Wolf Pack and three of the Montgomery brothers were either working on laptops or talking on their phones. David was nowhere in sight. Was he asleep?

Elliot came toward her. "Here." He handed her a travel mug. "Compliments of David."

Her heart melted. David Montgomery was the best thing to ever happen to her. "Where is he?"

"Waiting for you on the deck. He thought you'd be waking up about now. David's taking a short break."

Emma stepped outside the back door and drew in a deep breath. After the harrowing events of the night before, the air was crystal clear and pleasant. The calm after the storm, she mused.

She found David sitting on the outdoor couch at the far end of the deck, sipping what was probably coffee from his own travel mug. A small bag sat near his booted feet.

He glanced over and smiled. "Feel better?" When Emma sat beside him, David wrapped his arm around her shoulders.

"I do. I can't believe I slept that long."

"Tough night. Any nightmares?"

"A few."

"About Jerome?"

She sipped her tea. "Actually, the dreams were about Marty escaping from the hospital and coming after us again."

"He's handcuffed to a hospital bed with Agent Mayfield in the hallway and Agent Jordan at his bedside. Marty won't escape."

"Is Marty talking?"

David kissed her temple. "He's holding out for another deal."

She frowned. "Will he get one?"

"Not if I have anything to say about it. Marty expects his family's money to buy him out of trouble again. That won't happen, either. However, I don't want to talk about Marty or his posse of killers."

"Something on your mind?"

"Several things." He set her mug and his on the deck and picked up the bag. He reached inside and pulled out a small, velvet-covered black box with Chase Jewelry stamped across the top.

Emma's breath caught. "David?"

"I planned to wait until the Hunt Club was behind bars to do this, but I want people to know you're mine." He knelt in front of her and opened the box. Three diamonds nestled in a gold band sparkled in the morning sunlight. Grasping the ring, David held it poised at the end of her ring finger. "I love you, Emma Tucker, and I want a lifetime with you. Will you still agree to marry me?"

"You are my greatest gift, David. Yes, I still want to marry you."

He slid the ring on her finger and kissed her, a long and lingering expression of his love for her. By the time he broke the kiss, Emma's cheeks were wet with tears. "Good tears?" David whispered.

"Very good. How did you buy the ring? Chase Jewelry isn't open this early."

"I called Ryan before the sun rose and told him what I needed. He agreed to go to the shop and get what I wanted for you." He suddenly looked uneasy. "If you prefer a different ring, we can exchange it for something else."

Emma shook her head, her heart overflowing with love for this amazing man. "I love the ring. It's perfect."

"How soon can I convince you to marry me?"

"I don't want to wait, either."

"As soon as we run the Hunt Club to ground?"

"Depends. How soon will that happen?"

"Hopefully, tonight. Tomorrow night, at the latest."

Emma's eyes widened. "Are you serious?"

David smiled. "It's a good thing Jon and Zane work for the good guys."

"What about Agent Jordan? He thinks he's part of your plan."

"He is. Jordan is going the slower legal route. He got the names of the other hunters from Marty. While he learns more details and handles the red tape, my brothers and I will partner with Fortress. By tomorrow night, our local law enforcement partners and the FBI will receive anonymous phone calls about the locations of the detained Hunt Club members." He brushed her mouth with his. "So, Emma, how soon will you make me the happiest man on the planet?"

"What's on your schedule for Saturday morning?"

His eyes gleamed with heat. "Nothing is more important than marrying you. You're sure, baby?"

"No doubts."

"Guess it's a good thing I also bought the wedding bands this morning, too."

She grinned. "I guess it is. How soon will you and the others leave?"

"Two hours. Think you can be ready by then?"

Emma blinked. "I'm going with you?"

"We're driving to Nashville to meet at Fortress headquarters with the operatives. Maddox has arranged for an operative to watch over you while my brothers and I are gone."

"You're still worried about my safety."

"That, and I'm concerned Agent Jordan might whisk you off into protective custody while I'm gone."

Returning to FBI protective custody wasn't high on her list of things to do. "Excellent points. I'll be ready."

David stood and held out his hand to Emma.

Hopefully, this nightmare would end soon, and she and David would be able to start their life together with the darkness behind them.

CHAPTER THIRTY-THREE

Emma's hands clutched the end of the seat in the waiting area of John C. Tune Airport as she watched the night sky for the telltale lights of the last Fortress jet. She wasn't surprised that David was with one of the last teams to return to Nashville. He, Elliot, and Levi had left the city two days ago with Ethan Blackhawk to track down one of the teams hunting in the desert outside Las Vegas. Since the area was remote and well-known to Ethan, Brent Maddox had requested his help.

Caleb patted her shoulder. "Shouldn't be long now."

"You said that an hour ago."

"Chill, Em," Owen said, his tone mild. He and his brother had landed two hours earlier after the successful capture of their assigned team of hunters. They had been sent out with two members of the Texas unit. "If there was a problem, we'd know by now."

Not necessarily. Something in David's voice worried her. Before she could ask what was wrong, he'd had to board the plane.

Three hours and counting. Unable to sit still, Emma paced the length of the private waiting area reserved for Fortress operatives and their families.

Brent Maddox strode into the room. After shaking hands with Caleb and Owen, he approached Emma. "How are you holding up?"

"To be honest, not as well as I thought I would." She wrapped her arms around her middle. "I didn't have this much trouble when David was deployed with his SEAL team."

"This is different, more personal. He went after one of the teams that targeted you." Brent studied her a moment. "But that's not the problem, is it?"

She shook her head. "I know something is wrong. I heard it in David's voice when he called to tell me they captured their assigned team."

A slow nod. "You're right. The mission was a difficult one in rough terrain. David and Levi are a little banged up. They'll recover."

"What happened?"

"Ask him when you see him." Brent laid his hand on her shoulder. "If the injuries were serious, I'd tell you. I don't hide the truth from my operatives or their families."

Her eyes widened. "Your operatives. He and his brothers have agreed to work for you?"

"Not yet. They will. They won't be able to help themselves. We're all adrenaline junkies. The question is, will you be able to live with his decision?"

"I love him. If working for Fortress makes him happy, then I'll find a way to deal." She may be spinning tons of yarn and knitting like crazy, but she would get through his absences. To love David Montgomery and have the privilege of calling him hers would be worth every lonely hour she'd face.

His lips curved. "David told me you were a rock. I can see he's right." He glanced out the window. "The jet's on final approach."

Relief washed through Emma. Thank God. She hurried after Brent as he strode toward the door leading to the tarmac.

The jet landed smoothly and soon slowed to a stop. Brent kept his hand on her arm until the cabin door opened and the stairs were lowered.

Elliot exited the jet first carrying two bags, followed by Levi who limped down the stairs. Ethan came next with his duffel slung over his shoulder.

When David appeared in the doorway of the jet, Emma broke away from Brent and ran across the tarmac. David wrapped his arms around her and kissed her as if he'd been gone for two months instead of two days.

Breaking the kiss long minutes later, David cupped her face between his roughened palms. "All the teams were captured and left trussed up like presents for teams of local law enforcement and FBI agents. It's over, baby. You're safe now."

"Will I still have to testify?"

He shook his head. "Jordan and the Grisham attorney convinced Marty that he'd receive a better deal by pleading guilty to multiple murder charges and rolling on the other members of the Hunt Club."

She frowned. "What kind of deal?"

"He gets to live."

Brent walked up and shook David's hand. "Good job. Have you decided yet?"

David chuckled. "We talked. You've got yourself another team. Give me a few weeks to hire two more deputies to cover for us when we're gone." He smiled. "And take Emma on a honeymoon."

"Excellent. As we discussed, expect to be deployed once a month. Short-term missions only. Welcome to

Fortress. I'll email the offer and forms to each of you by tomorrow morning." He started to turn, paused. "By the way, Emma's a sharp lady. She knows, buddy." With a nod at Emma, he walked toward the terminal.

David looked at Emma. "Who told you?"

"No one. I heard something in your voice. How bad is it?"

"Perp got in a lucky swipe. I have a few stitches in my side. The doc said I'll be as good as new in a couple of weeks."

"How many stitches, David?"

He flinched. "Fifteen. I've had worse injuries."

Fifteen stitches? Oh, man.

"The good news is the injury won't stop me from marrying you in three days." He grinned. "We'll have just enough time to get our marriage license and round up a few cupcakes for the reception. I hope you don't mind, but I invited Wolf Pack to the wedding."

"Of course I don't mind. I like all of them. Mrs. Grady, Gigi, and I have been planning while you were hunting the bad guys. You'll have more than cupcakes to eat."

He shrugged. "All that matters to me is sliding my wedding band on your finger and having you to myself for two weeks."

"Sounds like a great plan." Two weeks would also give him time to rest and recuperate.

David placed a gentle kiss on her lips. "Let's go home, Emma." He slung his bag over one shoulder and draped his other arm around her waist. "It's finally time for us."

ABOUT THE AUTHOR

Rebecca Deel is a preacher's kid with a black belt in karate. She teaches business classes at a private four-year college outside Nashville, Tennessee. She plays the piano at church, writes freelance articles, and runs interference for the family dogs. She's been married to her amazing husband for more than 25 years and is the proud mom of two grown sons. She delivers occasional devotions to the women's group at her church and conducts seminars on personal safety, money management, and writing. Her articles have been published in *ONE Magazine*, *Contact*, and *Co-Laborer*, and she was profiled in the June 2010 Williamson edition of *Nashville Christian Family* magazine. Rebecca completed her Doctor of Arts degree in Economics and wears her favorite Dallas Cowboys sweatshirt when life turns ugly.

For more information on Rebecca...

Signup for Rebecca's newsletter: http://eepurl.com/_B6w9

Visit Rebecca's website: www.rebeccadeelbooks.com

Made in the USA
Monee, IL
01 September 2020